Praise for Tricia Jones' *Satin Lies*

"well written and well paced..."

~ *Rocio Rosado, Ecataromance*

Rating: 4 Blue Ribbons "Emotions become real and tangible in the heart wrenching SATIN LIES ...passionate, powerful, and a wonderful way to spend an afternoon."

~ *Sarah W, Romance Junkies*

Look for these titles by

Tricia Jones

Now Available:

His Convenient Affair

Satin Lies

Tricia Jones

A Samhain Publishing, Ltd. publication.

Samhain Publishing, Ltd.
577 Mulberry Street, Suite 1520
Macon, GA 31201
www.samhainpublishing.com

Satin Lies

Print ISBN: 978-1-60504-172-8
Digital ISBN: 978-1-60504-044-8

Editing by Heidi Moore
Cover by Dawn Seewer

First Samhain Publishing, Ltd. electronic publication: June 2008
First Samhain Publishing, Ltd. print publication: April 2009

Dedication

For Nan—who introduced me to "Love Books" and taught me that love will always find a way.

Chapter One

"Please, Mummy, wake up!"

Faye didn't want to. She wanted to drift back to the blankness, the nothingness. But the edge of panic in the young voice and the tremble of fear pulled her up...up...up...

Her eyes felt heavy. Incredibly heavy. But she willed them open.

"Mummy!"

Slowly, the blur cleared and Faye looked into a child's eyes. Dark and beautiful with fear glittering in their long-lashed depths.

As Faye tried to shift, an arrow of heat shot down her spine and into her leg. Where was she? Who was this distressed little girl beside her bed?

Mummy. The word echoed around Faye's empty, throbbing head. *Mummy...*?

She closed her eyes. What was happening? Where was she? She was supposed to be getting ready to go to university. She was studying... Oh God, what was she studying?

The little girl sobbed again.

Oh, please. What was happening? There had been some mistake. How could this child be hers? How could she have a daughter? She wasn't even married...

"Where..." Her voice was husky and it hurt to clear her throat. "Who...?"

"Mummy, it's me. Melita!"

The wrenching sobs tugged at Faye's heart, and instinct more than desire forced her eyes open again. She turned, that same instinct preparing to console, but pain leapt between her shoulder blades and forced her head back to the pillow.

"It's all right, little one." A deep, headily familiar voice filled the room. "Your mama just needs to rest now."

Slowly and tentatively, Faye turned her head. Tears flowed down the child's face, her button-nose red and running. Behind her stood the blurred outline of a man, his head tilted, his big hands resting on the child's tiny shoulders. Recognition shot through Faye only to disappear before she could grab hold of it.

A nurse hurried into the room as Faye's brain spun violently. Flashes and colors, then a hazy fog. A million questions all demanding answers. But panic clawed at her throat, tore through her chest, and she couldn't speak.

"Welcome back, Mrs. Lavini." The nurse's steady hands checked tubes and bones. "We hoped a visit from your daughter would bring you around. You've given everyone quite a scare."

Mrs. Lavini? Her stomach hitched. *Lavini? Your daughter?* Something inside shifted, a glowing sun piercing through the shadows.

Enrico. Oh, sweet, sweet heaven. Enrico.

When the child's head settled gently on her chest, Faye lifted her arm to stroke away the long strands of raven hair, damp with the little girl's tears, as they fell across the white sheet.

Mrs. Lavini... Mummy...

Even the pain of moving her arm, the steely pierce that dug

into her ribs, couldn't stop the deep joy threatening to swamp her as she hugged the child close. *Their* child.

Faye felt like her heart might burst. Through the fuzz of her brain, the discomfort of her aching body, all she knew, all she cared about, was that they had married and she was his wife. This was their child.

A flurry of activity at the doorway brought a doctor into the room. "Mrs. Lavini, how are you feeling?" The doctor flashed light into her eyes. "You've been away from us for quite some time."

Faye blinked away the moisture triggered by the bright light. What was she doing in hospital? What on earth was happening to her?

As the doctor moved away and out of her line of vision, Faye's eyes refocused.

It was then she had her first clear view of him. Standing behind the little girl, one reassuring hand still on her shoulder, he oozed that attractive but dangerous combination of formidability and breathtaking allure.

Enrico Lavini. Tall, proud and arrogantly handsome. Powerful owner of the Lavini vineyards in the beautiful Tuscan hills. He'd started his own business straight out of university, determined not to become another "yes-man" in his domineering father's banking conglomerate.

Enrico. Her heart tumbled.

Melita stayed close, her concentration fixed on the doctor who cradled Faye's head and proceeded to move it from side to side. "Are you better now, Mummy? Does that hurt?"

Watching the concern flash over her daughter's face, Faye's heart ached more than bone or muscle. "No, it doesn't hurt," she lied. "I'll be all right." Lord, how could she not remember this beautiful child? How could she not remember how this angel felt in her arms? How could she not remember being Enrico's wife?

Through the tears threatening to blur her view, she saw Enrico's large hand engulf Melita's tiny one, his aura of authority slicing through the sterile air. "Go with the nurse, *carina.* Your mama needs to rest now. You can come back tomorrow." He waited while Melita plopped a wet kiss on Faye's cheek, then guided her toward where the nurse waited at the door. When he returned to stand beside Faye's bed, his hard charcoal gaze whipped over her face. But he said nothing.

The doctor moved forward. "Do you remember the accident, Mrs. Lavini? Do you remember what happened?"

Accident? No, she didn't remember an accident. She shook her head, wincing when the movement sent pain into her neck and shoulders. "Was...was anyone hurt?" Her voice, though scratchy, was stronger now.

"You've been in and out of consciousness for almost two days," the doctor said, ignoring her question. "Do you remember anything?"

"No." Faye fought back the escalating fear and gnawing vulnerability. Why hadn't Enrico touched her, kissed her, whispered words of comfort? Why hadn't he even smiled at her?

"Melita...?" Some innate protective instinct whispered through her and she tried to lift her head from the pillow. Had she caused this accident? Had her child been hurt in some way and she hadn't noticed? Please God, no!

"She's fine." The doctor pressed a hand to Faye's forehead, easing her head gently back against the pillow. "Tell me how you feel."

"I'm okay." Though her head felt like it might explode. "My back hurts a little and my chest feels tight."

"You have some heavy bruising to your back and chest but

miraculously there's no permanent damage. And you have a concussion, of course."

"W...what happened?"

She saw the doctor glance anxiously across the bed to where Enrico stood, his expression grim as he watched her.

Tiny pieces—flashes, glimpses—fired through her brain. Memories. Enrico. Somehow they all involved Enrico. But why hadn't he touched her? Why hadn't he kissed her? Her fingers ached with the need to touch him.

"You were in a light aircraft traveling back to London and the plane experienced problems during landing." The doctor lifted her eyelid and shone his pencil torch around the circumference of her eye. "Are you able to tell us what happened?"

"No." Faye whispered. "I don't remember."

"Can you tell me the last thing you do remember?"

Faye closed her eyes. There were those pieces again. Mere impressions really. Something about a wedding, a hotel, a room...she was with Enrico. They were together.

"I...I'm not sure..." She opened her eyes and looked straight at Enrico. "I remember packing for university and then...then there was a wedding."

Enrico's wide shoulders drew back, his jaw tightened, then a deep groove appeared between his eyebrows.

"Faye?" He addressed her for the first time, his voice low and tight. "Do you remember you have a daughter? Or that you live in London?"

No. She didn't remember they had a daughter, she didn't even remember they were married. How on earth would she have forgotten her child or that he was her husband? He was the most important person in her life. She loved him. Had always loved him. First with the naïve crush of a schoolgirl and then with the passion of her teenage heart. And why were they living in London? Enrico hated London.

She shook her head, noticing that the pain had eased a fraction. Most likely the result of the injection the doctor had administered. "I don't remember."

"Now, I don't want you to worry," the doctor assured her. "This is a common enough occurrence after a traumatic experience. You just rest, let the memories return in their own good time."

"I don't want to rest." Faye turned to Enrico, reached out her hand. "Tell me what happened. Rico, please tell me what happened." *And tell me why you won't touch me*, she pleaded silently when he looked down at her outstretched hand. *Tell me what I've done to make you treat me with such indifference.*

When at last his fingers curled around hers, she almost wept with relief.

"The doctor is right, *cara*. You should rest now." He gave her hand a light squeeze. "When I bring Melita to see you tomorrow we will make plans to take you home."

"Yes," she gripped his hand like the lifeline he was. Or tried to grip. She didn't seem to have the strength, and her lids felt heavy again. "Yes, Rico," she managed, as his handsome face faded. "Take...me...home..."

"She's lost about eight years." Enrico pushed back his jacket, and slipped his hands into the trouser pockets of an immaculately cut suit. He stood looking out over the London skyline glittering in the late spring sunshine. The specialist's office was on the top floor of a prestigious Mayfair clinic where Enrico had arranged Faye's immediate transfer upon hearing of the accident. He'd flown straight over from Tuscany, taken

Melita out of the crummy excuse for a flat she shared with her mother and moved her into the penthouse apartment he kept for his compulsory business trips to London—and when the time was right he'd investigate just what the hell was going on.

"She'll remember more every day," the specialist assured him. "We'll perform more tests, of course, but there seems no indication of any permanent damage as a result of the concussion. There's no reason to suggest her memory loss will be permanent."

Enrico turned from the window. He rolled his shoulders, trying to dislodge the ache that had settled there during the past two days. "She has to be told. I do not want her finding out from some tabloid or a well-meaning remark from one of your nurses. The shock might set any recovery back. I need to be with her when she finds out, when she has to tell Melita."

The specialist, a world-authority on retrograde amnesia, sat back in his chair. "I agree. Do you want her to attend the funeral?"

Pain stabbed at Enrico's heart. "That is her decision to make." Not that he doubted what that decision would be. Whatever the circumstances surrounding Matteo's death, he knew Faye would want to say goodbye—and, God forgive him, if acknowledging that didn't deepen his own grief.

But he had no right to these feelings. He'd given up that right long ago. Now his only claim was as protector. Technically, in his role as head of the Lavini family, she was his responsibility. He might have forgotten that once, but he would never do so again. Faye was his duty and responsibility. Anything he once felt for her had to finally be buried...along with his brother.

Chapter Two

Faye sat at the small window table in her hospital room, surrounded by colored pencils and paper. Melita was tucked into her side as both of them drew pictures.

"And this is our house." The seven-year old drew the standard box house with the equally standard front path and trees. "And this is Blaster and this—"

"Blaster!" Faye laid her hand over her daughter's, currently outlining a shape in green. "Blaster's our cat."

Two enthusiastic arms shot around her waist. "Oh, Mummy, you remember!" Then she pulled back, face crumpled with concern as Faye winced. "Does it still hurt very much?"

Faye drew her daughter back into her arms, despite the fact her ribcage felt like it had gone a few rounds with a steamroller. It had taken only a heartbeat to fall in love with the child who chatted constantly about school and dancing classes. Had brought in virtually every book she owned to read to Faye. Drew pictures relentlessly trying to spark memories.

"No, it doesn't hurt very much," Faye assured her daughter. "And I do remember Blaster. He's black and has green eyes with two white rings around them. Teo bought him for you." Something inside her twisted. Some remote yet important memory, although why it should involve Matteo...

Dear Teo. He had helped her pack for university. She was

upset and they had shared too much wine and—

"Time to go, little one." Enrico stood in the doorway, his shoulders almost as wide. Faye's stomach gave one long unsteady roll. She hadn't forgotten that underneath the crisp Italian suit his muscles were long, lean and hard. His body had always been a source of fascination for her. Ever since she had snuck a look one summer when, believing he was alone, he'd stripped off and gone swimming in the lake near the Lavini's Tuscan villa.

He'd always protected her, sometimes making her feel like his younger sister. But there was nothing sisterly in the way she felt about him. And if they were now married and had a child together, he obviously no longer felt that way either. If he was cool with her, if he was distant, then it was most likely because he felt as anxious and uncertain as she did. She might be getting snatches of her memory back, but it was fragmented, patchy. Only natural they were skirting around each other like strangers.

Melita gathered up her things and with a tug at Faye's heart, left with her temporary nanny.

Enrico pulled up a chair and sat opposite Faye. Her pulse tripped as his knees bumped hers, the blood flowing warm in her veins when he leaned forward. This was the first time they had been alone together since she awoke from the accident. Maybe now it would be different. Enrico wasn't a man given to public displays of affection, in fact, he often found it hard to show affection even in private. Which was why she shouldn't be surprised at his reserve now. The characteristic was integral to the man he was. Even as youngsters, while she and his half-brother Matteo had whooped and jostled around the lush gardens of the Lavini villa, Enrico had distanced himself from their antics. As if it was beneath his dignity to indulge in such behavior. As if the natural birthright of childhood games and adventures were never his to claim.

"I have something to tell you and you must be strong." His grim expression matched the steel in his eyes. "The accident happened when you were flying back from a trip to Edinburgh, do you remember?"

Faye shook her head, the growing sense of foreboding only marginally diminished as Enrico took her hands in his.

He stared down at their clasped fingers as if gathering himself. "Matteo was piloting the aircraft." He looked up, held her gaze. "He was killed, Faye."

She stared at him, long and hard. Part of her expecting him to laugh, to say he'd been playing a cruel joke. But this was Enrico. He was tough, uncompromising. But never cruel.

"Faye…?"

She squeezed her eyes shut. What? What had he said? Matteo? Matteo dead?

From a long way off she heard a door open, then close. When she opened her eyes she fastened them on Enrico, saw the deep grooves cut into his forehead. Vaguely, as she struggled to process what he'd said, she was aware of someone sitting beside her.

"He died instantly, Mrs. Lavini." The doctor's voice came to her through a fog. "Your husband would not have suffered."

Husband? What was he talking about? Enrico was her husband. He was sitting here. Right here in front of her.

She squeezed her fingers around Enrico's tightening grip, her gaze locked to his as if to reassure herself he was indeed living…breathing. Then she snatched her hands away. "Just what exactly is going on?" she demanded. "What's this all about? Teo is…" Her head was spinning, but something wasn't right. There was something not right. She hadn't thought she wanted to cry, but tears spilled down her cheeks before she could stop them. "It's not true. Teo and I weren't—"

"You were married for almost eight years, Faye." Enrico spoke with quiet force. "You had a daughter together."

"No." Faye moved her head slowly from side to side, as if the movement would jog her brain back into gear and allow all her memories to come tripping back. "It's not possible." But something in the grim seriousness of Enrico's expression assured her it was.

"I've made arrangements to—"

"No!" Faye's head thumped, her mind reeling. What sort of nightmare was this? "This is all some hideous mistake. It's not true. There's no way Teo..."

Enrico grabbed for her hands, held on tight when she would have pulled them away again. "Faye, you must be strong, for Melita's sake as well as your own."

Faye stared at him. At the short hair framing that ridiculously handsome face, the formidable jaw, the charcoal eyes softly shadowed with his own grief.

How could this be? Teo dead? Her husband? She would never have married Matteo. She loved him dearly, but like a brother, a beloved friend. Not as a husband. For her there was only one man...just one. And he sat opposite her now, watching her with such grim intensity as he attended to her grief while ignoring his own.

"Oh, Rico." She sobbed it out, her shoulders slumping as she gripped his hands in return. "I don't understand what's going on. Please tell me this isn't true."

He watched her for long moments, then swallowed. "You are not to worry about anything, *cara*. You and Melita will be taken care of. I promise you."

Somehow Faye knew that being taken care of was the least of her problems. Enrico had always looked out for her...and for Teo. Enrico was always the strong back supporting the Lavini family. He had lost so many people he loved. First his mother when he was a mere toddler, then his beloved grandfather, now his younger half-brother. The brother he had always shielded and guarded.

Something fluttered at the edges of memory, but Faye didn't try to grasp for it. She wanted to console Enrico, wanted to wrap her arms around him. Wanted his arms around her. For mutual comfort, mutual support? No. Much more than that. She loved him. Had always loved him. She may, for some obscure and incomprehensible reason, have married Matteo, but it was Enrico she ached for. Even with her memory impaired that much she knew. Would always know.

"After the service you will come home to Tuscany with me." Enrico's tone signaled that was non-negotiable. "I've arranged for your things to be packed and shipped to the villa. Melita will attend the local school. Thankfully her Italian is adequate, despite the fact she has known only England as home."

"Is...is she all right?" Lost in her own desperate grief, Faye suddenly realized that her little girl had lost her father. Melita should be here now, with her.

"She doesn't know." Enrico's expression was grave. "We thought it best she heard it from you. She will feel more secure hearing it from her mother."

Oh God. This was all so surreal.

Yesterday she had woken in a hospital bed, learned she had a child, a husband. It didn't seem possible. She was Faye Benedict. She was seventeen. She was going to study business and law. When had she married Teo? Why? When she loved Enrico, always Enrico. Yet, here she was preparing to tell a child she didn't know that she had lost a father, a man Faye couldn't even remember marrying.

Oh God. Faye squeezed her eyes shut, as if she could as easily shut off the questions swirling around in her head.

"How am I supposed to tell her?" She opened her eyes and stared at Enrico, excruciating pain gripping her heart. "What am I going to say?"

"You will find the words." He gave her hands one last squeeze, then released them. "I will bring her to visit early this evening. You can tell her then."

The doctor stood and, after a reassuring pat on Faye's shoulder, discreetly left the room.

The room seemed to spin as Faye continued processing the horrible facts. An involuntary shiver had her hugging her arms around her chest.

Then she was lifted effortlessly into Enrico's arms. "You should rest." He carried her over to the bed, where a shaft of afternoon sun streaked across the pillow. "You must not worry, *cara.* I will take care of everything." He held her there in his arms for endless moments. Faye wanted to drop her head on his shoulder and let his enveloping arms hold her safe and secure forever. Make every awful thing go away. But then he lowered her slowly onto the crisp white sheets.

"Sleep now," he said, the softness in his deep voice a temporary balm over her troubled thoughts. "I will see to it you are not disturbed."

He walked to the window and lowered the blind enough to block the sun from Faye's eyes. Then he left. Without a backward glance.

Alone, Faye let the tears flow. A myriad of emotions battled in her chest and beat against her tender ribcage. Teo. Sweet, wonderful Teo. She could grieve for him as a dear and trusted friend. Love him as such. But as her husband? It wasn't possible.

Because it was always Enrico. Since that day when her parents had first taken her to holiday in Italy with the family of her father's new business associate, it had been Enrico. She was ten and he a surly seventeen. Yet she had idolized him on sight. Had wanted to follow him around like a puppy dog. Would have, if Teo hadn't claimed her attention. A gentle, kind boy, Teo became an equally temperate man. Unlike his intense half-brother who had a whip of danger about him. True, that dangerous edge was underpinned by a steely control, but that somehow made him even more exciting.

Not that her adoration was reciprocated. He had never been interested in her. Not as a girl and not as a woman. Except...

Flashes and snippets again. That wedding...

She couldn't bear to even try and grasp for it. There was much to cope with right now. Too much. She didn't want to remember. Didn't want to feel. She wanted to drift back into blessed unconsciousness, to slip back into the nothingness. Where there were no memories. No pain. But she couldn't. Wouldn't. She had a child to think of. A child who needed her mother to ease the loss of her father.

Faye lifted a heavy hand, stroked it across her wet cheeks. Melita needed her. She would focus only on her child. Everything else could fade into oblivion, to be dealt with at some later date. In private. Then she would grieve for Teo. Would try to remember. But right now she didn't care about her own feelings. Couldn't. All she cared about was making a safe, secure future for her fatherless child. That was her one—her only—priority.

For all she knew Enrico had also married. Hadn't she lost her memory of the last eight years? Anything could have happened. He might have children of his own.

As a sharp pain needled beneath her ribs, she turned her aching head into the soft comfort of the pillow. And wept.

"I know what you're going to say, Mummy." Melita's lovely eyebrows drew together as she sat on her mother's lap and tightened her arms around Faye's neck. Her daughter's reassuring tone had the back of Faye's throat contracting. "I heard the lady who's looking after me whispering to the man who drives Uncle Rico's car," Melita explained. "They said Teo died."

Faye swallowed, then stroked her hand over Melita's hair, pushing back long strands of silk. Beside her, Enrico shifted in his seat. "Yes, darling." Faye fought to keep her voice from trembling. "That's right. Teo was killed when he tried to land the aircraft he and Mummy were flying in."

Faye thought it strangely touching that her daughter referred to Teo by her own nickname for him. But she pushed it away, wanting only to reassure and protect Melita—to soften her child's heartache and alleviate the pain of losing a parent.

It was something she remembered only too well. The excruciating sense of loss. The fear. The loneliness. That was something her amnesia hadn't dispelled.

She drew her daughter close as memories of her own father's fatal stroke snapped at her heart. Still painfully raw—although she supposed it was now well over nine years since he'd died—the loss sat like a heavy weight in her soul.

She'd been only a few years older than Melita was now when a debilitating illness had finally claimed her mother shortly after the family began holidaying at the Lavini villa. Enrico had found her that summer, crouched behind some bushes by a stream. She'd gone there to be alone, to grieve for her mother. She was crying, weeping buckets, but he'd said nothing. He had simply settled himself down beside her, put his arm around her shoulders and held her while she'd sobbed.

But such memories were too dangerous to indulge in right then. With him sitting beside her, his presence at such a time both a blessing and a curse. She ached to have him put his arm around her now, to comfort and console her. Just as she was trying to do for her daughter.

"Is Teo in heaven now, Mummy?" Melita's eyes, those questioning Lavini eyes, looked into Faye's. "Will he know we miss him?"

"Yes, he'll know we miss him, but we have to be very brave. We'll be brave together, all right?"

Melita thought about it for a few seconds, then nodded. "I think he'll be pleased we're going to live with Uncle Rico."

"Yes," Faye agreed, even as something nudged at her that the sentiment wasn't necessarily true. She pushed the feeling away. "It will just be until Mummy is feeling much better, but will you like that?"

Melita gave another nod, slightly more enthusiastic. "He said there are horses at his villa and I can ride one. And the sea's not very far away and we can go there sometimes to swim and sail on his boat."

"Won't that be wonderful?" Faye smiled down into her daughter's face, the pure wonder on it tugging at her heart. Not that Faye thought it would be wonderful at all. She had mixed feelings about moving in with Enrico as it was. Although reason told her it provided a short term solution until her memory completely returned, and she and Melita could go back to whatever life they had been living, Faye knew she had to safeguard herself and her daughter. She didn't trust her feelings, her emotions. Until she knew, until she remembered what had happened—why she had married Teo—she had to keep some sort of distance between herself and Enrico.

An hour later, when Melita's nanny had taken her home for the night, Faye took the opportunity to voice her anxieties to Enrico. "I appreciate everything you're doing, but there's really no need for us to stay with you. It's better for Melita to get back to normal as soon as possible, to be with her friends, to go to school. She needs familiar things around her, so do I. On reflection, I think it's best if we just go home."

Enrico stood at the window gazing out over the London sky. "And where is that, Faye?" He turned to her, eyebrows raised, his mouth grim. "If I am not mistaken you do not even remember your address." The tension in his jaw had a lone muscle flickering. "Rest assured that what I can offer will be an improvement on your previous accommodation."

"I don't understand."

His accusatory gaze held hers for long moments, then he shook his head. "You are my brother's widow, and as such it is my duty to protect you and your daughter. You are both my responsibility."

"I don't want to be anyone's responsibility." Both because he had said it with such cold resignation in his voice and because she suddenly felt helpless and frighteningly vulnerable. Memories nudged, but she couldn't quite focus. Perhaps because some instinct warned they wouldn't be good ones.

"The matter is settled," Enrico shrugged. "When you are recovered and your memory returns in full you may do as you wish. Until then I will assure your welfare." His tone indicated he did not expect to be challenged. But then he rarely was. That much Faye did remember.

"The specialist assures me you will be well enough to attend the memorial service by Friday, so I have arranged it for then. We will fly to Tuscany later that evening."

His imperious manner made her bristle. "I'm not sure I appreciate your tone or the way you seem to think you can just take control of my life." Faye eased herself from her chair, pleased to discover her legs felt stronger. "I have things I need to do, all manner of things to arrange. For one, I need to pack our clothes, to arrange for someone to look after Blaster."

"Everything is taken care of. You can purchase whatever you need in Italy." He turned, making for the door. "You should rest now."

"Enrico!" Her sharp tone made him turn slowly to look back at her. "I'm grateful for everything you've done, but please don't treat me like a child and presume you know what's best for me. I'd appreciate being informed of the arrangements you're making on my behalf before you actually make them."

He flicked back his jacket and slipped his hands into his trouser pockets.

Faye swallowed, unsettled by the way he looked at her, as if he was weighing up whether to challenge her remarks or let them go. Then he came toward her.

She made herself hold his gaze even though her knees felt weak again and she wanted to sink back down into the chair. But the haughty arrogance in the sharpened angles and planes of his face made her stand her ground as he moved up close.

"You have lost your memory," he said, as if she needed reminding. "You have bruised ribs and a concussion. You have suffered the death of your husband and need to comfort your child." His nostrils flared as he drew in a deep breath. "If I presume to make arrangements on your behalf, it is because I consider you have other priorities at this time."

God. He made her feel like an ungrateful idiot.

He raised his hand and traced his finger along her left

cheekbone, where the remnants of a vicious bruise still lingered. Her stomach trembled at his touch. A crazy part of her willed him to take her in his arms, to as easily stroke away the pain of her inner bruises.

He drew in another long breath and dropped his hand. "Now, get some sleep, *cara*. Allow me to take care of the practicalities. It is my duty at this time."

Faye watched him stride out, her throat tight and a niggling ache in her chest.

She didn't want to be his duty. Didn't want to be his responsibility. But that was all she was to him, and knowing it made her heart break even more. How could she have married Teo when her heart belonged to Enrico? How could she have slept with another man when her very soul belonged to Enrico?

Faye looked down at her hands, at the wedding ring she couldn't remember Teo slipping onto her finger. Had Teo known she was in love with someone else? Had he realized her heart could never be his? That their child—the child she wished with everything she had belonged to...

As her head throbbed with merciless persistence, she touched her fingertips to her temples. *Why* couldn't she remember? Then she could go home...back to *her* home, wherever that was. Make a life for herself and for her daughter. Then she wouldn't have to stay with a man who made her pulse race, her heart thump, her legs tremble. A man who could give her the world with a rare smile and snatch it back with a not-so-rare frown...and for whom she was merely a duty.

Faye enjoyed little rest that night. Or for the next three. She tossed and turned as best her bruised body could manage before slipping into an exhausted sleep. More than once she considered pressing the red call button and giving in to the offer of a sedative. But she had wasted enough time not knowing what was happening to her body, to her mind. She didn't need, or want, to add to the void.

Enrico came by twice each day, with Melita in the afternoons and by himself in the evenings. Tonight he'd arrived later than usual. Faye knew because she all but counted the minutes between his visits.

She braced herself for the sharp punch of awareness whenever he entered her room. Today the dark grey business suit was an exact match for those perilous eyes, and the immaculate tailoring showcased his broad shoulders to perfection. Tall, commanding and agonizingly masculine. Every cell, every fiber of her body seemed to want him.

Tonight he did what he always did. Asked how she was feeling and if she needed anything. Assured her Melita was okay at his apartment.

"My neighbor came by to see me," Faye told him, leaning forward in her chair as Enrico popped another pillow behind her. "Thank you for contacting her."

"Melita was worried about your cat." His brief, if unexpected, smile sent Faye's pulse racing. "Your neighbor said she will take care of him."

"Yes." Faye had discovered that she and the amiable woman were friends. "She was very worried about us. She said she'd also take care of our flat while we're away. The flat—"

"Good," he said with brusque efficiency. "That is good. But there is no reason to concern yourself with any of that now."

She wanted to tell him she had a job. Her neighbour had told her she worked part-time at a bookstore and that she rented the flat above it. It seemed her boss had been trying to contact her. When she'd rung him from the hospital he'd been very understanding. He'd assured her the job would still be there when she was fully recovered, as would the flat. As the rent was deducted from her salary, Faye had been worried she couldn't pay it until some sort of sick pay kicked in. He'd told her not to worry.

Enrico pulled up a chair beside her, his tone brisk and clipped, his expression stern. "Do you have everything you need for tomorrow?"

For Teo's memorial service he meant, though neither of them seemed to want to acknowledge it as such.

Faye nodded. "Will your father be there?"

Enrico had told her—reminded her—that several years ago his father had married for the third time and after handing over the reigns of the family banking business to his eldest, had retired to the shores of Lake Geneva on doctor's orders.

Enrico's expression turned to stone. "He's flying in from Geneva in the morning."

And no doubt flying right back out again in the afternoon, Faye realized, reading Enrico's seasoned attempt to batten down anger and contempt.

"Tell me more about your vineyards?" she said in a voice that sounded far too bright. She had always hated the way Enrico went into brooding mode at the slightest mention of his father, but get him talking about the land and you were on safe territory.

"What do you want to know?"

"Anything. The number of staff you have, any plans you have to expand, that sort of thing." Faye was clutching at straws because he'd already told her that he'd been expanding over the years, that his vineyards now encompassed most of the valley and surrounding area. But she wanted him to talk. Wanted *them* to talk. There was only a short while left of visiting time and she wanted him with her until the very last minute.

Guilt tugged at her conscience. She should be grieving for her husband, not craving the company of his brother.

Enrico rubbed his jaw. "I'm always planning to expand, but my father's retirement put many of those plans on hold. Banking leaves little time for the hands-on work of running vineyards."

Faye felt for him. He had always been active and never minded getting his hands dirty. It was one of the reasons he'd refused to join his father in the family business and ventured off on his own. Despite that, she knew he would never allow the bank to fall into anything other than Lavini hands. It had been built from nothing by his adored late grandfather who, on the couple of occasions Faye had met him, was as devilishly good-looking as his equally beloved grandson.

So, Enrico had taken on the role of international businessman, leaving the day-to-day running of his vineyards to a management team. Faye could never imagine Rico spending his life behind a desk. Not that the role didn't suit him, physically that was. He looked every inch the civilized businessman.

"Now you must rest, *cara*." Enrico stood, straightening his tie. "Tomorrow will be a long day."

He gave her a chaste kiss on the forehead, then left without a backward glance. As he always did.

That night her mind was more active than usual. Strange tingles and fizzing sensations erupted in her head, which she put down to being off her feet for so long—courtesy of Enrico's insistence she rest as much as possible.

Faye lay awake, her gaze tracing a curve of the ornate ceiling. The plasterwork was strangely familiar, and not only because she'd spent the last few nights becoming acquainted with it. No. There was something about a brown water stain in the corner of another ceiling, a patch of damp over a fireplace...

Then an image of Melita in a lilac party dress, her eyes sparkling and her hair falling onto a cute little white collar...

Another image—no, not an image. A recollection...a sound. Teo. He was shouting something...her name...

"*Faye... I can't get control...*"

Faye snapped her eyes shut, as if the action would cut off the piercing memory.

It didn't. The whole room seemed to shake, to shudder. The sound of an engine droning, sputtering...

"*Faye...*" Teo's image materialized beneath her closed lids. "*I'm sorry...*"

She squeezed her eyes until they hurt. Her insides spun against the sickening terror, her heartbeat so fierce she feared it might leap from her chest. Her skin felt clammy, but at the same time icy cold.

She didn't want to think. Didn't want to remember. *Think of something else,* she ordered herself. *Think of something else*!

With her eyes shut tight she trained her thoughts on Melita, and began repeating her little girl's name over and over—a silent, comforting mantra.

Melita, Melita, Melita...

Several times the memory wanted to squeeze between the syllables of her daughter's name as Faye kept up the silent repetition, but she wouldn't give it the opportunity. She wouldn't give it the power.

Slow and steady the vicious physical sensations of panic began to subside.

Melita, Melita, Melita...

At some stage she drifted into a fitful sleep, but even her dreams were packed with images and impressions. When she woke with a start, memories of the eight years she'd lost battled for recognition at the forefront of her mind. It was like a surge of energy—violent and unrelenting, frightening and inescapable.

No comforting mantra could help her now.

She lay there, her muscles tight, her flesh slick and clammy.

Powerless to stop the flood of memories, she let them come.

Minutes later she had the pieces. All she had to do was connect the dots.

Faye stared into the dark, letting her vision adjust until she could pick out the familiar shapes and curves of the room. She needed something to hold on to, something solid and familiar, as memories slid together. *Keep calm,* she ordered herself, while panic skittered along her spine. *Breathe. Just breathe.*

She pulled in several deep breaths, her throat burning as she forced air into her lungs. First, she concentrated on the rise and fall of her chest, then her child. Her Melita. During the past few days, while getting to know her daughter, Faye had fallen in love with her child all over again. But now, as the memories swamped her, she felt an almost unbearable surge of love for her baby. She wanted her here now. Wanted to wrap her arms around that perfect little body. Wanted to touch her, smell her. To hold tight to the one thing in her life that had made the last eight years bearable.

Her child.

Hers and Enrico's.

Chapter Three

Somehow, she got through Teo's funeral. Even with the weight of truth reverberating around her anxious mind, she got through it. Before she left the hospital that morning, in a smart black suit Enrico had arranged to be delivered, along with equally stylish hat, shoes and handbag, she told both him and the specialist that more fragments of her memory had returned. She still couldn't remember the accident or the few days leading up to it, but the specialist assured her the details would return in their own good time and she was not to force things.

Now, as the sleek black limousine sped toward the airport where Enrico's private jet would whisk them to Tuscany, Faye cuddled her sleepy daughter close. She hadn't told Enrico that her recovered memory had brought into sharp focus the fact that the child sandwiched between them was the wondrous result of their solitary union. Nor would she. Ever. Not when moments after she'd come apart in his arms, he'd told her so cruelly that the whole thing had been a mistake.

"You are very quiet." Enrico's hushed deep tones resonated across to her. "You must be exhausted. As soon as we are on the plane you should sleep." He glanced down at Melita, whose eyelids had lost their battle with gravity. "She is handling it very well."

"I don't think she's taken it all in yet. She doesn't

understand the implications, and she's too young to have to cope with the loss of...someone she loved." Faye couldn't bring herself to say "her father". There had already been enough lies between her and Enrico and, while she never intended for him to know the truth, she wasn't prepared to deliberately build lie upon lie any more.

"It is hard to lose a parent at any age." Enrico reached for a rug on the back shelf of the limo and slipped it around Melita. "You were only a little older when you lost your mother."

"And you were much younger." Faye pointed out.

"Too young to remember."

A mere toddler, Faye thought, still learning to walk on those sturdy legs of his. "But we had fathers who loved us," she said with care. "That was a blessing."

Enrico considered that. "For you and I maybe." He turned then, looked out into the Friday evening London traffic, his formidable jaw clenched, eyes narrowed. She knew he was thinking of Matteo, and how difficult Ruggerio Lavini had made his younger son's life. Ruggerio had made no secret of his adoration of his first-born, given to him by his equally adored first wife. While Matteo, the progeny of his devious second wife, was barely tolerated. As expected, Ruggerio and his third wife had flown in that morning for the funeral and had as quickly flown out again.

Faye's heart ached for both Lavini sons. For dear, sweet Teo, ignored by his father. For tough, uncompromising Enrico, whose love for his half-brother had often brought him into harsh conflict with his father. As far as Ruggerio was concerned, his youngest son was weak and submissive, while his eldest son was the epitome of everything the Lavini name stood for. Strength, honor, integrity.

Ruggerio and Enrico. They were so alike, Faye thought, as

she studied Enrico's harsh profile. Both wickedly attractive, proud, arrogant, demanding. Both possessing a dangerous masculinity, with a ruthless edge shimmering beneath the cloak of civility. Both unshakeable in their belief that power and success was their birthright and family honor was worth dying for.

How she would have loved to have told them that Matteo had valued family honor enough that he'd sacrificed himself for it. But that would mean revealing secrets. The very secrets Matteo had died trying to protect.

They arrived at the Lavini villa just before midnight. It had changed little since her last visit eight years ago, and Faye felt a poignant warmth remembering the wonderful, carefree summers she'd enjoyed there. There was the villa itself, with its huge secluded swimming pool, the beautiful Italian gardens where she and Matteo had played hide and seek as children, the stables where she had ridden her first horse. Then there was the delightful town of Lucca a few kilometers away, where her father had treated her and Matteo to massive ice creams that melted before you could eat them. So many wonderful memories.

She sighed as the limousine purred along the wide, sweeping drive lined with cypress and olive trees. The sixteenth-century, three-storey villa was enchanting. Diffused lighting shimmered from the deep Italianate windows, throwing the villa's terracotta walls into deep and romantic shadow. Water sprang majestically from the fountain in the centre of the circular driveway, while the scents and sounds of the night seduced with their magic.

"It has been a long time." There was a slight accusatory edge to Enrico's voice as they pulled up at the entrance. "But you will find little has changed."

"It has been too long," Faye agreed, too tired to rise to his challenge or look too deeply into the reasons she had stayed away. The main reason being the man who lifted her sleeping child from the back seat of the car, cradling Melita against his chest as he carried her into the hallway.

Faye's heart tumbled at the sight of father and daughter...and froze with guilt that neither would ever know it. As weary as she felt, it didn't stop the surge of self-reproach. She tore her gaze from Enrico's back and followed him into what she always thought of as a small ballroom rather than a hallway. Cream marbled floors and soft terracotta walls glowed from lighting cast by the Murano glass chandelier dominating the wide space.

Enrico stopped briefly to nod and mutter something in Italian to the couple who had bustled forward as they'd entered the villa, then climbed the stairs with a still sleeping Melita in his arms.

"Welcome back, *Signora* Faye." Carla Gianni, wearing her customary black dress and perpetual expression of woe, grabbed Faye in a bear hug, jolting her still-sore ribs. "Oh, such a dreadful thing. But we take care of you, Giovanni and I." She waved a hand to where her husband was in the process of retrieving their bags from the car.

"And your poor *bambina*," she continued, her arm still around Faye who she hustled toward the staircase. "Oh, such a tragedy. But we take care of you both."

Faye forced a smile. She loved the old couple who had been with the Lavini family since before Enrico was born. They were loyal, trustworthy and kind.

"Then we're in the best possible hands," Faye said, and gave one of Carla's a squeeze. "How are you both?"

"We do well enough. But," she began, in a conspiratorial whisper. "*Signor* Enrico, he work too hard. It no good for a man to work all the time. Now you here you must take him in hand. He always did take from you what he would take from no other."

Faye turned to Carla, but before she could reassure her that Rico never took anything from anyone, they entered a charming, feminine bedroom. Custom-made to satisfy a little girl's every desire, with its soft pink bedspread and floaty white voile curtains. Dolls were propped against the pillows, as well as on the white sofa with its fluffy pink throw. On a dressing table lay an ornate silver brush and comb set surrounded by colorful baskets and tins. A bookcase housed a small library of children's books, while a state-of-the-art computer sat with DVDs and games piled high.

"It's beautiful," Faye said to Carla as she moved into the room. "Who does this belong to?" She already knew it wasn't a child of Enrico's. During one of his visits to her at the clinic she'd asked him outright if he'd married or had a family. With her recovered memory came the realization that although he'd answered in the negative, there had been many women eager to share his life and provide him with heirs. Faye had kept abreast of that both in the tabloids, where his name was linked with various actresses or supermodels, and via an old school friend who lived for a while in Florence.

"*Signor* Enrico arrange for room to please the little one. The decorators they left just a few hours ago." Carla bustled forward to help as Enrico lay Melita on the bed. "Now, you let me put the *bambina* to bed," she said, nudging Enrico out of the way. "You go down to kitchen and enjoy late supper I prepare for you. Go," she instructed, when neither of them moved from the bed, but stood staring down at the sleeping child.

Faye couldn't bring herself to leave Melita. She was tired,

she told herself. That was why she felt vulnerable and somehow superfluous as Carla undressed her daughter, cooing words of comfort as Melita whimpered in her sleep. It was only Enrico's gentle touch on her arm that made her move with some reluctance from the room.

In the kitchen he pulled out a chair and motioned for Faye to sit. She tugged in a breath. "This is all very kind of you, but it's too much."

Enrico pushed a plate with tomato bread and olives in front of her. "What is too much?"

"Melita. You had a room decorated for her." Faye waited until his gaze met hers. "We're here just until my memory returns in full, Enrico. Until I can get things sorted out. I don't want us to be a burden and I certainly don't want Melita getting used to having everything she wants. It's not realistic and...well, there need to be boundaries."

"For her or for me?" His eyes held hers in challenge.

"For all of us." She made herself hold his gaze, wondering if like her, he was remembering their one night together. With not-quite-steady hands, Faye reached for the pitcher of Carla's specialty hot chocolate and poured some into two white mugs. "This is temporary, Enrico. A few weeks at most."

"Then the child will have plenty of time to enjoy her room." A flicker of annoyance crossed his face. "You cannot take proper care of Melita until you are fully recovered, Faye. As much as you hate me, even you must see that."

Her eyes widened. "I don't hate you."

"Why else do you find it so hard to let me help you?" When she didn't answer he folded his arms across his chest. "It makes sense that you remain here until you can tell me about the accident that killed my brother. I want to know why a great deal of money was found in the wreckage. I want to know why you were both flying back from Edinburgh alone, without your daughter, who it appears had been left with some stranger." His nostrils flared slightly. "I want to know, Faye."

"I...I can't tell you. I don't remember." Her heart tore with fear and frustration. "But I know I would never leave Melita, and as for the money, what money? I don't know what you're talking about."

"Enough money to have gotten you out of that stinking flat."

Beneath the confusion and anxiety pumping through her system, Faye felt the slow burn of indignation. "That *stinking flat* is our home. Some of us don't need every luxury money can buy to be happy, and my daughter *is* happy and deeply loved, she doesn't need her head turned by solid silver hairbrushes and dolls that cost the earth. I don't want her discontented when we return to London."

"Discontented?" Enrico repeated with ominous calm. "Because she is living in some dingy apartment with no heating and damp, cracking plaster?" Slowly, he shook his head. "My, what a *prima donna* you have raised."

His heavy sarcasm deepened her anger. "There is heating." She kept her voice deliberately low. "And for your information the bathroom ceiling is being repaired."

"The whole place should be condemned," he muttered, his expression fierce.

Faye wanted to retaliate, but a sudden weariness swept over her. She knew from experience that to argue with Enrico required strength. "I don't have to justify any of this to you, it's my business. I understand you want to know about the accident and as soon as I remember anything I'll tell you." Well, she'd tell him what she could afford to tell him. "Now, can we please talk about something else?"

"Like what?"

Faye's fingers tightened around the mug as she took a sip of chocolate. "Like how wonderful this is," she said, grasping for something, anything, to stop the clutch of guilt tightening her chest. "Perhaps I can convince Carla she's known me long enough to give me her secret recipe."

Faye glanced up from sipping her drink and saw Enrico fingering the edge of a plate. The shuttered expression made him look tired. Which was hardly surprising, seeing as he'd been running his business from London this past week, arranging a funeral, visiting the hospital twice a day, supervising Melita's schedule, making arrangements for them to come live with him in Tuscany... Not to mention grieving for his brother.

She felt ungrateful for questioning his kindness and almost forgiving of his arrogant ways. It would have been hard, impossible almost, if she'd had to manage this past week without his help.

"I didn't mean to sound ungrateful, Enrico. It's just—"

"I understand." He pushed away the plate he'd been fingering. "It is late and you have had a long day. Go to bed."

The curt, non-negotiable dismissal had her temper at simmer point again.

"I'm more than capable of making that decision for myself, thank you." She sounded like a petulant child, but her excuse was she felt frighteningly vulnerable and alone. Scared. Unbalanced. Like she had to grasp control of something. Anything. Even a childish retaliation.

"Of course." He said it with such reasonable calm it made Faye's antenna pick up. "Because you are very good at decision-making are you not, Faye?"

"What does that mean?"

He raised his eyebrows. “Choosing to live in squalor rather than sorting out your differences with my brother for one.”

“Teo and I decided to live apart a long time ago.” Faye put down her unfinished mug of chocolate. “It was easier for me to move out, and I wanted to stay close to Melita’s school.”

“Even if it meant living in an area infested with drug dealers and God knows what else?” Exasperation made his eyes glitter. “Tell me why the hell Matteo did not find you somewhere to live. It was his duty as a husband and father. Or were you trying to make a point, Faye? Trying, as you always do, to show how independent you are? Which is fine if you are the only one to suffer, but you had a child to consider. You should have put your child first.”

Faye stared at him, all weariness burning away as her chest thumped with the injustice of that accusation. “I always put Melita first. And the flat wasn’t in a bad area, on the contrary, people were very kind. It might not have been a palace but it was...” All she could afford, she wanted to say. A place where her child could be safe.

How she’d love to wipe that superior sneer off his face, make him swallow his words. But to do that would mean revealing things she could never reveal.

She snapped her lips together.

“If you were too stubborn to demand Matteo’s financial support, why the hell did you not come to me?”

Because I would have had to tell you the truth, she thought miserably. Because you would have pushed and prodded until one revelation led to another...then another...

“I didn’t need anyone’s support. I managed by myself.”

“So I saw.” He cursed under his breath. “It is unthinkable for a Lavini to live in such a place.”

The sheer arrogance in his tone snapped her restraint. "I see eight years has done nothing to rid you of that unbelievable conceit. Do you really think I would have come to you? Do you honestly think I would have lowered myself to ask you for help? Come crawling on my hands and knees just to hear you say..."

"Hear me say what?" he prodded, when she remained silent.

"That it was your *duty* and *responsibility* to help me." A dull ache settled in her chest, a deep longing for something she would never have. His love.

He would have helped her had she come to him, that was never in question. But she wanted more from him, more than he would ever be able to give her.

The harsh reality of it tightened her throat and she swallowed.

"You expect me to act in a different way?"

"No." She let out a resigned breath, stroking her hand over her hair. "Because that's who you are, isn't it, Enrico? Always the honorable, dutiful man. You'd always do the honorable thing, wouldn't you? Whatever the cost to yourself."

His brows drew together. "I am not sure you intend that as a compliment."

Faye laughed softly as she got to her feet. She was bone tired and wondered how her legs were able to hold her up. "I'm not sure what I'm saying right now, or what I mean. Just ignore me."

She took the remains of her drink to the sink and bent to slip the empty mug into the dishwasher. As she straightened she felt him come up behind her.

"You are exhausted," he said. "I will show you to your room."

The scent of him, musky and male, trickled over her, pushing long ago memories to the surface. It was tiredness that made her feel dizzy, she reasoned. It was the aftermath of traumatic events that made her sway.

"Easy now." He caught her, his fingers curling around her upper arms to steady her. Gently, he turned her around. "Are you all right?"

She couldn't look at him, couldn't chance he would see the need swirling in her eyes. It was exhaustion making her feel this way. After all this time, with everything that had happened, surely she should be over him.

But, as her pulse raced and her skin burned, it seemed she wasn't. Not that she would ever let him see. Ever let him know.

Avoiding his gaze, she stared at his throat. That big, solid, muscular throat. "Yes, I'm all right. I don't know what's the matter with me."

When he showed no signs of releasing her, she looked up. In his eyes she saw understanding, mixed with a tenderness that made her throat constrict. "You buried your husband today," he said. "Whatever happened between you doesn't change that."

Tears threatened, and she wished he would release his hold and put a stop to this ridiculous and inappropriate need whipping through her. But even when he did, the feeling remained.

"Now," he sighed, stepping back. "At the risk of being reprimanded, I would venture again that you are tired and need to go to bed."

Recognizing the nearest he'd get to offering an olive branch, she flickered him a watery smile. "I'll let you get away with it," she said, turning toward the door. "Just this once."

Her room was next to Melita's. Just as feminine, if more

adult, in soft blue and cream. Enrico stood at the threshold, looking as if one step across it was tantamount to decadence. "You have everything you need?" He waited until she nodded. "Then get a good night's sleep."

Faye listened as he went down the hallway. When she heard his door close, she hurried next door.

Melita was in her usual deep-sleep position, arms sprawled over the pillows, one pajama-clad leg outside the duvet. She looked peaceful and content and Faye thanked God for it. She was also thankful for the relationship her daughter had known with Matteo—casual and occasional, but loving and kind. At first Teo had taken on the role of surrogate father with an ease and affability that befit his caring nature. But the deception had eaten away at him, serving to make Faye feel guiltier with each passing year. Until...

Leaning forward, she brushed renegade strands of shoulder-length hair from her daughter's warm forehead, hair as dark as her own was fair. Melita believed Teo was her father and the knowledge of that weighed heavy on Faye's conscience as she watched her child sleep. Teo's visits had become shorter and the duration between them longer, something else Faye was now grateful for. At least Melita wouldn't have to mourn the loss of them.

With a gentle kiss on her sleeping child's cheek, Faye went back to her room. She looked at the cases Enrico had arranged to be packed and shipped over but, lacking the strength or inclination to sort through them, sank down onto the bed.

She shuddered in a deep breath and let it out again. She felt drained and desperately alone.

The sense of desolation was a mystery. She and Teo hadn't shared anything these last few years. Not even friendship. It wasn't something they had decided, something they had sat down and discussed. But the slow, insidious destruction of their friendship had begun, she believed, from the moment they agreed to deception. It had eaten away at them both, each in different ways, but none less potent than the other. They had come to resent each other, and each other's secrets and lies.

The very thing they wanted to protect had become their nemesis.

For Teo, the protection of his secret proved worse than the outcome he feared. And for her? Retribution came when she was at her weakest. When there was nothing left but to face her demons...even as she battled to hide them.

She only prayed that fate, and Enrico, would allow her to continue living the lie.

Chapter Four

"And I swam across the pool twice and Uncle Rico said he would teach me to swim underwater." Face flushed with pleasure, Melita chattered happily as Faye poured her more orange juice. "And I can almost do a backstroke, can't I, Uncle Rico?"

Opposite Faye at the poolside breakfast table, Enrico nodded before taking a swig of black coffee. The child was a delight. Happy, enthusiastic and eager to learn. He'd planned an activity-packed day for her, hoping to keep her young mind off the tragedy of the past week. Aside from a couple of references to Matteo, she didn't seem unduly affected by her loss. He found it strange she referred to her father as Teo, but these days it wasn't unusual for children to address their parents by their given names—even if he didn't care for it.

His gaze slid to Faye. Whatever had gone on between her and his brother, it was obvious his loss hit her hard. Her eyes, that beautiful lavender blue, mirrored her every emotion and had always pulled at some protective part of him. It was no different now, he realized, because he wanted to shake the shadows from them. Make her understand that as long as there was breath in his body she would be taken care of. Although they could never become close again, not after...

No. He would not think of that night. Not now. But he

would make damn sure she and her child wanted for nothing. It was little enough, but he could do that for her. For his brother.

What in heaven's name was Matteo thinking allowing Faye to take his child from him? How could his brother simply discharge his responsibilities to his family? Allowing them to live in that hovel of a flat.

Matteo had loved Faye from the moment he'd seen her, and realizing that, he himself had steered clear. Until she'd turned from gangly schoolgirl to... Well, whatever in hell she had turned into. All he knew was one summer she had swept into his orderly world and sent lust spiraling through him, pushing him down a slippery path that eventually caused him to betray the brother he'd spent most of his life protecting. The brother who'd lived in his shadow, wanting nothing but recognition and acceptance from their father. The brother who'd demanded so little from life...until he'd seen Faye.

Enrico's thoughts were interrupted by his housekeeper bustling across the patio, her sights set on the little angel whose welfare had overnight become her most pressing concern.

"Come, *bambina.*" Carla swamped Melita in a fluffy white towel. "If you are to go riding we must get you dressed."

Melita, who'd instantly taken to Carla, put up no argument. Her eagerness for the riding sessions Enrico had arranged with his stable staff had her tugging Carla toward the house.

Faye pushed back her chair. "Excuse me. I have to go and help Carla."

"No need." Enrico sipped his coffee. "She is capable enough."

Faye bristled at the mocking tone. "I'm not suggesting Carla isn't capable, just that Melita has never ridden before and I want to make sure she knows what the ground rules are."

He lifted a straight eyebrow. “Ground rules? For riding?”

“I don’t want her to get hurt. She needs to know there are certain things she mustn’t do.”

“And my staff will ensure she knows them.” He settled back in his seat and pushed a hand through hair still damp from his swim. Faye felt her stomach curl. There had always been something incredibly exciting—dangerous—about Rico when his hair was wet and slicked to his skull like that. It made his eyes even more powerful, edgier, like honed steel. And his cheekbones...the hard line of his jaw...

“And what about me, *cara*?” Those powerful eyes narrowed. “Do ground rules apply to me?”

Faye watched a renegade droplet of water trickle from his hair, along his throat, tangling in a whisper of chest hair before disappearing beneath a black tee shirt.

She hadn’t meant to swallow. But somehow, all she could think of was how magnificent he was, how wonderful it had felt when she was in his arms that one time. Just that one time...

“Well?”

She shuffled in her chair. “This is your home and we are your guests. Ground rules apply only to my daughter and myself.” The sun burned into the top of her bare arms and she ran her fingers over her warm flesh. Her insides fluttered as his gaze followed the light stroke of her hands.

It was mortifying he unsettled her this way. On some level she still felt like the naïve girl she’d been eight years ago. Still reacted to him the way she had on that night when he’d taken her to heaven, then shattered her heart.

If she allowed herself to react to him that same way now, she had only herself to blame. Her focus during this enforced time with him should be on ridding herself of these ridiculous and inappropriate feelings once and for all.

Of course, he wouldn't tolerate being shut out of her life again. Not anymore. Not with her and her daughter being his *duty*, his *responsibility*.

How she hated those words.

But if duty and responsibility were his only reasons for wanting her here, then two could play at that game.

"Perhaps we ought to spend a few moments confirming what your rules are," she said lifting her chin. "Just so there's no misunderstanding."

Frowning, Enrico put down his cup. "No rules apply here. This was Matteo's family home and as such becomes yours. The fact you saw fit not to visit since your marriage makes little difference."

She hadn't remembered his gift for easy sarcasm, but could hardly blame him for it. Not only had she stayed away from the villa, but had asked Teo to instruct him to stay away from her. For the sake of her marriage.

In truth, she'd played on his remorse, his inevitable self-reproach. But in her desperation she'd convinced herself it was for Enrico's own good. That her deceit was justified on moral grounds. A nice fat lie tied up with a shiny bow. *Satin lies* her mother used to call them. Not intended to be malicious, or meant to cause harm, but untruths just the same. And wrong. Very wrong.

Her mother would be mortified...ashamed.

Unable to face him, Faye lowered her head.

He stood, pushing back his chair with the scrape of steel against stone. "The doctor will soon be here. We should—"

"Doctor?" Faye looked up. "I don't need to see a doctor, not for a couple of weeks. The specialist said I would be fine as long as I didn't overdo things." In fact he'd said how lucky she was, that her physical injuries were light and with rest she should enjoy a rapid recovery. Her memory, he considered, would return when it was good and ready.

Enrico moved behind and held the back of her chair. "Your blood pressure needs to be monitored and your injuries examined on a regular basis. There is no point protesting, *cara*," he added, as she looked over her shoulder at him and started to do that. "He is already en route."

She stepped away from him as he went to catch her arm. "Oh, right. There are no rules I see. Just as long as I do what I'm told, is that it?"

He caught her anyway, wrapped his fingers around her upper arm and steered her forward. "You have suffered a major trauma. Do not expect me to apologize for wanting you observed." His low voice echoed off marble as they stepped into the villa's air-conditioned hallway. "You would do best not to fight me on this as you will not win. Best save your energy for other battles. No doubt there will be many."

His patronizing tone grated over her, giving her the strength to shake away his grip. She whirled to face him but the sudden movement, fuelled by a surge of angry energy, made the hallway tilt a little. Her vision blurred and again Enrico gripped her arms.

When her eyes refocused, she found herself looking into his steady gaze. She blinked a few times, allowing the queasiness to settle. "I think I moved too fast," she said, aware of how close they were standing. His breath brushed her face, his chest a warm and solid sanctuary. With considerable reluctance, she tried disengaging herself by planting one hand on his chest and applying pressure. Heavens above, it was like trying to dislodge granite.

"I'm fine now," she lied.

For long seconds he watched her. "And I intend to make sure you stay that way, which is why the doctor will continue to call on you until I am satisfied you are indeed recovered."

Faye bit down hard on her lower lip, rattled not only by the arrogance of his statement but more by the way his physical contact unnerved her. "There you go, talking to me like I'm incapable of taking care of myself." Like she hadn't been taking care of herself and her child since Melita was a baby. Like she hadn't made the decision to put her toddler daughter in day care in order to take a job and earn enough money to provide them both with the basic needs of life.

"You are recovering from a major trauma," he said, releasing her. "What happens if you suffer some sort of relapse? What happens to your daughter?"

The bastard knew just where to hit for maximum effect, and with a grudging acceptance Faye had to admit it made sense to get checked out. She *was* recovering from a major trauma, and she had to keep herself fit and healthy to continue to provide for Melita. She was well on her way to regaining full physical strength and her memory would return soon enough. God, she didn't want to think what might have happened to her child had she suffered more serious injuries. Although that wasn't true. She knew what would have happened. The exact same thing that was happening now. Enrico would have taken over.

Which was the reason she was trying to act like she didn't need a doctor. Why she wanted to pretend everything was okay. Because then she and her daughter could get home to London, she could start living her life again. Without him in it.

Then he'd never find out...

"I'll see the doctor," Faye said, lifting her chin. "But while I'm grateful for your hospitality, you will not issue me orders and you will give me the courtesy of letting me make my own decisions for my own welfare."

His hands slid into his pockets. "Having evidenced the outcome of some of your decisions, it seems your welfare might best be left to my control."

"*Your* control?" Heat stung her cheeks. "Just where do you get off? You really are the most arrogant..." Faye shook her head. "I'll see the doctor, Enrico," she said, before turning and heading for the stairs. "But afterwards I'm packing our bags and taking my daughter back to England."

His voice, low and accusatory, drifted to where she was halfway up the stairs. "How will you live? My brother's estate will be tied up in legal red tape for some time. There needs to be an investigation into the cause of the accident before the insurance company pays out and until then his assets will be frozen. I repeat, how will you live?"

Satisfied he couldn't see her face, Faye allowed herself a wry smile. Matteo's *estate* likely consisted of a myriad of debts to some less-than-salubrious characters, and if any kind of insurance existed, it would be a complete surprise to her. Not that she'd give Enrico the satisfaction of knowing any of it. She owed Teo that. She would keep his secrets. As he'd kept hers.

Her fingers curved around the banister. In truth, she wasn't sure quite how she'd manage. It still hurt to lift her arms and her ribs were far too sore to heft boxes and stock shelves. But she could go back to work and maybe do admin and ring up sales.

Prepared to tell Enrico to mind his own business, she turned to face him. He stood at the bottom of the stairs, his hand on the newel post, one foot on the second tread. How she'd like to wipe that arrogant expression off his face by telling him his half-brother had long ago gone through all his assets and had been reduced to borrowing from…who knew where? But promises made between friends went deep. Enrico Lavini wasn't the only one who knew about duty and responsibility.

"How I live is my business." Faye turned back to climb the remainder of the stairs. "You might feel responsible but you don't have to. I have a good job and I'm more than capable of taking care of myself and my daughter."

She hadn't heard him negotiate the stairs but he came up behind her, his fingers around her wrist halting her. "A job?"

Faye looked over her shoulder, his position two treads down from her making them at virtual eye level. She looked to where his hand encircled her wrist, but when he didn't remove it she met his gaze. "There's no need to look so horrified, Enrico." Sensing that for once, she had the upper hand, she kept her voice low and controlled. "Women do work, you know, it's the twenty-first century."

"You have a child." His face was thunderous. "You should have let Matteo provide for you. There was no need for you to work."

She laughed then. Couldn't help it. Both because she had most often been the one doing the providing, and because Enrico was so hopelessly old-fashioned in his appreciation of a woman's wants and needs.

"You shouldn't concern yourself." She gave him a sweet smile, resisting the urge to pat his cheek. "I enjoy my work and Melita attends an excellent school with good after-school facilities."

He swore, something harsh and not for delicate ears. Her Italian wasn't bad, but she was certain she'd never heard that particular word from him before. Perhaps just as well if the heat shooting from him was anything to go by.

"We need to talk about this." His fingers tightened around

her wrist. "After the doctor's visit we will discuss it. But there is no way you will return to England, neither will you work. As for my niece attending after-school facilities..."

He glared at her as if she were proposing child slavery, then with an abrupt turn went back down the stairs. Faye stared after him. He was the most exasperating, egotistical, supercilious...

"No you don't," she warned, gripping the banister as she hurried down after him. "Don't you walk away from me. I've had enough of this. I'm sick of your demands, of your arrogance. Who the hell died and made you—" Her hand shot over her mouth as he wheeled to face her. "God! I'm sorry. I didn't mean..."

Faye moved back against the railing. How could she have said something that crass? "That was a stupid thing to say. I didn't think...didn't mean..."

All color drained from his face as he stared at her. Then he looked away, half turned, then faced her again. "I am trying to act in your best interests, Faye. Why do you keep fighting me?"

Because she wanted him to act for other reasons. Reasons that weren't primarily duty and responsibility. Reasons that didn't remind her of the words he'd flung at her that night. The night he'd shattered all her hopes and dreams.

"Because you don't listen to me," she said, hating the somber look that had crept into his eyes. "You refuse to even consider what I think."

It was hard to give the words weight, especially when he looked so shattered. She hadn't noticed the pale, sunken skin beneath his eyes before, or the hollow beneath his cheekbones—the marks of his grief. How could she have made such a tactless comment?

After several moments, he gave a weary smile that twisted

her heart and tugged on it for good measure. “Very well, we will talk.” He drew in a breath as if preparing to say something momentous. “I promise I will listen.”

Well, it was momentous all right and Faye’s mouth twitched in response. “I never thought I’d hear those words from you.”

He shrugged. “Stay and you may well hear others that surprise you, an incentive if ever there was one. How can you pass up such a rare opportunity?”

His uncharacteristic humor had her insides melting. Strangely, Enrico in this sort of mood was as dangerous and exciting as Enrico in one of his tough, uncompromising moods. Perhaps even more so.

What on earth was happening to her? Why was she feeling this way? Technically, she was a new widow and feelings like this were inappropriate to say the least, even if her marriage had been a sham.

Yet it was hard to feel anything but a sick yearning as Enrico watched her. He moved closer, not a deliberate movement, more a simple lean. The ground shifted again as his scent—that musky male scent—shimmered over her. She wanted to close her eyes, draw it in, but instead offered a shaky smile. “When you put it like that, how can I refuse?”

The Lavini family doctor checked her out, satisfied she was recovering as well as expected. Faye remembered the gruff old physician from her summers at the villa, from when he’d attended scraped knees or sprained limbs. His grumpy exterior hid a marshmallow centre and Faye promised she would take things easy and call immediately if she needed anything.

Contrary to Enrico’s demands Faye insisted she be allowed to see the doctor alone. She also insisted on joining Enrico and

Melita for lunch in town a couple of days later, arguing the change of scenery would do her good. As he drove them past rolling Tuscan hills, with their patchwork green landscapes and the sun hazily caressing the peaks and valleys, Faye knew he brooded over having his authority challenged and guiltily, she had to wonder if that was why she'd dug her heels in deeper.

As they drove, she made polite conversation. He made polite conversation. Somehow the formality between them felt worse than complete silence or heated disagreements.

Faye was grateful for her daughter chatting happily in the back seat. She had to admit Enrico was good with Melita, tirelessly answering her zillion questions and pointing out interesting landmarks along the way. Some of the tension between them melted a little as they exchanged a wry glance at Melita's tendency to pepper every conversation with horses. She had *really* enjoyed her very first riding lesson ever and hoped—*really* hoped—she could have another one.

Giving in to her infectious enthusiasm Enrico finally assured her that, yes, she could have another riding lesson whenever she wanted and, yes, if she wanted one every day that would be fine.

With a roll of her eyes, Faye turned to look out at the passing scenery. So much for them talking. So much for him listening.

When Melita plugged herself into her private stereo and began singing along, Faye faced Enrico. "You're back to making unilateral decisions, I see."

He glanced over, eyebrows raised. "We agreed she would have riding lessons."

"We didn't agree she would have them every day. Or did we and I just missed it?"

"Now, now, *cara*. Sarcasm does not sit well with you."

Although she fought it, her mouth twitched. “No. You’re right. It sits much better with you.”

Theatrically, he clutched his chest, making her smile.

“Why are you such a control freak, anyway? Don’t you get tired of always running the show, always being right?”

He pursed his lips, as if to consider. “No.”

It made her smile again. “A psychologist could have a field day with you.”

“Or with you.”

She turned and looked out of the passenger window. “I’m not into control.”

“Yet constantly you remind me you need it.”

“A healthy dose of it, not bordering on obsession like yours. I’m a mother. I want what’s best for my child. It doesn’t feel right, having someone else make decisions about her.”

And that was it, Faye realized. It had been just the two of them for so long it was hard to allow anyone else to take over. Let alone Enrico. What if he found out? What if he had the slightest inclination Melita was his? If he was controlling now, believing Melita his niece, the heavens would rock if he found out she was his daughter.

Not that he’d wanted children of his own. He’d made that clear enough.

The truth of it had plunged her into a fraudulent marriage.

“Fair enough.” Enrico looked away from the road just long enough to nod his head toward the back seat. “Perhaps you would like to tell her arrangements have been changed and she is no longer able to take riding lessons.”

Faye’s laugh was mocking. “And be bad, cruel mummy? I bet you’d just love that. Well, as it happens I think it would be good for her to have riding lessons, and had I been given the courtesy of making that decision for myself, I would have been in complete agreement with what you said."

"So, we are having this conversation because...?"

"Because you're a control freak and I'm a doting mother," she said sweetly. "And we're not having a conversation, we're having an argument."

His mouth curved. "But we are in agreement. You have sanctioned my decision, therefore there is no argument."

She wanted to scream. Was there no winning with this man?

Faye was still gritting her teeth as they entered the small town. She welcomed the imminent escape from his restricting presence. She wanted to get out of the car and drag in some restorative, calming oxygen from the tranquil Tuscan countryside.

Melita danced alongside Enrico as they made their way to the restaurant, the two of them chatting with ease and affability. It suited Faye just fine, as it took his attention from her for valuable seconds, giving her the opportunity to massage her still-painful back and ribcage. Rubbing, she watched father and daughter getting to know each other and if her eyes and ears didn't deceive her, getting along amazingly well. As guilt tugged at her conscience, Faye focused on the pretty little terrace of the popular restaurant where the manager greeted them and led them to their table.

Tired and aching, Faye struggled to find an appetite. Even lifting her coffee cup was an effort. When Enrico suggested heading back to the villa she didn't protest. During the journey home, with the sun playing through the windows onto her face and the lull of Melita's happy chatter in the back, Faye dropped her head back onto the cool leather headrest and let her lids drift down.

It felt good to relax, to enjoy the warmth, the gentle rocking of the car. To let go for a while...just for a while...

“I am nothing like my father.” Enrico glared at her, his eyes slits of pure venom. “Nothing.”

She was only seventeen but Faye held her ground, wanting to salvage something from the awful confrontation between Enrico and his father. Ruggerio had said the most dreadful things.

“I just meant that the two of you are both as stubborn,” Faye used her most placating manner. “Why can’t you just sit down and discuss things? I’m sure he didn’t mean it.”

“He meant it well enough. He has always taken any opportunity to hurt Matteo, but this time he has gone too far.”

He looked at Faye, then turned and strode back toward his father’s study. Faye raced after him, fearing yet another altercation. Enrico pushed open the door, stalked to the desk and slapped his hands on its polished mahogany top. With ominous intent, he leaned across it and faced his father. “You apologize to Matteo,” Enrico demanded, his face sharp angles and planes as anger stretched his skin. “You take back what you said and you rewrite your will, or I swear I shall make you regret it.”

Faye came to a stop beside Enrico, placing a tentative hand on his arm. She snapped back when he shook it away and continued to glare at his father. Fear trembled through her, not because she was frightened for herself, Enrico would never hurt her. No. She was frightened at the tension crackling between the two headstrong and volatile Lavini men. Neither of whom would be prepared to back down.

Ruggerio sat back in his leather chair, puffing on his fat cigar. “I’m doing only what your grandfather intended. Leaving the company to my first-born son."

"He never intended Matteo be denied his share, that is your doing."

Ruggerio shifted his powerful frame. He was a big man, his muscular body firm and athletic. He took another long puff on his cigar. "Matteo will have what is rightfully his. Nothing."

Enrico showed his teeth. Faye saw the muscles of his forearms rope as he leaned forward, his hands pressing into the desk. "He is your son!" Barely leashed anger thrummed in Enrico's harsh tone. "Your own flesh and blood."

Ruggerio shot from the chair, mirroring his eldest son's stance as the two faced each other across the desk, nose-to-nose. "He's the product of a scheming woman with one eye on a fortune and the other on any man who promised her a good time," Ruggerio said in a voice thick with scorn. "If it wasn't for a DNA test I still wouldn't believe that weakling is *my* son."

"Believe it," Enrico shot back. "He does not have the streak of mean that runs through your veins, but he has inherited all the good attributes from our grandfather which obviously skipped a generation and completely bypassed you."

"He's a weakling," Ruggerio taunted. "A lightweight who can't fight his battles without his big brother to help him."

"Most of those battles have been at your instigation. You have hated him since the day he was born."

"*Si*, and I'll hate him until the day I die. He'll not see one lira of my money and I've placed a clause in my will to ensure it."

As Enrico grabbed his father's shirt, Faye lunged forward. "*Rico*," she screamed, pulling at his arm. "Don't."

The two men glared at each other, Enrico's fingers showing no sign of releasing their death grip on his father's shirt. Faye gave his arm another tug.

After endless moments, and still glaring at his father, Enrico released his grip and shoved back from the desk. "What kind of man blames his son for his own shortcomings, for his inability to see a woman was playing him along right from the start?"

Ruggerio laughed. "Any kind of man, my son," he said, straightening his shirtfront. "Women will suck you in and then bleed you dry. You won't even see it coming. Do you think for one moment I would have *married* that scheming witch if she hadn't gotten herself pregnant? Do you believe I would have allowed her to milk me of millions of lire in paternity payments? No. At least by marrying the harlot I ensured she got only what I intended she have. Which wasn't much after I tricked her into signing a prenuptial with very small print."

He laughed again, and Faye hated the cruelty in the sound. She stepped forward and wrapped her fingers around Enrico's wrist. This time he didn't push her hand away.

"Rico," she said in the gentlest tone. "Let's go."

She was more than a little surprised when he let her lead him from the study, through the marbled hallway and into the gardens.

He sank down onto a stone bench and laid his forearms across his thighs. "Bastard," he fumed. "I will not let him get away with this."

Faye sat next to him, letting her jean-clad leg brush his. The contact sent a thrill through her body. His profile was strong—the straight Roman nose, the thick black eyebrows, firm jaw—she wanted to trace her fingers over every wonderful feature. Instead, she laced her fingers together in her lap as the breeze whipped her long, blonde hair across her mouth. She brushed the strands away, continuing to watch Enrico.

He turned to face her. “I will not let him get away with this, Faye.”

“I know, but arguing with him won’t help.” She gave a tentative smile, hoping to ease some of the tension emanating from him. “Why don’t you wait until after the wedding next week, he’s probably a bit tense with the build up.”

Enrico scoffed. “More probable he is wondering how he can ensure Alana is in fact what she professes to be. Barren.”

“Rico!”

He raised his eyebrows. “Why so shocked, Faye? That is the only reason he is marrying for a third time. Because his bride-to-be cannot have children.”

Faye shook her head. “Your mother was the love of his life,” she said. “He never wanted children with anyone but her.”

Enrico’s own laugh held all the bitterness he felt for his father. “*Dio*, Faye, you are so naïve.” When the breeze sent hair across her face again, his gaze softened as he followed the movement. “So sweet.”

He lifted his hand and she held her breath. Her pulse raced as his fingers brushed her mouth and caught the renegade locks of hair.

“I’m not sweet,” she said, trembling as he tucked her hair back. “And I’m not naïve. I know what it feels like to be in love and not want anyone else.”

“Indeed?” He dropped his hand and leaned back, considering her. “And who is this lucky man?”

Her cheeks burned under his intense scrutiny, but she wasn’t about to let this chance pass her by. If she didn’t tell him now, she might never get another opportunity. “Someone I’ve loved forever,” she whispered, willing him to see into her heart. To take her in his arms and say the words she’d dreamed of hearing him say.

When his face transformed into that shuttered mask that signaled the emotional barrier was coming down, the realization tore at her heart. He'd seen the signs, recognized that the words she'd spoken were for him, but he wanted none of it.

He didn't want her.

He would never want her.

He would...never...want...her...

"Mummy!" Faye woke to a gentle nudging against her shoulder. "Mummy, are you awake?" Melita stood at the open car door beaming down at Faye. "We're home now."

Her child's smile was warmer than the sun and sleepily, Faye smiled back. "Mmm. Yes, darling, I'm awake." Pushing away the remnants of memory sleep had invited, Faye prepared to haul herself out of the car. She winced as her ribs squeezed and her back tightened.

"Uncle Rico said you've got to go to bed because you're very tired and he's taking me shopping to buy me some new riding clothes."

That got Faye's eyes open. "I don't think—"

"A few clothes, Faye." Enrico appeared at the car door, his hand reaching for hers. "Call it an uncle's indulgence."

Dio! He'd been afforded precious little opportunity up to now. But seeing Faye's pale complexion and the way she tried to hide her physical discomfort, had the accusation sticking in his throat. He'd noticed her rubbing her ribcage and how she'd tried to hide how exhausted she was during lunch. Maybe he shouldn't have forced the issue of riding lessons.

He couldn't imagine how unsettling memory loss could be, especially for someone with her independent spirit. Plus she was dealing with grief, with fear, with a loss of control. He'd whisked her from her home, from her life, without a thought for anything other than he wanted her with him. Truth was he didn't trust anyone else to watch out for her.

But the woman didn't make it easy.

She agreed to rest, but was steadfast in her refusal to go to bed.

"I can rest just as well on the veranda," she argued. "The fresh air will do me good and the sun loungers are as comfortable as a bed."

With some reluctance, he gave in. The fresh air *would* do her good and perhaps put some color back into that translucent flesh. He also gave in because he didn't want her tiring herself any more by arguing with him.

She was still asleep when he and Melita returned from their shopping trip. He pressed a finger to his lips, steering his niece toward the villa where Carla waited for them. Melita skipped off with her many shopping bags, desperate to show off her new riding gear. Enrico made to follow, stopping to lift the light throw that had fallen from Faye's shoulders. Her pale skin glistened, clear and soft and he fought back a flicker of lust as he covered it with the throw. He let his finger skim across the base of her neck, easing away the soft blonde hair that caressed her collar bone. A few itinerant strands lingered at the edge of her mouth.

Dio, that mouth.

Memories stirred, threatening to swamp him. He'd spent a night with her. Just one night. But it had ruined him for any other woman. Perhaps that was his penance.

She had been fresh and innocent when he had taken her, willing enough in her naiveté but hardly old enough at seventeen to consider the implications of it. Just one week before, following an argument with his father, she'd sat next to him and confessed her love for another man—for Matteo—sending a fierce and crippling envy barreling through his system.

Her hair had been much longer then, the silky lengths feathering across the swell of her small breasts, then spearing down to her waist. But her mouth was rich and full, just as it was now. Her cavernous blue eyes had drawn him in like a siren's lure—as they did still. He remembered the way her long legs felt around him, the way her scent had invaded his system, the way her soft breath whispered over his flesh as she'd gasped out his name.

What the hell had he been thinking? He didn't know then, and he didn't know now. His only excuse was that he hadn't been thinking at all. Anger and alcohol had proven a deadly mix.

But now fate had given him the chance to make things right. Of sorts. Maybe by taking care of Matteo's widow and child he could make reparation to his dead brother.

Spellbound, he continued to gaze down at Faye's sleeping form, the lines and curves of her body visible beneath the soft throw. He couldn't stop the memory of how those curves felt beneath his hands, beneath his body. How she'd reached out to him in sensual pleasure, how she'd begged him to take her...pleaded...

Fierce guilt burned through his system, coupled with a brutal desire for this woman who had belonged to his brother.

He fought the images that warred in his treacherous mind. Had she reached out to Matteo in the same way? Had she begged...pleaded...?

He ordered himself to stop before he drove himself into a frenzied hell.

He had no right to these thoughts. He'd had even less right to Faye. All those years ago, when he'd allowed anger at his father to fuel his lust for her, when she'd comforted him, tried to appease him. And how had he repaid her generosity?

With one night of hot, raw sex.

Shame washed over him. *Dio,* when he screwed up he certainly pulled out all the stops. In that one night, in the space of hours, he had broken a promise to Matteo's mother, gotten himself involved in a bar brawl, punched his own father...

And stolen the virginity of his brother's future wife.

Chapter Five

Dining on the terrace the following night, Faye realized she felt much better. She'd slept right through the night and dozed on and off during the day. Her chest was still sore but the pain in her back had eased.

Her insistence on being allowed to help Melita with her bath, read to her and tuck her into bed felt like a small victory and now, sitting across from Enrico, she let a smile play across her mouth.

"You look rested, *cara.*" Enrico sat back, the sleeves of a black silk shirt rolled to his elbows showcasing tanned forearms. His fingers played idly along the stem of his wineglass. "Make sure you do not overdo things."

Faye felt the light evening breeze flutter over the top of her bare arms, then skim across the skin left exposed by her white linen shift dress with its scoop neckline. "I won't overdo things." She sipped sparkling grape juice. "But I am feeling better and I want to do things for Melita. I need to reassure her, heaven knows what's going through her little mind right now." Her words gained a frown from Enrico. "I wish we didn't have to argue about that."

He watched her with that steady gaze of his, the one that made her feel like he knew everything she was thinking while at the same time guarding every one of his own thoughts. He continued the slow stroke of his glass stem. “And I wish we did not have to argue about my wanting what is best for both of you. You are my brother’s widow and Melita his child. If you expect me to back off, to watch you exhaust yourself, you are heading for disappointment.”

Faye looked away as her stomach somersaulted. She should be grateful he readily accepted that Melita was his brother’s child, even if she would spend the rest of her life racked with guilt over her deception. For if he had the slightest inclination Melita was his, Faye’s life would no longer be worth living. If he was demanding and controlling while believing the child he protected was his niece, how on earth would he react knowing she was much more than that?

But how could he not know? Was she the only one who saw Enrico in her—their—daughter? The same sharp eyes that missed nothing, the same proud set of shoulder, the same frightening tenacity. Surely he must have noticed that Melita didn’t share Matteo’s rather timid and unassuming nature.

But then she and Teo had gone to great lengths to make sure he would never have cause to doubt Melita’s parentage. They married almost as soon as Faye knew she was pregnant, making it easy to plant the lie that Melita was conceived on their wedding night and delivered prematurely.

What had she done?

Faye rolled the edges of her napkin as shameful warmth spread across her cheeks “I know you want what’s best for us, and I know you want to protect Melita. Just as you always protected Matteo.”

His scoff had her gaze lifting to clash with his. “It’s true,” she dropped the napkin. “You always looked out for him, despite everything that’s happened you always looked out for him.”

"Which is why he told me to stay away from you both," he mocked. "Or perhaps he was concerned my brand of *looking out for him* would involve taking his wife to my bed again."

Faye felt the flush creep down to her throat. "Don't be ridiculous."

"What? Are you going to deny he warned me to stay away from you? That he did not know we had slept together? That he did not want to beat the hell out of me?"

"And if he'd beaten the hell out of you, would it have made him more of a man in your eyes? Perhaps then he would have reached those high family standards, perhaps then he would have been a true Lavini."

"Well, I am sure if my future bride told me another man had just taken her virginity I might have delivered a punch or two."

Faye was trapped and she knew it. If she lied and said Teo didn't know they had slept together, Enrico would demand to know why his brother had instructed him to stay away from Faye. But if she confessed the real reason, that Teo had suggested marriage to their mutual advantage and demanded that Enrico keep his distance in order to protect the secrets at the heart of their pact... Well, she couldn't confess that.

Although her heart pumped, she made herself meet his gaze. "I'm happy to say your brother wasn't like you."

"Evidently not." He sat back, sipping his wine as he subjected her to that fierce scrutiny at which he excelled. Then his accusatory tone resonated through the Tuscan night. "I assume he did know about us?"

Faye raised her chin. In this, at least, she didn't have to lie. "Yes. He knew."

His nostrils flared, then he gave a slow nod. "And I was banished from your lives."

Faye smoothed her palms over the soft white linen of her dress. "You were hardly banished, and you said yourself it was natural enough for Teo to want to retaliate somehow. He chose to avoid trouble, rather than confront it. That was just his way. He thought that asking you to stay away from us would avoid further unpleasantness. That was his way of handling the situation."

"Perhaps more effective than a physical blow." His eyes narrowed, but he kept them on her. "Had I been wise enough to adopt his approach, to avoid trouble rather than confront it, events might have taken a different turn. Had I walked away, the repercussions might have been less dramatic."

One look at his expression and Faye knew he was referring to the night he had thrown a punch at his father, the night she had gone to placate him. The repercussions he referred to had nothing to do with being instructed to keep away from her, and everything to do with the night they'd had sex.

Had I walked away...

As her throat contracted, she reached for her water glass. "Your father provoked you," she said, wanting to put the emphasis on the argument with his father, rather than what came afterward. "You were just sticking up for Teo."

Silence reverberated through the clear night. The cool water she sipped made Faye's flesh chill. She had to stop where her mind wanted to go, stop the memories of being in Rico's arms, of how his tough body felt against hers, the play of muscle, the feel of skin, his special scent...

"What I did was unforgivable."

Faye couldn't look at him. It was as if he'd read her thoughts, been able to see into her mind. She shook her head and looked down.

He was about to apologize. To confirm that what they'd

shared had been a mistake. She couldn't bear that. Couldn't bear to know he had spent all those years regretting it.

Had I walked away...

"It's all history now," she said in a determined tone, reaching out for the crystal water jug. "None of it matters."

Her hand wanted to shake as she poured herself water, but she wouldn't allow it. How dare he think to apologize? She didn't want it then, and she didn't want it now.

"I'd like a tour of your vineyards," Faye said, returning the jug to the table with a not-too-gentle thump. "Perhaps tomorrow, if you can spare the time."

Something rustled in the bushes near the terrace, but neither one of them looked toward the direction of the sound. When Faye looked up, Enrico was eyeing her through narrowed slits. "I'll be flying to London tomorrow." He draped an arm across the back of his seat. "I have a meeting with the lawyers to go through Matteo's affairs."

Although she had anticipated the legalities, she hoped for later rather than sooner. "What time will we leave?"

His black brows drew together. "We?"

"Of course." Her own eyebrows lifted. "Teo was my husband and I'm responsible for putting his affairs in order." She offered up a silent prayer that those affairs wouldn't be as bad as she feared they would, although common sense—and past history—indicated otherwise. She'd wanted to do this on her own, at least then she could safeguard her husband's privacy. But some part of her knew Enrico would insist on accompanying her.

Carla hurried toward them with coffee and a silk wrap for Faye. She fussed over them before bustling back to the villa.

Enrico eased his coffee toward him. "You are not fit enough to travel, and there is nothing to be gained from taxing yourself further by dealing with legal matters. I will handle anything that arises."

Faye's stomach jumped. Would he? Would he handle knowing she had lied to him for years? Kept the cruelest of secrets? Would he handle knowing that his brother had gone through every penny of the inheritance Enrico had fought for on his behalf, and then some?

Going through Matteo's affairs would raise all sorts of questions. Questions Faye didn't know if she would be able to answer.

"I am fit enough to travel. Besides, the flight to London might jog my memory."

"The flight over here had no such effect."

"No, but I feel better now, stronger and—"

"Melita needs you here. You said yourself she is feeling vulnerable and needs her mother. Your leaving her now will do little to restore her peace of mind."

Oh, the sneaky bastard. "Then I'll take her with me. We can drop by my neighbor's and check on the flat, and Melita can visit with Blaster. In fact, there's absolutely no reason for you to be involved at all." One glance at his tight features indicated she had a fight on her hands. "It's *my* business."

His eyes flashed. "It is family business. *Lavini* family business."

"And I'm a Lavini, and Teo was *my* husband."

"In name only, it seems."

While Faye ignored the comment, she had less success ignoring the ripple of muscle as he shifted, folding his arms across his chest. She chastised herself, then focused on the matter at hand. Silently she acknowledged that there was no point in insisting she be allowed to handle Teo's affairs on her own—Enrico would just wear her down. If she was honest, she wasn't sure she was tough enough to handle both him, her physical recovery and all the legalities just yet, so she would have to settle for having him involved.

"What time will we leave in the morning?" she asked with a sigh.

He didn't say anything as he came around to hold her chair. Faye glanced back at him as she stood. "What time, Enrico?"

He caught her wrap as it slipped from her shoulders, his fingers brushing hers as she reached for it at the same time. The sharp thrill of contact made her legs weaken. His mouth was inches from hers and she was powerless to stop her eyes zeroing in on its fullness. She remembered how wonderful his lips felt on hers...warm, firm and determined... How easily they had taken her from trembling teenager to wanton woman.

Was it her imagination, or did he keep his hand on her shoulder a moment too long? Did his eyes darken as they looked into hers? Did his mouth part slightly?

His fingers pressed into her flesh as he positioned the wrap on her shoulder, the movement breaking the spell her imagination was weaving. She suddenly felt awkward, embarrassed and...ridiculously aroused.

As he stepped back, Faye pulled the wrap tight around herself. Not that she needed it. Her body was burning up. But her pride needed it. Especially when he lifted his chin in an arrogant sweep, an imperious expression shadowing his face.

She raised her own chin. "You didn't answer my question," she said haughtily. "What time do we leave?"

He pushed his hands in his pockets. "When we are ready."

Exasperated, Faye mumbled a goodnight and headed upstairs. Once in her room she made for the French windows.

Leaning on the balcony rail, she looked out over the gardens toward the vineyards.

Having Enrico there when the lawyers delved into Matteo's affairs was not an enticing prospect. He'd poke and pry into every single thing. While she might be able to fudge around some things, there was no way to avoid others. Especially those things best left alone. Enrico's finding out about Teo's lack of financial savvy might well prove the least of her worries. But she would make sure Teo came out of it with some dignity.

Faye clutched her wrap as the cool night breeze skittered around her. She drew in a breath, wishing her full memory would return so she could find answers to the questions that haunted her.

Why had she been traveling to Scotland with Teo? What was that money for?

Another business deal gone wrong? But where had the money come from?

She pressed her fingers to her temple. If only she could remember.

Then she would take her daughter and go home. She'd be happier away from Enrico, happier when she could get on with her life without him in it.

Faye tried to disregard the pesky inner voice that taunted, *Liar.*

Right now she had other things to focus on. Enrico believed she and his brother had married for love, that they had a child together, had built a life together...

If only he knew the truth.

But he never could. Never would. She'd make sure of that. Going to London tomorrow would help to finalize this whole mess once and for all.

Motivated to protect secrets and lies, Faye prepared for bed.

Downstairs, a lone lamp cast a solitary glow over the papers on his desk as Enrico leaned back in his chair and sipped brandy. Hearing Faye confirm his brother knew about them had torn open that slice to his heart that had never really healed. The sick feeling in his stomach that came from betraying the brother he had vowed to protect.

He'd always known Matteo knew the truth. Why else would he have insisted Enrico stay out of their lives? Faye would have told his brother. Lying would have played on her conscience, eaten her up. Her total lack of guile was something he admired most about her.

He tipped back his glass, but found the brandy did nothing to quell the emptiness coiling in his stomach.

How his brother must have hated him. Not only had Matteo lived with the injustice of paying for his mother's devious nature, but also with the unfairness of birth order that made his elder brother the lone beneficiary of the Lavini wealth. And then, as if that were not enough, he'd suffered that same brother's treachery. All the years spent trying to shield Matteo from the wrath of their father had come to this.

The protector had become the destroyer.

Enrico stared down at the empty glass in his hand, remembering how he and his father had argued in this very study where he now sat ruminating. On the eve of Ruggerio's third marriage to a woman barely old enough to make it legal.

He'd tried one final time—unsuccessfully—to get his father to recognize Matteo in his will. He'd been on the verge of threatening to boycott his father's wedding, realizing as he opened his mouth to do so that he was in danger of pressing his father's most volatile of buttons.

Blackmail.

In the quiet familiarity of his surroundings, Enrico scoffed. It seemed he had more of his father in him than he cared to admit. Hadn't he dug his heels in when his last lover had tried to coerce him into marriage?

He'd been on the brink of going along with it, knowing that the terms of his father's will passed the Lavini wealth only to the first-born child of each subsequent heir. If he failed to produce such an heir, the family assets would pass to a syndicate when he died.

Ruggerio knew Enrico would never allow his beloved grandfather's company to be scattered, broken into pieces and strewn amongst strangers who cared nothing for honor and integrity. The very attributes upon which his grandfather had built the foundations of his fortune. So Ruggerio had ensured that Enrico danced to his tune, and the clause in his will meant Matteo would never assume the mantle of heir even if the unthinkable happened to his first-born son.

Enrico stared at the photograph on his desk. His grandfather's face smiled back at him, a lifetime of morality and decency etched into the noble lines of his aged skin. A lifetime of love for the grandson who held his heart.

While he would fight tooth and nail for the company his grandfather had built, Enrico knew the old man would never condone his grandson accepting a marriage of convenience to keep it. His grandparents had adored each other. Perhaps it was an awareness of that love that had stopped Enrico entering into a marriage that would provide anything less, although he'd cared deeply for the woman who'd shared his life for the best part of a year. He'd told himself it was because she'd pushed too hard, because she'd tried to trap him with constant reminders of Ruggerio's will. In truth, he'd refused to admit to himself that the real reason he withdrew from the marriage plans had more to do with his feelings for Faye.

Enrico raked his free hand through his hair. *Dio,* the number of times he'd wanted to go to her in London. The number of times he'd talked himself out of going to her.

Keeping away was the hardest thing he had ever done. Harder still after he'd received news of her separation from his brother. But he'd kept away.

Guilt was his restraint. The knowledge that he wanted to steal from his brother the one thing Matteo ever had that was truly his.

Matteo hadn't wanted a share in the company. Ruggerio had done a good job over the years, convincing his youngest son that his mother's trickery and deceit gave him no right to a share of the Lavini wealth. But Matteo had wanted Faye.

Enrico stood, taking his empty glass to the cabinet where he set it on the silver tray. It was no use brooding on what might have been. All he could do now was ensure Faye and her child were secure and that involved investing whatever assets Matteo had left. Faye couldn't refuse to use any of the money now that Matteo was dead, as she obviously had done when he was alive, the stubborn woman. No. He'd make sure she didn't have to work, that she was settled somewhere better than that excuse of a place where she currently lived. This was the last thing he could do for his brother, and by God in heaven he'd do it right.

He walked back to his desk, switched off the lamp and headed out of the darkened room.

Standing in the kitchen just after eight the next morning, Faye ordered herself to stay calm.

"He leave even before I can arrange his breakfast." Carla

said, shaking her head as she answered Faye's question as to Enrico's whereabouts. "I get up early because I know he is flying to London, but he is already gone."

"He's *gone*?"

"*Si.* Giovanni, he drive him to the airport." Carla lifted her hands in exasperation. "What about his breakfast? I ask Giovanni. But, no—" She shook her head again. "What does it matter? What does it matter if he does business on an empty stomach?"

With a click of her tongue, she busied herself getting Faye coffee and preparing a place for her at the huge rustic table.

"And the little one," Carla continued, obviously in full flow as she waved a hand for Faye to sit, "a typical Lavini. She is up with Enrico, chattering of horses and such things. Not a thought for food. But with her I put my foot down. No horses until you eat, I say. So she eats."

While she was grateful her daughter had been cared for, Faye could barely contain herself. Her mind went into overdrive as anger battled with anxiety. How dare he leave without her when she had told him she was going with him? What secrets would he unearth without her there to smooth the way?

"Can Giovanni drive me to the airport? I need to be at the meeting with the lawyers."

Carla shook her head. "It is not possible. You are still weak and Enrico he said you must rest."

"I feel fine." And right now she didn't give one hoot about what Enrico said or wanted. "Is Giovanni able to drive me?"

"Vanni is in town doing errands. He will not be back until later this evening when he collect Enrico from airport."

"Then I'll have to drive myself." Faye stood, anger and panic making her face burn. "Can you ring and check on flight times to London while I go and get Melita?"

Carla visibly paled. "This is not possible."

Faye froze on her way out of the kitchen. "Why not?"

"Enrico, he said not allow you to leave villa today."

"He said what?" She made herself take a breath when Carla's big eyes widened. "Well, Enrico doesn't get to say where I go or what I do." Of all the pompous, arrogant... "Don't worry Carla, I'll tell him you couldn't stop me from—"

"He has taken the keys to his car and has forbidden anyone to drive you or to arrange a taxi," Carla said in a rush, then snatched up a tea towel and frantically wiped the worktop. The tremble of her hands had Faye's anger deepening. How dare he do this? And how dare he put poor Carla in the firing line of what he knew would be her outraged reaction?

With considerable effort, Faye damped down her temper. She'd store it, then let it erupt when she was face-to-face with the one person who bloody well deserved it.

"Very well." Her throat ached with barely leashed rage. "In that case I'll just ring the lawyers and cancel the appointment. If Enrico has a wasted journey, that's his problem."

But a call to the offices of Streetman and Jarvis did nothing to appease her simmering fury. The meeting was scheduled in a location Nathanial Streetman's PA couldn't—or wouldn't—reveal to Faye. Although the PA promised to get a message to Mr. Streetman and Mr. Lavini, if Faye would like to leave one.

Oh, she'd like to leave one all right. But it wasn't for this young woman's ears.

Realizing she'd get no satisfaction from being able to talk to Nathanial Streetman directly, Faye left a message demanding that the meeting regarding her late husband's affairs be postponed until she could return to London and deal with the matter herself.

She spent the day anticipating either a furious phone call from Enrico, or one from Streetman and Jarvis rescheduling the meeting. Neither call materialized.

Although anger was her constant companion, Faye damped it down to make way for pride as she watched her daughter ride, swim and chatter away about things in general. Then it would erupt again. What kept her sane was the thought of confronting an equally furious Enrico on his return home from an aborted meeting and a wasted trip to London.

Tough.

He should have thought of that before taking it on himself to stick his nose into her affairs.

As the clock in the library struck nine Faye heard the rumble of tires on the drive. She put down her book and went to the window. Enrico stepped from the car saying something to Giovanni before striding across the portico and into the villa.

Faye met him in the entrance hall, his footsteps echoing eerily across the marble floor as he made straight for the stairs. He still wore his suit jacket, but the knot of his tie was loosened, his white shirt open at the neck. Shadows played around his jaw sending his chiseled features into relief.

She snapped his name as she stormed after him.

"Not now," he barked, shrugging off his jacket and throwing it across his arm.

A sick dread swallowed her temper as she watched him effortlessly negotiate the stairs two at a time. His body, broad and muscular, always emanated an aura of power and strength, but now there was tension and ferocity in his movements that shot panic through her body.

Faye's stomach rolled. She'd expected him to come home

annoyed, irritated. But not this. This was exactly the reaction she anticipated if he ever discovered what she had kept from him for all these years. He wouldn't shout, or make demands. It was too huge for that. No. He would go into that place inside himself where nobody else could reach. The place where he needed to shuffle and sort his feelings into something he could control and manipulate. Only then, from a position of strength and power, would he react.

Faye pressed a hand to her stomach. He'd found out. Somehow he'd found out.

But he couldn't have, she assured herself, hurrying up the stairs after him. There was no way. Nobody else knew. Only she and Matteo had known.

A chill swept through her, freezing her in place as she reached the top of the stairs. What if Matteo had put something in his will? A confession of sorts, a final act of conscience.

Craving the sanctuary of her room, but knowing she wouldn't have a moment's rest until she knew for sure, Faye headed for his bedroom.

Her heart pounded against her ribcage as she knocked on his door. Without thinking she opened it before he answered.

His jacket had been flung across a leather settee in the alcove by the window, the sheer disarray of it confirming the aggressive action. He stood at a small desk, glaring at his laptop with such venom that Faye expected the power raging from his eyes would be enough to boot it up. Her legs weakened as she watched him yank at his tie and toss it away. It flew missile-like and landed on his jacket.

Faye swallowed through a dry throat, forcing herself to stay where she was while every instinct screamed at her to run. His tense energy flicked over her like a sharp whip, increasing her desperation to escape. But she wouldn't. What helped her own courage was the fact he must have known she was there but chose to ignore her.

Attack, she remembered, was the best form of defense.

"You had no right to take off like that without me." Because her arms had started to shake she folded them. "This is my business. It wasn't for you to interfere without my agreement which you know you didn't have."

Enrico yanked out the chair in front of his desk. "In the morning," he warned, an icy edge to his tone. "I do not want you here right now." He sat, scooting the chair closer, and began tapping at the keyboard.

His curt dismissal proved the last straw in a day where her emotions seesawed between anger, anxiety, frustration, worry, hurt. You name it. She had experienced it all and now everything combined into this swirling maelstrom burning in her chest.

"You won't dismiss me like I'm one of your employees. Nor will you treat me as if I'm a stupid woman who needs someone more capable to take care of her affairs."

His fingers continued to fly over the keyboard. Still he didn't look at her.

As heat pumped into her face, she took a step forward. "You won't ignore me. I demand an explanation and an apology."

Only the sound of the tip-tapping of the keyboard echoed in the large room.

"Enrico!" She stormed forward to stand in front of his desk. "Do you hear what I'm saying?"

He continued to glare at the screen, but his fingers stilled. In the silence Faye heard the thump of her heartbeat, the creak of leather as Enrico straightened and folded his arms. When he looked up his eyes pierced right through her and made a mockery of his seemingly casual pose. She remembered that look, and her insides pitched aggressively.

She had been witness to a real loss of Enrico's temper only twice in her life. Once, one long-ago summer, when she and Matteo had snuck off from his charge and gotten hopelessly lost during a visit to nearby Lucca. They eventually wandered into a local police station and asked for help, only to have Enrico storm in an hour later and tear them to pieces. It had upset Faye for days after that, although she'd never let Enrico know how miserable she felt having experienced the full extent of his wrath.

The only other time she witnessed his fury unleashed was...*that* night...when he and his father finally came to blows over Ruggerio Lavini's cruel dismissal of his younger son. She'd hated seeing Enrico so incensed and had tried to console him. That very act of consolation led to the reason she now stood in front of his desk, trembling a little as he glared at her while settling back in his chair.

Surely his mood meant only one thing, Faye realized with sickening dread. That he knew. Somehow he had found out.

"I have no intention of debating the issue of your hurt feelings at this hour." Enrico advised in a menacing tone. "I have other matters to attend to. As I said, we will talk in the morning."

"No!" Faye slammed down the lid of the laptop as he made to start work again. "You talk to me now." *I've been out of my head with worry all day*, she wanted to say. *I've been out of my mind you've somehow found out.*

His eyes narrowed as he stared at the laptop, then he made a show of examining the fingers she'd almost severed. "If it is that important to you then go ahead. Talk."

The unexpected capitulation took the wind out of her sails and for a moment Faye couldn't think of a word to say. It was obvious he expected her to start things rolling because he sat there with a look of strapped tolerance on his face.

That look helped Faye find her voice. "I want to know why you went against my express wishes. Why you prevented me from settling my own affairs. None of this is Lavini business, it's personal, and you had no right to exclude me."

He ran long fingers over his shadowed jaw. "I did not consider you were sufficiently recovered for such an ordeal. As I could handle things without your attendance I decided not to put you through it." He folded his arms again. "In any event it was a wasted exercise."

Merciful heaven. Her message had got through. The meeting had been cancelled. His bad mood had nothing to do with discovering the truth and everything to do with an aborted journey and the waste of his time.

Faye breathed easy for the first time that day. "I'm sorry you've had a wasted day but you deserve it. When I reschedule the meeting with the lawyers I don't want you there."

Pushing away from his desk Enrico stretched out his legs. "It seems we are at cross purposes. I've had a very productive and informative day."

"Informative?" The chill returned, sweeping through Faye's limbs.

"Your message was received but was of little consequence. As executor of Matteo's will my attendance was a prerequisite and in the light of your current memory loss—"

"You're the executor of his will?"

"I am." He fixed her with a steady gaze. "Is that so surprising, Faye?"

Surprising didn't come into it. "I find it almost unbelievable." He was the last person Faye would have expected Teo to choose as executor of his will.

"Unbelievable? Because he dismissed me from your lives, warned me to stay away from you?" Enrico's brow tightened. "Yes, perhaps unbelievable in that context. But Matteo's inheritance following his mother's death required that he make a will. He was eighteen if you remember and at that time we were on speaking terms. Hence my role as executor. I gather he never found reason to change that." The look he gave her was pure contempt. "Is seems he considered my bedding his future bride of secondary importance to my expertise on legal matters."

Faye wrapped her arms across her chest as an invisible knife plunged into her ribs. "That was uncalled for and...cruel."

"Not cruel." He pursed his lips, considering. "Realistic."

He stood and came around the desk, still watching her. He faced her, leaving mere inches between her thumping heart and his broad chest. "Why didn't you tell me, Faye?"

Oh God.

The juxtaposition of his soft voice and hard expression made her insides tumble as anxiety churned with dread. "T-tell you?"

He moved sideways, making her shift until her back was against his desk, in effect boxing her in. "You must have known I would find out at some stage. What did you hope to achieve by keeping it from me?"

Because her legs felt hollow and her heart was about to jump right out of her chest, Faye reached back, gripping the edge of the desk. "I...I thought it was... I thought..." She cursed the way fear made her voice tremble, stealing the words from her head. She was scared, terrified. There was no escape. Not from him, with his big body all but pressing against her. Nor it seemed, was there any further escape from the past. From the truth.

"You thought?" Enrico prompted, lifting his eyebrows. When she shook her head he blew out a breath. "I cannot believe you would protect Matteo when he would see you destitute."

Faye swallowed, her mind playing through all the questions niggling in her head. What would happen now that he knew he was Melita's father? And what did it have to do with Teo leaving her destitute?

"That was bad enough," Enrico went on. "But to have made no provision for his daughter's future." He turned then, walking over to a walnut cabinet in the alcove by the window.

His departure gave Faye much needed breathing space to fathom out what he was saying. Did it mean...? Yes, yes, it did. He didn't know. Relief poured through her as she eased herself away from the desk. He hadn't found out. He didn't know he was Melita's father.

She closed her eyes and took a steadying breath. When she looked up again he was lifting a decanter from the cabinet. He turned, holding it up to her.

Faye nodded. A shot of brandy would go a long way to settling her nerves, and her jumpy stomach. The worst of his mood seemed to have passed, but she wasn't fooled it couldn't just as quickly flare again.

He came over carrying two glasses and motioned her toward the leather settee. Faye scooped up his jacket, folded it and set both jacket and tie neatly across the back of the settee. Then she sat, accepting the brandy he offered.

Enrico took the wing chair opposite. "It seems there's no estate left to execute," he said, contemplating the amber liquid.

"No money. No property." His gaze lifted accusingly to hers. "But then you already knew that."

Unable to face his reproach, Faye looked away. It was awful Matteo's memory was tarnished by such a legacy, especially when he'd tried so hard. But what could she say? How could she handle this to make sure she left Teo with some pride, some respect?

Enrico seemed to read her thoughts. "Perhaps you should start from the beginning."

She expected to see contempt as she looked back at him, at the very least a kind of mocking challenge. If she had, she might have insisted it was none of his business, that she didn't have to explain anything to him. But instead she saw understanding, a flicker of compassion, and it had her throat constricting.

She took another sip of brandy and lifted her chin. "Everything was fine at first. Teo used his mother's inheritance to dabble in relatively successful business projects, not wildly exciting but we ticked over. Then he got involved in plans for this huge leisure centre which included a multiplex cinema, shops, wine bars. It was a disaster from the word go. There were numerous delays in planning applications and tender documents, then there were construction problems and staff difficulties. Teo wouldn't give in." She looked up, ventured a tentative smile. "You know what he was like, gently stubborn and even a little reckless when he had the bit between his teeth."

Faye waited, hoping for some sort of acknowledgement, but Enrico's serious expression didn't flicker. She took a breath and went on.

"It was soon obvious to everyone involved that the project needed a complete rethink, but Teo believed in it and insisted on plying good money after bad. His business partner lost interest. Teo was given very poor counsel and his accountant wasn't up to much." Again Faye waited, but it seemed Enrico wasn't yet ready to fully sympathize with his brother's plight.

"Then his partner decided to pull out and Teo thought he could do better on his own." Faye's insides shook as she remembered that worrying time. "For a while he did and things seemed to settle down. Then interest rates went up and he had borrowed heavily. He had no option but to sell some of our assets and, well, he tried hard to make things right—"

"He sold your home? He put his wife and baby at risk?" Enrico shook his head vehemently. "No business is worth that."

"He was desperate." Faye felt the heat in her chest. If only Enrico knew how hard Teo had struggled. He was no businessman, despite his Lavini blood. He was an artist, a poet. She felt hugely responsible for allowing that gentle soul to take on her problems. "He had nowhere to turn."

Enrico's nostrils flared. "He could have come to me."

"You know he would never do that."

Enrico stood and went over to the window. "He could have told me he was about to plunge himself into bankruptcy," he said, with his back to her. "That his wife and child were about to be put out on the streets." He turned, glowering at her. "*Dio*! Why didn't you come to me? Why didn't *you* tell me the truth?"

"I couldn't. Things were bad enough between Teo and me. Had I come to you—" which she wouldn't have done in a million years, "—it would have made things even worse. And you keep exaggerating things. We were never destitute, or about to be put out on the streets."

"What happened to the rest of the money?" Enrico demanded. "While he lost an extraordinary amount of his inheritance on questionable business projects, it doesn't account for the whole of it. I saw the paperwork, Faye, so do not try and deceive me." He placed his hands on his hips. "I want the truth."

Faye toyed with the finger that once held her wedding ring. "Please don't insult me. You already know, or have at least guessed. It was one of the reasons you fought with your father..." She was about to say *that night* but stopped herself. "Why do you insist on dredging it all up now? It makes no difference to anything."

"He was a damn fool, and you were no better."

Faye's chin shot up. "I beg your pardon."

"You knew he had a gambling problem. Why the hell did you not safeguard your own security by insisting money be placed in your name?"

"For the same reason you fought with your father on his wedding day and demanded that Teo share your inheritance. Weren't you as foolhardy? You knew of his gambling and yet you still insisted your father sign over the bank to you both on equal terms."

"That was different. It was a matter of family integrity."

"It was no different. You felt responsible for Teo, you always have. You wanted—demanded—your father put Teo's name in his will and when he refused you...you hit him."

The color drained from Enrico's face. "The subject under discussion is that of your late husband's recklessness."

She wasn't about to let him off so easily. "Then why did you insist your father bequeath the business to both of you if you knew Teo was likely to gamble away his share of the profits?"

"Because it was fair."

"And because you always felt guilty that your father favored you. You felt you owed something to Teo."

"And you, Faye? What did you owe my brother? Perhaps you were stricken by guilt that you gave me what should rightly have belonged to him, and therefore allowed him *carte blanche* where money was concerned."

Faye swallowed down the lump that lodged in her throat. "That had nothing to do with anything," she lied, painfully aware it had everything to do with everything. But she wasn't about to argue the rights and wrongs of the loss of her virginity right now. "It was only fair Teo be allowed to handle his own inheritance. It was his mother's money. You seem to forget that I came into the marriage with very little."

"Your father was a victim of the stock market. He had sound enough business acumen but was unlucky. It was totally different from consciously gambling away your family's security, both on the card table and through questionable business projects."

Faye curled her fingers tightly around the brandy glass. "There's nothing to be gained from debating all this now. What's done is done."

"On the contrary. Just what are you planning to live on when you return to England? There was no insurance, Faye. No endowments. Nothing."

"Then I'll manage the same way as I have for the past few years. I have a good job and I might even start my degree. I can do it by distance learning and my employer said he would sponsor me."

"Where will you live? Surely you don't intend to remain in that—"

"It's perfectly adequate. And our neighbors are lovely."

He shook his head. "I will arrange for something more suitable."

"You will not. It's my choice where I live and I will make the decisions I think are best for myself and my daughter."

"Melita is my niece and a Lavini. In the absence of a father she is my responsibility. As are you."

A determined fierceness lit his eyes and Faye almost crumbled beneath it as guilty pressure pressed against her heart. *In the absence of a father...*

"I understand you want a part in Melita's life and I won't deny you that," Faye offered, knowing she had to appease his sense of familial duty. "But that means something like seeing her at Christmas, taking her on trips to the zoo."

Enrico's laugh was short and cruel. "I want more than that. Melita is my blood."

With an even stronger bond to him than he could imagine, Faye thought miserably.

She nodded, then swallowed the last of her brandy. "Perhaps we can iron out the details another time," she offered, knowing full well she was too tired, too emotional to argue with him and come out on top. Her hands shook a little as she placed her empty brandy glass on the table. "I'd like to take Melita shopping tomorrow. We need some things."

He stood when she did. "I will arrange it."

"Thank you." Faye stepped around the small table at the same time he did. Their bodies collided. Instinctively Faye reached out for the safety of his chest, her palms hitting hard, solid muscle. His hands gripped her arms.

"Oh." It was all she managed as she was drawn into him, his fingers tightening and digging firmly, but gently, into her flesh. She stared at his throat, at the small hairs escaping his unbuttoned collar. All at once she remembered how that dark hair arrowed down his torso, sheathing lean, honed muscle. How wonderful his abdomen felt beneath her hands, the strength of him, the power of him...as he'd thrust into her...

What was she doing?

Her legs weakened at alarming speed, her lungs tightening to such an extent she barely drew breath. She tried to push away, or maybe she just thought she did, because she was still held tight against him and, heavens above, it felt amazing.

Better than her memories, better than her dreams. Here. Now. He was all she ever wanted. All she ever would want.

But it could never be, because if he knew the secrets she kept hidden he would despise her. She couldn't bear that. Couldn't bear for him to hate her.

"Rico..." she whispered, watching the storm rage in his eyes. She ached to press her fingers to the hard line of his jaw, to trace the fullness of his mouth.

"It has been a long time since you called me that," he said gruffly. "A long time."

He pulled her closer, gripping her so hard she would have winced, except then he would have let go. She wouldn't chance that.

"Yes," she murmured, letting her hands creep up his chest. "A long time. So much has happened."

His gaze slid slowly over her face. "Too much, perhaps."

"Perhaps." Faye reached up, brushed the back of her fingers over his cheek feeling the rough graze of stubble. "Rico."

He looked at her mouth, drawing closer and closer. "I am undone when you call me that."

A delicious shiver swept over her as she watched his mouth descend, imagining the warmth of his full lips as they covered hers. She lowered her eyes...waiting...waiting...and felt...

Nothing.

Just a cold emptiness as Enrico pulled back, locking his arms to his sides. "I apologize." His face went hard. "That was inappropriate. I can only assure you it will not happen again."

Desire, tempered with embarrassment, burned her face. "Don't apologize." Because I can't bear it. I can't bear your cool assurances. "We're both tired and things are hardly normal right now."

Enrico rammed his hands in his pockets. "As my brother's widow you command my respect."

"Well, nothing happened, did it?" Faye snapped, irritated by his stoical forbearance while she felt like falling in a puddle at his feet. "Certainly nothing to reproach yourself for."

He scoffed. "I have spent the past years reproaching myself. Do you think I have forgiven myself for what happened between us? You were young and innocent. Barely a week had passed since you told me you were in love with my brother. I had no right to seduce you."

God. When she'd confessed to him she was in love with someone, he thought she'd meant Teo. "I knew what I was doing," she snapped, confusion and irritation making her head spin. "I knew exactly what I was doing."

"You meant only to placate me, but I took advantage of the situation. Do not think I hold myself above reproach for the breakdown of your marriage. I am to be held accountable."

"Why would you believe that?"

"You told Matteo what happened between us. It is not something a man can easily forgive, the knowledge that his bride slept with another man, his brother, on the eve of their wedding."

"It wasn't the eve of our wedding. Teo and I never planned to marry." It was out before she could stop it, and the flash of Enrico's eyes alerted her to her error. "I mean, when you and I...we...Teo and me, we hadn't actually set a date. I could hardly be termed his bride." She averted her gaze as guilt whipped at her flesh. "You had nothing to do with the breakdown of our marriage."

"How easily you lie, *cara*," he said gently. "Something you learned in the years we have been apart?"

Yes, oh yes, and she hated it. Hated all the lies. All the deceit. But whatever she did, she couldn't win. She might agree that, yes, he was responsible for the breakdown of her marriage, although not in the way he thought. Then he could keep her on that pedestal, the one that exonerated her from any wrongdoing in their lovemaking while placing all the blame at his own door.

But if she confessed her marriage was a sham, a mere marriage of convenience, she would have to reveal the reasons for it. That finding herself pregnant with his baby had made her determined to keep her pregnancy from him. Hadn't he told her that he would never allow himself to be tricked into a loveless marriage the way his father had been? That he never wanted a child of his to be subjected to the excruciating pain of knowing how much his parents hated each other? How much his father loathed his mother?

Aside from all that, she would have to reveal Teo's secrets. She would never do that. It was the one thing that had terrified Matteo.

Well, Enrico would never hear the truth from her lips. Teo had kept her secret for all those years. She would afford him the same privilege.

"I'm not lying," Faye told him, as her heart squeezed painfully. "You had absolutely nothing to do with the breakdown of our marriage."

Chapter Six

For the next few weeks the days slipped into an easy rhythm. When Enrico was around, Faye was forced into recuperation mode and when he wasn't she kept busy helping Carla with light duties around the villa or spending her time in the library. She had taken on the task of cataloguing the extensive and enviable Lavini collection of first editions and rare volumes into some sort of order.

A call to her employer back in England informed her all was well and she was to focus on her full recovery. Several calls to her neighbor confirmed her flat was okay and Blaster, much to Melita's relief, had settled in his temporary home quite happily.

Melita was virtually glued to the horses and spent all available time helping out in the stables. Enrico had arranged for her to start at a local school the following week. Although only a few weeks remained before the summer break, he thought it best she attend school rather than be tutored at the villa, as she was missing her friends back home. It was one thing in which they were in absolute agreement, although Enrico insisted on footing the bill for the exclusive private school. Faye had put up a fight but, realizing she was hardly in a healthy enough financial position to argue, eventually gave in. But it niggled at Faye, who secretly vowed she would find some way to repay him for everything. As soon as her full memory returned, and she was given a clean bill of health by the doctor, she would get back to her real life. Then she would set about paying Enrico back. Every single euro.

Although he spent an inordinate amount of time away on business, when he was around, Enrico addressed Faye with a polite courteousness that belied the underlying tension between them. They were rarely alone, but when they were, he cited business as an excuse to disappear into his study.

Late one Friday afternoon Faye closed the leather-bound catalogue and rubbed her eyes. A cool breeze from the library's French windows whispered around that part of her legs not covered by white cropped trousers. She hadn't done too well with the cataloguing that day, constantly distracted by the knowledge that Enrico was returning from a four-day trip to Vienna. Her stomach gave that familiar, if unsteady, roll at the thought of seeing him.

She looked around the large library with its floor-to-ceiling books, drank in the smell of polished leather and the scent of pine drifting in on the breeze. Faye closed her eyes. It was in this room that she'd tried to placate Enrico after that awful fight he'd had with his father mere hours after Ruggerio's wedding. Guests had mingled on the patio, in the gardens, and early evening scents drifted through the open doors and windows. Faye remembered how she'd tried to close them, how she'd wanted to keep Enrico's furious ranting from reaching the wedding guests.

But he wouldn't have any of it.

"Leave them open," he'd demanded, his anger fuelled by the whisky he'd downed. "Let them all hear what a complete bastard he is."

Faye hurried toward the doors anyway, smoothing down the silk of her lilac shift dress as she went. Her hand reached out for the brass handles when Enrico came up behind her. Growling, he threw his arms around her waist, pulling her back sharply against the rock-hard strength of his muscular body.

"I said leave them open."

He tugged her backward into the library, kept his arms around her waist as he rasped into her ear. "Stop trying to protect him, *carina*. Let his illustrious guests know the kind of monster he is."

All Faye's senses were on full alert, her chest tightening until she managed only tiny gasps of air. As Enrico's warmth pressed up against her back, she was aware of several things simultaneously—the solid wall of his muscled chest, the feel of his powerful arms encircling her waist, the way her bottom fit so easily into the cradle of his hips and—oh my—the rock hard length of him pressed tight against her.

Faye prayed he wouldn't let her go, because there was no way she would remain upright at that moment without his support. She wanted him. Wanted him to keep holding her like this. "He...he's not a monster," she managed, choosing words she knew would provoke him to keep hold of her and maintain that exquisite heat melting her system. *His* heat. She lifted her hands to her waist and placed them over his. "Rico..."

He spun her around, so fast she felt dizzy with the movement. "The bastard wants to deny his own flesh and blood what is rightfully his. Whose fault was it he let himself be manipulated, tricked into marriage by a woman who used whatever means she could to trap him? If he was unhappy with the arrangement, too bad. He had a duty to the woman he impregnated. Even if he felt no love for her he had no right to take it out on Matteo."

Faye had never seen him so incensed. She'd been party to arguments between him and Ruggerio before, too many times for comfort, but she'd never seen him like this.

He stared down at her, his chest heaving as he pulled in breaths. Fury shone in his eyes while his skin stretched tight across his face, highlighting all those sharp angles and planes.

She wanted to reach out to him, stroke her fingers across the angry jut of his firm jaw, smooth back the silky black hair that fell bohemian-long to touch the crisp white collar of his shirt. But then he gripped her arms, so tightly she jerked back. "Be on my side for once, Faye." He'd lowered his voice, but anger still roared through it. "Just once."

"I...I'm always on your side." Her voice trembled as she stared into the depths of those charcoal eyes, the whip of danger about him only serving to increase the sharp thrill of anticipation. She wanted to tell him how much she loved him, that whatever happened she was his. Always his.

But he scoffed, released her, then strode over to the drinks cabinet in the alcove.

"When you can tear yourself away from my brother." He lifted a crystal tumbler and filled it with whisky. "I am surprised you did not leave with him after the ceremony, go back to London. Do you not have some packing to do?"

Faye ignored the sarcastic taunt. "I don't leave for university for three more weeks. I've got plenty of time to pack." She wanted to go to him but didn't trust herself. She wanted him too much. Wanted to help him curb some of the anger that still pulsed through him. "You don't need any more to drink," she said softly. "Rico, you've had enough."

He turned, saluted her with the glass and watched her with fierce insolence as he downed the contents. "I am just getting started." He turned back to the drinks cabinet. "Who knows, I might just get mad enough to give *Imperatore* Lavini another punch he will remember."

Fearing he might do exactly that, Faye hurried over to him. "Rico, stop it!" She pulled the glass away from him, then the decanter, placing them both down on the silver tray with a firm snap. "That's enough. You're acting totally out of character and you have to stop now!"

She saw heat flare in his eyes, saw him steady himself as he swayed then his whole face softened as one side of his mouth kicked up. At that moment, he looked sexily rakish. His ruffled hair teased his collar and the sight of all that jet-black silk against the white fabric made her mouth water. He'd long ago disposed of his tie, and a sprinkle of dark chest hair escaped from the unbuttoned gap at the top of his shirt.

"Well, well. *Mio uccello del fuoco.*"

The way he said it, the heat in his hooded gaze, how he leaned in her direction, made Faye's pulse skip. But he was just teasing. If she really was *his firebird* she might have had a chance with him.

Suddenly, she couldn't stand his mockery. "You need strong black coffee." Faye busied herself by placing the top back on the decanter and wiping the spill of whisky against the tray. "Come with me into the kitchen and we'll get some down you."

He caught her wrist as she moved past him. "Stay with me, Faye." His fingers tightened gently around her flesh. "I do not want to be around other people right now."

She looked up, captivated by his soft, almost pleading tone, and the steady grip of his hand on her arm. *I'll stay with you forever*, she wanted to tell him. *I'll do whatever you want.*

He smiled that drunkenly crooked smile and her heart shot right into her throat. "Yes, well, it's probably best we stay away from the kitchen anyway. The staff will still be fuming from the extra work you've given them clearing up the mess you made in the bar, and administering first aid to the unfortunates who got caught in the fray."

"What did you expect me to do? Stand there and let him get away with it? He insulted Matteo."

"Technically, he insulted Teo's mother."

"Same thing." He ran his fingers through his hair. "The woman was his wife, Faye, not *a scheming whore,* and she was Matteo's mother. The dead demand respect as much as the living."

He strode to the window, took a couple of deep breaths, then closed the French doors. Faye watched as he slipped the lock and pulled across the sheer gauze curtains, effectively blocking the outside world. A quiet thrill skipped through her system. He wanted privacy. For them? *Stay with me, Faye,* he'd said. *Be on my side for once.* Surely that meant only one thing. That he wanted her.

Faye stared at his broad back, at the way his shoulders filled the white silk shirt to such perfection. She watched him rake long fingers through his hair.

A quiver of fear trembled its way through her body. She'd waited years for him to say he wanted her, to tell her all those things she'd dreamed of hearing from him. But now, as the silence buzzed between them, she felt years of longing and frustration tighten her chest.

Say something, she begged silently, as he stared through the sheer curtain toward the Tuscan hills beyond. *Say something, anything... As long as you don't break my heart and say you don't want me.*

Long moments passed until Faye could bear the silence no longer. "Rico?"

He pushed his hands into his pockets. "She asked me to

take care of Matteo," he said, without turning from the window. "She knew she was dying and she asked me to take care of him."

Faye tried to focus. "Teo's mother?"

"*Si.*" He turned then and faced her across the quiet space. "I promised her, Faye. She lay there, hours away from death, with the monitor flashing and tubes in her arms, and I promised her I would do everything in my power to ensure his happiness."

Which was why he fought so hard, Faye realized. Why he fought passionately against his father's treatment of Matteo. Why he wouldn't accept that he couldn't get through to his father, make him change his mind about refusing to give Matteo equal share of the family legacy.

Not only because he loved his brother, but because he'd made a promise to a dying woman.

In that moment her love for him soared to the heavens, threatening to burst her heart wide open. He was so honorable, so full of integrity. She had fallen desperately in love with the most wonderful man. And he was talking to her, *really* talking to her. Even though it was the drink loosening his tongue—the first time she'd ever seen him drunk—he was opening himself up, sharing his feelings with her.

Faye blinked away tears as emotion swamped her. She hated seeing this champion of injustice, this lone warrior against his father's treachery, disconsolate and morose.

Desperate to console him, she swallowed back her feelings. "You've done everything you can. You can't change your father's mind. All you can do now is make sure you give Teo what is in your own power to give."

His mocking laugh reverberated around the room. "My father has made certain I have zero power in that respect. He has put clauses in the contract which ensure I am powerless to give Matteo money from the estate."

"Well, Teo has his own inheritance from his mother," Faye soothed, watching Enrico's jaw sharpen. "He can invest that and—"

"It is little enough, and my father would strip him of that if he could. Besides, it is hardly the point. Matteo has a right to equal share in the Lavini fortune."

"Rico..."

"I am this close, Faye." He shot out his hand, indicating a small space between his thumb and forefinger. "*This close* to telling my father to go to hell."

But Faye knew he never would. He would never put the Lavini Bank at risk from outside predators. He would never allow his beloved grandfather's legacy, born of blood and sweat, to fall into the hands of strangers.

Enrico moved toward the drinks cabinet, but halfway there he stopped, sinking down onto a nearby leather couch instead. "I do not know what to do, Faye." He leaned forward and dropped his head in his hands. "I do not know what else to do."

Her heart felt heavy as she joined him on the couch. "Your knuckles are scraped," she said, noticing the red gashes on his right hand. "Let me have a look."

When she reached for his hand he waved her away. "It is nothing." He dropped his head back and closed his eyes.

She eyed his wounds, but didn't try to touch them. "There's nothing else you can do now. When it comes down to it, it's your father's decision. As wrong as that decision might be—" she added quickly, when his eyes snapped open, "—you have no choice but to accept it."

His nostrils flared. "I have a choice. Make no mistake about that."

Fear slithered down Faye's spine. "What do you mean?"

"My father's actions are driven by hate, the result of years spent in a loveless marriage with a clever and manipulative woman. That will not happen to me, Faye. I will not spend my life bitter and resentful because a woman played me for a fool. I will not be like him." He shook his head, his hair brushing against the back of the couch. "*That* is the choice I make."

The tone was matched by the grim set of his jaw, the sharp angles and edges of his cheekbones as anger tightened his flesh.

She kept her tone deliberately low. "Then your father's accomplished much more than denying Matteo his rightful inheritance."

He sighed deeply, all the fight seeming to leave him as he slumped back against the soft leather. "Like what?"

"He's turned you into a cynic, someone prepared to live his life looking over his shoulder to make sure he doesn't get duped."

His laugh was humorless. "That is just the way it is."

"No. It's the way you're choosing it to be." And she hated, loathed and detested what was happening to him. "What are you going to do, Rico? Vet everyone who comes into your life? Make them fill out a questionnaire so you can analyze their intentions, just to make certain they don't compromise your desire for self-preservation?" Faye moved off the sofa, aware her voice was rising until she was all but shouting at him. "And what about the people who care for you? Are we supposed to just stand back and watch you turn into some...some...embittered, lonely man who pushes away everything good in his life?"

One corner of his mouth kicked up in a wolfish curve. "I do

not plan on being lonely."

The slumberous heat in his eyes meant there was no mistaking his meaning, and with one simple statement he managed to ruthlessly quash all her hopes. Faye couldn't bear it anymore. Couldn't bear the mockery he was making of her stupid, naïve dreams. How could she have even thought for a moment that he'd wanted her, that he'd cared for her the way a man cared for a woman?

"Then I hope you'll be happy, Enrico." She hurried to the door, all her dreams crumbling as she went. "I hope you'll be happy with equally miserable women who feel the same way you do about using people."

She had to get away from him. Had to get away before she made a complete and utter fool of herself. But her traitorous eyes filled, the first tear falling as she reached for the handle.

She felt him behind her even before her bleary eyes focused on his hand as it reached to cover hers.

"Stay," he demanded. "I need you here with me."

Faye tried to tug at the handle, but his fingers tightened around hers and made any movement impossible. The tears flowed freely now and she didn't care. It was a toss up who she hated most at that moment. Him or herself. How cruel he was to put her through this. One moment telling her he planned to keep the company of as many women as it took to keep loneliness at bay, and the other telling her he needed her. And how stupid was she, knowing that and yet still wanting him so badly? How could she want nothing else than for him to take her in his arms and love her?

His hands closed over her shoulders, pulling her back against his warm muscled strength. Faye closed her eyes, lifting a hand to wipe the worst of the dampness from her cheeks.

"No, *cara*," he whispered, his warm whisky-scented breath

caressing her neck. "I do not deserve your tears."

Slowly he turned her to face him.

There was an odd sort of tenderness in his expression, remarkable perhaps because of the fierce tension vibrating from him. The combination thrilled her, making her lift her mouth to his in a primitive offering.

"*Cara...*" His thumbs brushed over her cheeks, gliding down to stroke along her expectant lips. "*Mia bella*, Faye."

Faye scarcely drew breath as she waited—silently pleaded—for his mouth to cover hers. An instant before he moved she did, so that her lips were perfectly slanted to accommodate his kiss. Gentle at first...brushing...skimming...then his fingers speared into her hair, dug into her skull as he held her head steady, took her mouth in an almost brutal possession that made her head spin. His lips tasted of whisky, reminding her in the little corner of her brain still functioning, that anger and alcohol drove his actions. But she refused to let the thought take hold, banishing it from her mind to let Rico take her where she'd always ached to go.

His strong hands slid down her back, over her waist, until they cupped her bottom. Faye gasped into his mouth. Her stomach spun mercilessly as he pulled her against him, angling her so she felt what he undoubtedly wanted her to feel.

Faye's response was to plunge her fingers into his hair, gripping handfuls of all that wonderful black silk.

He kissed her like she was his savior, his redemption. Like he couldn't get enough of her. Even when he reached out behind her and she heard the gentle snick of the lock being turned, he didn't stop kissing her.

Heat and chills warred against Faye's sensitive flesh. She plastered herself against him, knowing she could never get close enough. Knowing that part of her would die if he stopped now.

Not that he showed any signs of stopping. His hands raked over her hips, the sides of her ribcage, up between their joined bodies.

When his hands found her breasts, so full and sensitive through the thin lilac silk of her dress, Faye let her head fall back. "Oh, God. Rico..."

Then her mouth was beneath his again. A keening sound came from deep in her throat as he tugged at her dress and hiked it up. She pulled at his shirt, her fingers leaden as they fought with the tiny white buttons. His chest hair brushed against her fingertips, his muscles jumping with each touch of flesh against flesh. Everything inside her flared and heated.

Enrico mumbled something in Italian, something she couldn't make out. But before she could think about it his hands were around the edges of her panties, and with an unrestrained urgency he yanked them down.

Faye gasped, knowing she had to slow things down. As much as she wanted him, she wanted this, her first time—*their* first time—to be special. To last. But he was nudging her back against the door, closing his fingers around her hips, forcing his knee between her legs.

He pushed her hard against the door, using his chest to anchor her.

Faye clung on to him. It was all she could do. Everything was happening so fast. Too fast.

The air backed up in her lungs, until her frenzied gasps tangled with the erotic sound of Enrico's labored breathing. He gave a guttural groan and pressed his mouth against her throat.

When his teeth grazed her heated flesh, her eyes almost rolled back in her head. All her muscles tightened. But something screamed at her to stop him. This wasn't how things were supposed to happen between them. It wasn't meant to be like this. Fast. Harsh. Brutal.

She pushed her palm against his shoulder and tried to ease him back. But all it accomplished was a whisper of space between them that allowed him to slide his hand between her legs.

She opened her mouth to ask him to slow down, but the words came out on a cry as his fingers sank into her. Her head shot back, hitting the door with a thump. If there was discomfort she didn't know it. Sensation exploded through her, her pelvis convulsing with heat and fire as Rico brought his mouth down on hers again.

Beyond conscious thought, Faye sank against him. She slid her arms around his neck, trying to pull him closer. But he resisted, pulling back to make space between their bodies while his mouth continued its punishing assault on her. She heard the metallic brush of his zipper, trembled at the stroke of fabric against her heated flesh as his trousers slid down. She ached to have him inside her...fast...slow... She didn't care anymore.

I love you, Rico, she wanted to say. *I love you with all my heart.* But she knew he didn't want to hear that. She knew he'd stop if he heard that. And she didn't want him to stop.

The hard length of him nudging against her was almost too wonderful to bear, and she bit down on her lower lip. He gripped her hips, lifted her against him. With a groan he pressed forward. The pain was sharp and harsh, but the intensity of it lasted only for an instant. Then there was just Rico, and the exquisite sensation of him pushing into her.

She didn't try to stop the tears flowing. How could she? The man she loved was moving inside her, turning her from girl to woman. He filled her, stretched her...not only her body, but her heart as well. It filled until she thought it might burst from her chest.

Then she was incapable of thinking anything at all, as pleasure built—swift and excruciating. She gripped Enrico's shoulders as he pumped into her, over and over, harder and harder, until his own frenzied gasps mingled with hers as they catapulted toward oblivion.

In the aftermath she clung to him. The warmth of his skin and the scent of his passion flooded her senses as she burrowed into his neck. His chest heaved against her sensitive breasts, his labored breathing holding a hypnotic appeal as it rasped through the silence. She tried to breath with him, matching her rhythm with his. She was in his arms. They'd made love. Nothing else mattered.

From somewhere outside came the sound of a woman's laughter, and it seemed to break the spell. Enrico eased away. He didn't look at her, didn't speak, but reached out and pulled down her skirt. When he did look at her it was with a quiet intensity that signaled regret and apology.

Faye's heart twisted as tears threatened again. "Don't," she warned him, as he inhaled and prepared to speak. "Don't you dare apologize or say it shouldn't have happened."

"It should not have happened." He zipped his trousers, the cold whisper of steel a somber affirmation of the statement.

Humiliated and heartsick, she swiped her fingers across her cheeks. If he was going to start with the platitudes she wouldn't hear them while her face was stained with tears.

"So, what do you want to say, Rico?" she taunted, watching him button the shirt she'd almost ripped apart in her eagerness to get the slide of his flesh beneath her hands. "That you didn't know what you were doing? That you were drunk? Angry?" Her breath hitched, but no tears accompanied her outburst. She didn't feel like crying anymore. She felt incensed. Her body shook with it, her face burned.

"All of those things," he said, pushing his hair back as he watched her retrieve her panties. "This was a mistake. I should never have let things get out of control that way. What I did was unforgivable."

Faye struggled into her panties then smoothed down her dress. "Don't worry about it," she snapped, mortified at his words. "At least it did the trick. You seem to have sobered up well enough. Good to think I'm a better remedy than black coffee."

Desperate to get out, she turned toward the door. But she couldn't get the damned thing open. She pulled, tugged, cursed. The door wouldn't budge. What had Rico done with the blessed key?

"Open the door," she demanded, giving it another yank. "Please, just open the door."

"I never meant to hurt you."

"Well, you have." She drew in a long shaky breath. "How could you, Rico?" *How could you break my heart with such careless ease? Then throw away the pieces with a few meaningless words?*

"I am sorry, *cara*." He was behind her again. "I am so sorry."

Faye pulled at the handle of the door. "Just let me out."

"We need to talk about this."

"No. We don't need to talk. We have absolutely nothing we need to talk about." *All I need is to get out of here, away from you. So far away that you never get the chance to hurt me again.*

"I did not use anything."

His quiet tone seeped through all the anger and frustration and let her focus on the words. The realization, and its implications, brought her head up. She stared at the door, at the rich mahogany panels, and a myriad of emotions stormed through her. A crazy thrill...a reckless desire...a sharp and fearsome dread...

He hadn't used protection.

God.

"Faye?"

She swallowed. She couldn't talk to him right now. Not when she felt this vulnerable, this humiliated, this terrified. Not when he'd have all the right answers ready for her to hear. All the right suggestions. He'd offer to take care of her, take care of *things.* She couldn't bear to hear him say any of that, especially when he thought what they had shared had been a *mistake*, something to be fixed.

"It doesn't matter." She swallowed again, letting the lie formulate on her tongue. "I'm on the pill."

For long moments there was silence and Faye prayed he'd simply accept it, that he wouldn't question her, make her look in his eyes and say it again.

Her prayers were answered. He reached down and picked up a small brass key from where it had fallen on the richly patterned rug.

Faye watched through a blur as his long fingers turned the key in the lock. She kept watching as he reached for the handle.

"I am sorry, Faye," he said, before opening the door and stepping back.

Faye flew through the door, keeping her head down as she passed stray wedding guests meandering through the marbled entrance hallway and children playing on the huge curving staircase. In the sanctity of her room, she slammed the door shut and dropped back against it. She slid to the floor as her legs gave way.

And wept.

Later, cried out and furious with herself for being gullible, she'd grabbed a pillow and beaten it against the wall, cursing Enrico Lavini for the unfeeling beast he was with every thump of feather against brick.

Memories faded with the sound of gravel crunching beneath car tires, and Faye gave herself a mental shake. She hadn't meant to take the journey back to the past. In fact she'd promised herself over the years that she would never return to that part of her life. Ever. But many times she had. Not all the way, but certainly most of it, and she would feel Rico's arms around her, the way his mouth fit perfectly with hers...but she would always stop herself before...

Heavens above, she was about to do it again.

Dinner, she thought, and a shower. Melita and Carla would return from their shopping trip shortly and she wanted to start preparing dinner before they arrived. Despite Carla's protests that she should rest, Faye loved helping out in the huge rustic kitchen with its bang-up-to-date appliances and state of the art design.

As she slipped on her sandals she heard a richly accented voice giving instructions to his driver.

Enrico.

Her stomach leapt and then did the weirdest dance. It was because she had been thinking about—no, don't go there again, she warned herself. Don't *ever* go there again.

She ran her fingers through her blonde hair, aware she didn't have on a scrap of make-up. As she'd been on her own in the house the whole afternoon, she hadn't bothered with a bra beneath her clingy crimson tee shirt. Even more clingy since that trip down memory lane.

No way could she let him see her like this. Not in the very place it had happened. He'd know what she'd been thinking about. He'd take one look at her and know where her perilous thoughts had taken her.

Forgetting the catalogue on her lap she jumped up, intending to race for the stairs. Loose papers and notes scattered theatrically to the floor.

Faye muttered a curse as she bent to snatch up the papers. Her insides were still doing that ridiculous samba thing, which was stupid. He'd made his position clear enough, by action if not words. He didn't want to be around her, couldn't bear to be in her presence for more than a few moments without excusing himself. Didn't that speak for itself?

She cursed again as more notes scattered to the floor.

"Such language for a lady."

Faye jumped and spun around. Enrico stood framed in the French window, the sun at his back giving a surreal halo-effect to his muscular body. He looked like some sort of conquering warrior standing there, his suit jacket thrown casually over one shoulder and a black tee shirt displaying that solid chest. Faye stared for long moments.

"You're back," she managed, inwardly kicking herself for the redundant nature of her greeting. But then words seemed meaningless as she continued to stare at him. She could look at him all day and be left wanting more.

He strolled into the library, each step casting his face more clearly. Mouth-wateringly gorgeous in a rough, chiseled sort of way and, oh yes, she could look at him forever and still crave more.

"You have been busy."

He stooped, inches from her legs, and gathered up the loose papers.

Faye wanted to step back but kept herself rooted. Damned if she'd let him see he unnerved her like this. "Well, it needs doing and I enjoy doing it."

He rose, uncoiling like a snake, but twice as lethal. At least to her equilibrium.

She all but snatched the papers he held out, slipping them into the catalogue and hugging it to her like a precious child. She felt an acute and unsettling reaction to him—or rather her body did—shivering and shaking so badly he had to notice. She strengthened her stranglehold on the catalogue as her nipples tightened and her insides did a death-defying somersault.

Enrico tilted his head in the general direction of her predicament. "Ah, is this the infamous ledger?"

Faye drew it closer still, flattening her throbbing breasts. "Infamous?"

"I heard you have kept yourself busy rearranging the library. I only hope you have not taxed yourself unnecessarily."

"I haven't, and it was in need of some restructuring." Talk, she thought. It was easier when she talked. Then she didn't have to focus on the way her heart thumped. "Do you know you have first editions going to rack and ruin, not to mention collections that need only one or two books to complete them. Acquire the missing books and the value of the whole collection could most likely double in price, triple even."

Enrico listened with an indulgent glint in his eye. "Interesting." He pursed his lips. "But make sure you get enough rest."

Talking wasn't doing much good, Faye realized, as sensations sizzled through her. She gripped the ledger until her fingers hurt. "I'm bored silly just sitting around here all day.

Everyone watches me like a hawk, at your instruction no doubt. Besides, by doing this I feel I can pay you back in some way."

His brow creased. "Pay me back?"

"For your kindness in allowing us to stay here."

He threw his jacket over a nearby chair. "Please do not insult me, *cara.*"

Before she registered his intention, he'd snatched the ledger from her arms, his gaze falling to her breasts. "If I required payment from you I would demand it by more interesting means."

He dropped the ledger onto a side table where it fell with a resounding thud. Then, quick as a beat, he had her breath jerking from her lungs as he grabbed her arms and pulled her against him.

"And would you make such payment, Faye?" He caught her chin when she tried to turn away. "I wonder what price would my *kindness* be worth to you? Exactly how high a price would you be willing to pay?"

Hot blood raced through her, burning her veins. She looked at his throat, that thick tanned column that made her mouth water. He jerked her chin giving her no option but to look in his eyes.

"Stop it." She damned herself for the weakness in her voice. "I only meant—"

He gave her chin another jerk until their mouths were a breath away. "What exactly did you mean, Faye? Did you think that by insulting me, by offering me payment for your board and lodgings, I would keep my distance?"

His breath feathered over her lips, sending waves of awareness down her spine. "No, of course not."

Suddenly his arms were around her and she was pressed

against him. The hard, muscled strength of him seeping through her until her frenzied brain demanded he finish what he undoubtedly intended to start.

Kiss me, she willed him. *Oh, God, just kiss me.*

"Perhaps I have kept my distance for too long," he ground out. "I should have dealt with this years ago, made things right."

A mad joy hovered at the edges of her heart. "What are you saying?"

His eyes bored into hers, his voice deep and rough. "We made love," he said as if it was something that might have slipped her mind. "Here in this room. Then you went to London, married my brother, and I never had the chance to make things right."

The self-reproach in his tone poured icy water on her hopes. "What do you mean?" she asked her voice flat. "How did you expect to make things right?"

"I should have formally apologized to you for what happened, made sure you knew it was not your fault. That I—"

"Oh, for heaven's sake!" Faye shook herself out of his arms, not even trying to cloak her anger. "You apologized all right. In fact, that's all you did do, over and over. Told me how *sorry* you were."

"You belonged to my brother. I had no right to take from you what was rightfully his." He shook his head. "I had no right."

She poked a finger into his granite chest. "Get this, Enrico. I don't belong to anyone. And what I do—did—with my body is my business. It's *my* right to decide who gets what."

She stopped, dragging in much needed oxygen while she fought against the urge to tell him that if anyone had a right he did. He had every right. He was the father of her child. The only man she had ever loved. The man she loved still and always would.

"You are angry. You do not know what you are saying."

"I'm angry all right. Do you know why? Do you?" She poked him in the chest again. "Because I'm sick and tired of you insinuating I don't know who I am or what I want. I'm bloody fed up with you always telling me how I feel, what's good for me." She dragged in more air, her chest rising and falling with the effort. "I've had enough of this, Enrico. I've so had enough of this."

His expression darkened. Nostrils flaring, chest heaving. He glared at her as if she were the devil incarnate.

Then he swore...and his mouth came down on hers.

No tenderness. No tentative play of lips. Just possession. Fierce and brutal.

And she was more than a match for it. Her fingers spiked into his hair, pulling his head down to take more. She wanted more...more... She wanted to pour into their kiss every long, lonely, aching moment of those eight years without him.

Harsh breathing filled the air, punctured only by fractured mutterings of pleasure—of encouragement. Not that Enrico needed any. His body pressed against hers, the hard, muscled strength of his arms keeping her close, allowing her little space to move.

Possessive hands slid down her back, molding her curves. Those long fingers dug in, squeezing and lifting until her pelvis was cradled tight to his. She tried to shimmy, but he held her too firmly.

The heat was so intense she marveled that she didn't simply combust on the spot.

Without knowing why, she pulled back.

She gasped for air and watched him do the same. It was fear that had made her stop. She was scared. Though not of him. Never of him. It was the situation. The consequences.

She was scared of her lies, her treachery. What had they done? She and Teo. What had they stolen from Enrico? If they made love now she would have to tell him. She wouldn't be able to stop herself telling him. And once he knew the truth he might never forgive her.

If she loved him, and she did with all her heart, she had to tell him first. Then, if he still wanted her, he could have her. Body and soul. For always. Forever.

There could be nothing less for either of them.

Even though she'd pulled back Enrico still had hold of her. His arms hadn't slackened at all, if anything they'd grown more insistent.

"*Bellezza.*" He bent, trailing a line of kisses along her throat. "*Come sei bella.*"

Faye closed her eyes as her body flared beneath the onslaught of his mouth. Perhaps he wouldn't think her beautiful at all once he knew the truth. What if he didn't want to hold her, kiss her? What if he felt nothing but contempt?

It was vital she tell him first. Before they made love. For there to be any hope for them, she had to do it now. Now. She would make him understand, make him see that everything she had done had been... What? For the best? How on earth could she convince him of that? When right now she didn't even believe it herself.

She had lied to him. The cruelest of lies. She had kept his child from him, allowed that child to be raised by another man. His brother. A hard thing for any man to accept, but for an Italian? And for one as proud, as fierce a believer in honor and family and duty as Enrico? He would never understand her reasons. Never believe she'd done only what she believed best for everyone concerned. Even if he'd wanted nothing more to do with her, refused to marry her, abandoned her completely, he would never have abandoned his child. His own flesh and blood. Look how fiercely he insisted on taking care of Melita when he assumed she was his niece. How much more ferocious would he be in his protection of a daughter?

Her whole being ached with the weight of it all. With what she stood to lose by telling him. But, regardless, she had to do it.

"Rico." Forcing her eyes open, she eased her throat away from where it was currently being devoured by his mouth. "Rico, there's something I have to tell you."

But his mouth refused to release her throat and she was pressed up against him again. Oh, how was it that his hands seemed to fit perfectly around the curve of her backside?

"Rico."

He growled, low and harsh, as he reached one hand around to cup her breast. "No words, *cara mia.* Just let me touch you."

He tugged urgently at her tee shirt, slipping his hand beneath the soft cotton. Long fingers skimmed over her ribcage, making her naked flesh tingle and her stomach muscles clench. She whimpered as his hand curved around her breast.

Her mind emptied as her body craved, the heavy dragging sensation in her pelvis forcing her forward until she ground her hips against him in a desperate attempt to find relief.

He swore again, ripe and harsh, urging her back until she was trapped between him and the wall. "Is this what you want, Faye?" he asked, his mouth feathering along her jaw as he pushed her tee shirt up, exposing her naked breasts. "My hands on you?" He stroked his thumb across her nipple, making her arch. "My mouth on you?"

Oh, yes! This was exactly what she wanted, what she craved. His hard strength taking her where she ached to go.

But some part of her frenzied brain spun a warning that she shouldn't give in to this heady sensation of knowing—feeling—how much he wanted her, how much she still wanted him. How much she would always want him. Not before telling him, not before she... Heavens, she couldn't remember what she needed to tell him, not with sensation piercing every atom of her being as the man she loved slowly devoured her.

His mouth claimed hers in a punishing kiss and she made a purring sound, pushing her breast into his hand and grinding her hips against him. When he lifted his mouth from hers, she slid her tongue over her bottom lip savoring his taste. His gaze followed the path of her tongue, then his shoulders rolled back and his jaw went tight. Abruptly, he released her, bracing his hands on the wall either side of her shoulders and lowering his head.

"*Madre de Dio*! How is it you make me want you beyond everything I know to be appropriate."

He took several deep breaths before he looked up. The smoldering charcoal gaze had disappeared, replaced by that steely glare that lashed her heart.

"So, why don't you just apologize and get it over with?" she mocked, pulling her tee shirt down to cover herself. "While you're at it, why don't you just remind me that I don't know what I want or how I feel?"

He pushed away from the wall, turned sharply, and with his back to her snatched up his jacket. "You will receive no apology from me this time."

Some of the heat was back, Faye noticed as he faced her again, fire and irritation smoldering beneath the steel. He gave her a swift and mildly insulting once over, and slung the jacket over his shoulder. “From your reaction I take it you would have no objection to sharing my bed.”

Frustration and miserable embarrassment had her flesh burning as she pushed the tee into her waistband, wishing she could as easily tuck away her feelings for him. “I won’t be sharing anything with you. Ever.” Least of all the truth about her child. “I’m leaving.”

She pivoted, heading for the door with the intention of giving it a nice healthy slam to help vent some of the wretchedness. But he caught her, his fingers curling into the back of her waistband and yanking her back.

“You are not going anywhere until your memory has returned,” he growled.

Faye whirled on him. “You mean you want me to stay in this room until I can remember everything?” Venom laced her mockingly sweet tone. When his eyes narrowed she shook her head. “I meant I’m leaving this room, Enrico, not the villa. At least, not yet.”

“I want to know what happened,” he said, as if she hadn’t spoken. “I want to know why you and Matteo were traveling together. What was the purpose of your trip?”

“Like it’s any of your business.”

“I want to know if you intended to reconcile.”

Faye stared at him. “Why?”

The question seemed to unnerve him. Just imagine that, Faye thought, Enrico Lavini unnerved. But then her heart took a soaring leap with the realization there was only one reason he wanted the answer to that particular question.

“Why?” she demanded when he didn’t answer. “Why do you want to know that?”

He rolled back his shoulders. “Melita needed her father.”

Faye caught the reprimand, and gave herself an even sharper one for the stupid thoughts she’d been harboring.

Guilt surged through her, because he was right. Melita *did* need her father.

Him.

She was over a barrel. Damned if she told him the truth and damned if she didn’t. If she confessed the truth would he ever forgive her? Regardless, she couldn’t let things remain like this. Couldn’t let any more time go by allowing him to believe his daughter belonged to someone else, that *she* belonged to someone else.

“We would never have reconciled.” Her throat burned with the words but she had to say them. “Neither of us wanted it.”

Faye paused as her throat tightened painfully. She took in a breath, trying to think clearly, to formulate the words that would change all of their lives forever.

But the short pause allowed Enrico to say, “You cannot be sure, not until your memory returns.” He walked to a nearby chair and dropped his jacket on the back of it. “You were everything to Matteo,” he said wearily. “All he ever wanted in life.”

“That’s not true—”

“You married him,” he interrupted. “You chose him as your husband. There must have been something left between you, something you might have built on.”

“It wasn’t like that.” If she wasn’t careful he’d box her into a corner where her only possible escape meant revealing the true reasons behind her marriage to Teo.

“Facts are facts, *cara*.” He shook his head. “I only hope in some small way he forgave me for taking from him what was never mine to take. And that he would forgive me now for my lack of restraint around you."

"For heaven's sake, Enrico. There you go again. You're like something out of the Middle Ages. Making it sound like *I* have nothing to do with anything." Exasperated, she headed for the door. This was *so* not the time to be having a conversation about something as important as her daughter's paternity. The man had it in his head that she and Teo had been the love story of the millennium.

"And it was my *virginity*," she snapped as she waltzed past him. "Not the rights to the world's oil reserves or a bank of diamond mines in some undiscovered—"

"How flippantly you brush aside something so important to a man."

"To an Italian, maybe." She jerked as he reached out and grabbed her arm, then looked pointedly down to where his fingers curved around her flesh. "Be careful, Enrico. Who knows what unspeakable taboos you're violating by touching me."

It was a childish retaliation and she knew it, but he was just so ridiculously—infuriatingly—*Latin*.

"This I have already done," he said in a hard tone, "and have since lived to regret it."

If he'd wanted to hurt her more he couldn't have said anything worse. If there was anything in *her* life she had never regretted, would never regret, it was their one night together. But obviously for him it was a different story.

"Well, I'm sorry I was such a disappointment." Her heart lurched and she attempted to tug her arm from his grip. "Let go!"

He held firm, waiting until she glared up at him. Only then did he release her.

Faye hurried up the stairs, her feet barely touching the floor as she made for the sanctuary of her room. Heaven help her, it was almost a replay of the scene she'd been remembering. She slammed the door, sank against it and stared at the pillow.

Not this time, she thought. No tears this time. No pillows. No pining for a man who wasn't worth the effort.

That was one part of history that wouldn't repeat itself.

Enrico stepped from the shower and snagged a towel. How was it a woman could make a man feel like a complete bastard?

She'd misinterpreted him. She'd managed to twist everything he said.

Maledizione!

He shrugged on a clean white shirt and pushed it into his black tailored jeans. Maybe he'd been too rough on her. She was still recovering from the accident, still battling grief for all he knew. And what had he done? Kissed her—groped her—had her against the wall for pity's sake. Again. Then for good measure he'd insulted her. At least, that was her interpretation of it. What he'd actually meant was... *Dio*! She was probably in her room now, cursing him for the insensitive *Italian* he was. He grumbled under his breath, recalling the sneer in her voice as she'd accused him of living up to his heritage. The woman made it sound like it was a crime for a man to put value on virtue and purity.

He swore at the pompousness of his own thoughts. Perhaps she was right, he was something out of the Middle Ages. But then he wasn't about to apologize for having standards and living up to them. *Dio*, he wasn't.

He slipped his feet into black loafers and left his room.

Stupid, insensitive...*Italian*!

Faye braced her hands on the edge of the bathroom sink and stared at her reflection in the gilt-edged mirror. Enrico Lavini. Prehistoric man.

She tapped her foot, as if that would relieve some of the tension whipping through her system. Lord, she was *furious.* What century was the man living in, for heaven's sake? A woman's virginity was hers to do with as she pleased. She didn't need anyone else's permission, and she certainly didn't need the intervention of some...some...stupid idiot who acted like she wasn't qualified to make the decision for herself!

Heat flared along her skin, pumped through her veins. A shower. That was what she needed. Something to wash the idiot man and the memory of that kiss away.

Fifteen minutes later she was drying her hair when she heard a resolute knock at her door. She switched off the dryer and set it on the hook by the dressing table. Another knock came, even more determined. She knew it was Enrico. Even his knock had that imperious quality. Well, he could wait.

Faye tightened the knot in the towel still wrapped around her body.

Another knock. Louder. Any moment now he'd have the door off its hinges, and how would they explain *that* to the staff?

Determined to stay calm, Faye went to the door. When she flung back the door Enrico took a swift, almost imperceptible sweep of her towel-clad length, and if she hadn't been tuned to his every nuance she might have missed it.

"What do you want?"

His mouth hardened. "I came to sort out a misunderstanding."

"No misunderstanding as far as I'm concerned." She lifted her chin and faced him squarely. "I believe I know exactly where I stand and that's fine by me."

He stepped into the room. "May I come in?"

"Since you're already in, the question seems superfluous." She closed the door behind him with a nice, satisfying slam.

He turned slowly, raised a straight black eyebrow. "That snippy tone does you no justice, Faye."

She stuck her chin higher and waltzed past him to the dressing table, where she snagged the hairdryer. "Really? Well, just another misunderstanding on my part no doubt." She waved the appliance. "You don't mind, do you?"

The tiny arrow of heat along his cheekbones signaled he did, and she took a kind of grim delight in it.

"I want to talk to you. You will not hear me over that thing."

But she'd already pushed the switch and turned her back on him. The hum of the dryer blotted out any other sound in the room.

She knew it would provoke him. Which was exactly what she wanted to do. She wanted to hurt him, the way he'd hurt her.

But you didn't ignore a man like Enrico Lavini, and she wasn't the least surprised to find the dryer yanked out of her hand. The room was plunged into silence as the steady hum of the dryer ceased. The quiet air crackled with tension.

When he threw the dryer onto the dressing table, Faye followed the action with an expression of mock surprise. "Oh, dear, was that annoying you?" she asked sweetly. "You only had to say."

A harsh look flashed across his face and set his nostrils flaring. "Enough of this," he growled. "I did not mean to imply that I regret touching you. My only regret is that I hurt my brother."

"Because you *stole* my virginity?"

"Yes." His resigned, regretful sigh pierced through the anger and touched some part of her heart.

Faye's shoulders dropped as his did, and some of her temper evaporated. Even the tension in the room seemed to dissolve. Although her awareness of him standing there, big and masculine, didn't help with a different kind of tension assaulting her body.

She sighed. "You know. Here in the twenty-first century a woman's virginity is considered hers to do with as she pleases. It doesn't belong to a man." She tightened the knot in her towel, watching as his gaze tracked the movement. "I slept with you because I wanted to. It had nothing to do with anything or anyone else. It was my decision, and I don't regret it." There. At least she'd sown a seed of sorts, now all she had to do was water it. "I wanted you to be the first man I slept with because..." She swallowed, tightened the knot again. How did you tell a man he was the only one you had ever loved? That your beloved child was his child.

"Because?" Enrico prompted.

Blood rushed in her ears, and her chest thumped with terrifying ferocity. "Rico, I need to..."

Somewhere in her frazzled thoughts she registered her daughter shouting for her. Relief and frustration warred. She didn't want to tell him like this, not while she was half-naked and the air sizzled with unresolved business between them. Nor did she want to put it off any longer. Her nerves wouldn't stand it. He had a right to know.

She forced herself to hold Enrico's steady look as Melita came bounding up the stairs.

"Mummy! I'm going to—Uncle Rico!" Melita launched herself into his arms. "I thought you wouldn't be home until after I was in bed. Did you have a good time in...?" With her arms tight around his waist she turned her face up to his, her expression one of crumpled concentration.

"Vienna." Enrico smiled down, smoothing his hand over the crown of Melita's head to work back the strands of hair escaping her ponytail. "Yes, *carina*, I had a good time. Now, how would you enjoy a weekend at the sea?"

"Ooh, yes please. Can we go swimming?"

"We can indeed."

Outmaneuvered, Faye thought, watching her daughter's animated face gaze up at Enrico with something bordering adoration. He obviously hadn't taken on board anything she'd said about his tendency to assume he could take control of anything involving her daughter. But then she couldn't exactly take him to task over it, not when she had been close to giving him information that would ensure he took complete control over *everything* involving her—their—daughter.

"Can I wear my new swimsuit, Mummy?" Melita turned to Faye but kept her arms tight around Enrico's middle. "And you can wear yours." She focused on the towel Faye wore, her eyes huge. "Oh!" Her giggle was muffled beneath the hand she clamped over her mouth. "Mummy, you haven't got any clothes on!"

Faye felt heat pour into her face, even as her hands went to the knot again. "I know, and that's because people are keeping me talking about swimsuits and things." She laughed somewhat nervously down at her daughter, prayed she didn't look as embarrassed as she suddenly felt. But to hear her daughter spell it out, and see Enrico's gaze travel the length of her again—and again—made her feel uncomfortably decadent.

Her flesh heated, even beneath the towel. *Especially* beneath the towel, as he examined her with insolent ease. He lingered, it seemed, at the places not covered by fluffy cotton—the curved outline of her breasts, the middle of her thighs, her breasts again. Electric shocks sizzled through her veins, scorching her nerve endings until she thought she might cry out.

Enrico seemed in no hurry to leave. He looked at Faye as he addressed Melita. “Now, *carina*, may I have your permission to take your mother out for the evening? You need to have an early night if we are to go swimming and sailing—”

“Sailing?” Melita jumped up and down. “Oh, we’re going sailing.” She pulled away from Enrico, jumping in circles. “We’re going sailing.”

“I take it that is a yes,” Enrico said, as Melita chanted out her delight. Then raised straight eyebrows as if waiting for Faye’s agreement.

“So it would seem.” And Faye made a mental note to chastise her daughter about giving in that easily to a man’s request, but then she supposed that was a conversation for ten or so years’ time.

“I have a meeting with my vineyard manager in—” he turned his wrist glancing at a thick silver watch, “—one hour. I will arrange for you to have that tour you wanted and then we will have dinner.”

And no doubt pick up their conversation where they’d left off, Faye thought, as her stomach spun nauseously. But there was no going back now. It had to be done.

“I’ll just need to check that Carla can look after Melita this evening.”

“Very well.” He took another lazy appraisal of her towel-clad body, making her feel like he could see straight through to the flesh beneath. “I’ll leave you to get some clothes on.”

Chapter Seven

Faye hadn't remembered the vineyards were quite as stunningly beautiful and she sighed her appreciation as Enrico drove through the cypress-lined entrance to the management buildings.

"I take it my land meets with your approval." He shot her a glance.

"It does. You've done wonders with it. I can remember when you first bought it and it was just a patchwork of neglected plots."

"I cannot take all the credit, very little of it in fact. The success of the land is due to the dedication of the vinery workers and the expertise of my management team."

In recognition of their efforts he had set up an extremely generous bonus and commission scheme according to Carla, but Faye didn't mention it. She knew Enrico wouldn't appreciate hearing that his private affairs had been the subject of kitchen chatter.

While Enrico had a brief meeting with his manager, Faye was given a full tour of the operation. Later they drove into Lucca and enjoyed dinner at an exclusive restaurant, accompanied by wine direct from the Lavini vineyards.

"It must be difficult for you having to leave the day-to-day running of things to your manager," Faye said as Enrico topped off their wine. "It was your dream to work the land for as long as I can remember."

"We do what needs to be done."

"But you must hate having to devote the majority of your time to the family business. Banking never really interested you."

She remembered how fiercely he had battled to set up his own business, how determined he had been not to let his father dictate to him. That determination, coupled with the frustration of being forced to take on the mantle of chairman of the Lavini bank, had culminated in the fight with his father on the day of Ruggerio's third marriage. Seeing his brother's interests denied had fuelled his anger.

Faye watched him now as he sipped his wine. There was a somber look in his eyes, and the beginnings of a scowl shadowing his handsome forehead.

He leaned back. "At first I resented having to take over the bank, and will always resent the circumstances that led to it. But I focused on the fact it was my grandfather's business and as such it is my duty to ensure the continued success of the company he built." His jaw went as hard as his eyes. "In each generation it is the duty of a first-born son to uphold and protect the foundations, the traditions of the family."

Her stomach jumped but Faye asked, "What if the first-born is a daughter?"

He looked at her as if the very idea was preposterous. Then he shrugged. "The issue has never arisen, although as long as expertise is assured I see no reason for not having a woman as head of the Lavini Bank."

"Good heavens, Enrico." Faye lifted her wine in toast. "Don't tell me we've made a feminist out of you."

He returned the cautious smile she gave him. "I cannot

confess to having progressed that far. But if fate wills a daughter, then so be it."

They were skirting so near to reality, that Faye needed a fortifying swig of the one glass of wine she'd allowed herself. Perhaps now was the time to water that seed she'd planted. "You...you wouldn't mind a daughter? As your first-born child, the heir to your empire?"

He pursed his lips, considering it. "It is a moot point," he decided. "Lavini's tend to make sons."

"Not always."

His puzzled expression disappeared in an instant. "No," he agreed. "Not always. You and Matteo are evidence of that."

He watched her steadily and she had a moment of panic that somehow he knew. But he didn't of course, and this was the perfect lead-in she had been waiting for. All she had to do was say it. *Melita is your daughter.* It would be that simple. And that excruciatingly difficult.

Should she tell him now, in the restaurant, or wait until they were driving home? No, not when he was driving. Perhaps they could take a walk after dinner.

In an attempt to get her stomach to stop its wild pitching and tumbling, Faye tried to think of something innocuous to talk about. Before she could formulate her words a small, wiry man with a smile as wide as his shoulders bustled over.

"*Signor Lavini*," The man made a grab for Enrico's hand and pumped furiously. "An honor for our restaurant."

Enrico stood. "Mario, how are you?"

"Well, I am well." Having released Enrico's hand Mario wrung both of his own as his gaze darted around the crowded restaurant as if searching for something. "And you must allow me to seat you somewhere more appropriate." He made a tutting sound. "It is inexcusable I was not informed of your arrival. Inexcusable."

"Please do not trouble yourself, Mario. We are perfectly fine here."

A frown creased his pleasant face but he smiled at Faye before whispering conspiratorially to Enrico, "You would not wish for a table more...private?"

Enrico's wide shoulders drew back. "Mario," he said, with the same stiffness that had settled in his shoulders. "Allow me to introduce *Signora* Faye Lavini. My sister-in-law."

Color rose fast and deep on Mario's cheeks. He shook his head, mumbling "*Perdono, Signor.*" Then with a deep bow to Faye, "*Signora.*"

Faye smiled, touched at the depth of the man's chagrin as it mingled with the emptiness filling her chest at the way Enrico had stressed the term *sister-in-law.*

"Allow me to introduce *Signor* Mario Donetti," Enrico said, turning to Faye. "The owner of this rather magnificent restaurant."

With another deep bow and an expression of humility, Mario moved toward Faye. When she held out her hand he took it with such tenderness, laying a kiss on the back of it with equal care, that she smiled.

He kept hold of her hand as his expression turned somber. "*Signora* Lavini. You will allow me to offer my condolences on the loss of your husband."

The unexpected compassion grabbed at the place in her heart that hurt for Teo, and her eyes misted up.

"Thank you, *Signor* Donetti."

"Mario, please. And *Signor* Lavini, you must please allow me to send over a bottle of our finest brandy with my compliments, and my deepest thanks. I hope you are enjoying the evening's entertainment. It is Tuscany's finest, even though the pianist is my son and perhaps I am biased."

He gave Faye another infectious smile, muttered a further few words of thanks to Enrico and bustled off still wringing his hands.

"What was he thanking you for?" Faye asked, noticing several couples take to the small dance area as the music became louder.

Enrico shrugged. "Some business we did together."

"Does he buy wine from your vineyards?"

Another shrug, the type that indicated he didn't necessarily want to discuss the matter. "He does, has done for several years now. But he was referring to another matter, a loan. One he will repay in a quarter of the time we agreed on under the terms of the transaction if I know Mario."

Faye fingered the thin gold chain around her neck as she watched a young couple on the dance floor, their arms linked, eyes locked on each other to the exclusion of everyone else in the restaurant. Her heart fluttered with poignant longing.

Wishing. Hoping.

"You would like to dance?"

Enrico's question cut through the daydream she was enjoying of his arms around her, his gaze locked with hers.

She smiled, realizing that one out of two wasn't bad. At least if they danced she'd be in his arms. A glow of pleasure pushed its way to her skin. "Yes, I would."

Facing him on the dance floor Faye hesitated, not knowing quite where to put her hands. Enrico seemed just as uncomfortable, but then took hold of her hand and drew her in. She lifted her other hand, resting it on his arm. Their bodies barely touched, but her heart skipped fast against her ribcage. The dim lighting on the dance square hid the worst of the hot color that had to be scoring her cheeks, and if she pulled back a tad more he wouldn't be able to feel her heart banging a tune.

But *she* felt it. Oh yes, she felt it. Her lungs expanded with painful effort in their demand for oxygen, as her heart continued its resounding thump...thump...thump.

"Relax, *cara*." Enrico issued the instruction as he drew Faye into his arms. *Dio*. She was stiff and unyielding against him, trying to pull away. What had she to fear from him? Hadn't he apologized, made it clear that his restraint would now be assured?

She had never before felt rigid in his arms, never acted as if she was repelled by his touch. Earlier that afternoon she had welcomed his caress, molded against him like she too craved what they'd once shared. But now she acted as if he were a stranger, acted as if she wanted to put distance between them.

But how could he blame her? How? When earlier he'd pressed her to the wall and demanded her mouth against his, forced himself against her until she could be in very little doubt as to his intentions.

She deserved better and he owed her that. "I was rough today."

Her lavender blue eyes fixed him in their sights. "Rough in action or words?"

"Both." Her mouth was rich and full. If he kissed her now she'd have the taste of wine on her lips, made from grapes from his own vineyards. Beneath it would be the taste that was hers alone. The taste he'd never quite been able to purge from his memory.

May heaven forgive him.

It was right to keep space between them. She was his

brother's widow. His duty was to protect her, not seduce her. Again.

But sweet heaven on earth, she felt so good in his arms. So right.

He wanted to kiss her right there on the dance floor and be damned what anyone thought. If he himself was damned in the process, so be it.

Dio. May God help him. He was losing his mind.

He felt Faye stiffen against him and realized his grip on her had intensified along with the fevered thoughts spinning around in his head.

"I do not want us to argue," he said in a raw tone. "Perhaps we can declare a truce of some kind."

She didn't look convinced. In fact, she looked downright uneasy. But she nodded. "A truce would be good."

Then she turned her head away and shifted to put more distance between them.

When the music ended he led her back to their table. They needed to talk. There were things to discuss, much to resolve between them.

Mario's brandy sat between two crystal glasses. Next to it lay a platter of cheese, crackers and grapes, plus a *cafetiere* of coffee.

Enrico was half-conscious of Faye fussing with a flimsy wrap as he poured brandy for himself and coffee for Faye. Covering those soft bare shoulders, he realized. Using the delicate material to try and hide from him the milky curve of quite magnificent breasts, with their delicate buds that had been so receptive to his touch. He shuffled in his chair, discomfited.

"You've gone all quiet on me."

He looked up as Faye spoke and caught the questioning look in her eyes. "I have much to think about."

"Like what?"

When she caught the edge of her wrap as it slipped off her shoulder, he wanted to shuffle again. But he fought off the desire to move. He had to wonder if he was heading for disaster with what he was about to propose.

He cleared his throat. "It would be best if you and Melita move into the villa on a permanent basis." Watching her he sipped his brandy, the liquid burning as it traveled down his throat. "You have nothing in London you cannot have here," he continued, ignoring the way she caught her lower lip between her teeth. "It makes perfect sense all round."

She reached for her coffee cup, changing her mind halfway to fuss with the wrap again. She didn't look at him. "I have responsibilities, a job, a home. A cat. Melita has her friends."

"She will make new ones here. As for your cat, I will arrange—"

"It's not as simple as that." She looked up at him now. "There's my job for a start."

"Give notice."

"I... It's not that easy."

He watched all the excuses, all the arguments spin around in her eyes. Those expressive blue eyes had always told him more than her words ever could. He loved watching them flash with anger, soften with tenderness, sparkle with laughter, darken with desire.

"It is not that difficult," he lied, the memory of her sultry gaze making his libido bounce. "I will make all the arrangements."

"No, you won't." She reached for her coffee. Sipped. Sipped

again. "I've been independent for a very long time. I don't want to give that up. Anyway, I enjoy my job."

"If you insist on working you can find another job here." He was almost as shocked as she appeared to be as the words slipped from his mouth. "In fact, my manager informed me only tonight that he has been unable to find a suitable replacement for his assistant who leaves for Rome in two weeks' time."

Her eyes went wide. "Surely you're not suggesting I apply?"

"Why not? You have given me a salutary lesson in the need to change my medieval attitudes regarding working mothers, have you not?" He tried not to smile but his mouth quirked. "This is your chance to ensure I remain firmly committed to the principle."

His smile only widened as her expression turned wary. "I don't know anything about vineyards or working for the manager of a winery."

"I can teach you. The fundamentals of any business are the same. A manager requires assistance in the smooth day-to-day running of that business, someone to organize his day and generally ensure matters of administration proceed with the utmost efficiency. Of this I am sure you are more than capable." He waited as she stared down into her coffee, then decided to play his ace. "Unless the rendering of your own abilities have been grossly exaggerated."

She looked up. There was no flash of irritation as he'd anticipated, just a narrowing of her eyes. "I know what your game is. You expect me to get affronted and annoyed so I'll accept the job just to show you I can do it."

"Now, *cara*, would I be that devious?"

He gave her an expression of butter-wouldn't-melt but his eyes gleamed in challenge making her stomach spin deliciously.

Yes, he'd be that devious, Faye thought, watching as he cut

off some cheese and slipped it, along with a couple of wafer-thin olive crackers onto a plate. When he wanted something he'd use whatever means to get it. Right now that seemed to be her. Although not in the manner she wanted him to want her. No. He wanted to keep her here so he could do the manly thing and protect her and Melita. Because his sense of duty, of family responsibility, demanded it.

That was the reason, the only reason, he wanted some kind of truce between them.

He slid the plate toward her and began fixing one for himself. Faye watched him, unable to stop from thinking how much she wanted things to be different. She didn't want him to feel duty and responsibility toward her. She wanted him to want her. *Her.* She wanted him to ask her to stay because he needed her to stay.

"So." He tore off a stem of black grapes. "Do I get an answer?"

She wanted badly to say yes. Wanted more than anything to be near him. Not that she intended for him to know that, because if he did he'd use her feelings to ensure he got his own way on just about anything.

With enormous effort Faye fostered a bland expression. "My answer might not be the one you'd like."

He selected a plump grape and began rolling it between his forefinger and thumb. He studied it, pursing his lips as if formulating something in his mind. "For our wine we use the Sangiovese grape."

Faye tilted her head, her smile wry. "How interesting. Is that called changing the subject because it might not be going the way you want?"

One corner of his mouth hiked up. "On the contrary, the subject remains the same. I am giving you your first lesson in managing a vineyard."

"I can't stay, Enrico. It's not possible. I have responsibilities."

"Which is my point. I can offer you a better job than the one you have in London, more comfortable accommodation, an improved lifestyle for your daughter. Need I go on?"

She watched as he rolled the grape between his fingers. It was a sensuous movement and she bit down on the inside of her mouth as the urge came to lick her lips.

His voice, low and commanding, reached her from across the table. "Open your mouth."

"What?"

He held up the grape. "Open your mouth."

Reaction shot through her system, her nipples swelling against the delicate lace and satin of her bra before tightening to unbearable proportions. She tried to keep from watching his fingers rolling that grape, tried not to think about it.

But her lips parted as her gaze slid to his fingertips. He held out the grape until it almost touched her mouth, and waited for her to take it from his fingers. She looked up, saw the glint of devilment in his eyes as he continued to hold the fruit a mere whisper away.

Her skin burned, her senses spun and an innate self-protection urged her to pull back. He was playing games. And she wasn't entirely sure what they were. Was he trying to get his own way, making her agree to remain in Tuscany on a permanent basis? Or was he trying to provoke her? Playing sexual games so uncharacteristic for him that she thought herself insane just considering the possibility?

When she opened her mouth to challenge him he popped in the grape.

Her mouth clamped closed, catching his fingers. He didn't pull them away, even when she opened her mouth. Instead he slid a fingertip, light and sensual, over her lower lip before dropping his hand.

Faye shot back as if she'd taken a bullet. Her whole body hummed from his touch. She wanted to spit out the grape, to warn him to stop playing whatever games he was playing. Instead she chewed, swallowed, then glared at him. "I don't know what you want from me."

"I believe you do." His fingers, those perilous fingers, circled the rim of his brandy glass. "And I am still waiting for an answer."

"About the job offer, about staying in Tuscany?"

"Of course." He eased his chair back. "But I have more to say, and it is inappropriate to discuss it here. We should leave." Before Faye could respond he stood, holding out his hand to usher her from the table. On the way out he muttered something to Mario and received another deep bow.

Lucca's streets were filled with late-spring tourists enjoying the warm evening. Enrico slipped his hand on the small of Faye's back and led her away from the busiest area of the city, through a narrow, cobbled lane filled with colorful tubs of flowers and specialist shops selling decorative pottery and trinkets.

The lane opened to a large grassy area and they walked toward where a fountain trickled into a central pond.

"My brother has left you penniless, your daughter fatherless," Enrico said, without preamble. "I realize my offer to help on a more permanent basis is a futile exercise. Your need for independence will not allow it. But equally, my need to protect my family will not allow me to stand back and watch you struggle. So there it seems we have an impasse."

Because he was attempting to be reasonable Faye thought she ought to reciprocate. "I'm not trying to be difficult, and I do understand you want to help us. But I've been doing things my way for a long time now."

He turned and offered her a wry smile. "As have I."

Faye smiled back. "Then we're a couple of hopeless cases, aren't we?" *And how on earth will we agree what is best for our daughter*? Faye thought. *If we're both so used to doing things our own way, how will we ever agree*? She'd moved on a few steps, trying to formulate the right words to start the conversation she'd been dreading all evening, when she realized Enrico had stopped. She turned back.

He stood there, looking all the world like a man in turmoil. "I believe I have a solution that will appease us both." He held out his hand. "Come here."

Faye stayed where she was. "Why?"

He beckoned with his fingers. "Come here."

She moved forward, her legs heavy. With some reluctance she slipped her hand into his. Her heart tripped as his fingers closed around hers, then filled with disappointment when he continued to keep her at arm's length.

There was a weird look in his eyes. No fire, no heat. Just a sort of resignation. Her stomach dropped to her knees.

"We need to put what has happened behind us and focus on the future." He looked down at their joined hands, then back at her. "What I propose will provide the perfect solution to solve both our problems. You may remain independent and I will have the peace of mind knowing you and Melita are well provided for."

Faye tried to shake her hand free. "I won't accept any money from you. Don't you dare insult me."

With a humorless laugh, he tightened his grip on her fingers. “I would not dream of insulting you in such a manner. What I propose is marriage. That way you are legally entitled to a share of the Lavini wealth. As my wife you will benefit from what my father wrongfully denied you as Matteo’s.”

“What?” Faye’s heart shot back up into her throat, pounding with such ferocity she thought it might jump right out of her mouth. “Marriage? To each other?”

Enrico huffed with impatience. “Do not insult us both by feigning shock or offence, Faye. No doubt the possibility has occurred to you.” Abruptly, he let go of her hand. “Matteo left debts. How are you planning to cover those? You are hardly able to keep yourself and Melita as it is, how do you intend to honor your late husband’s creditors?”

“I don’t know, but I’ll manage somehow.” Faye spoke her thoughts aloud. Truly she hadn’t given a thought to having to pay off Teo’s creditors. “I can take another job, or get a better paid one. For your information, I keep myself and my daughter perfectly well. There’s no way I’d resort to your preposterous suggestion.”

“Hardly preposterous.” He took a step forward, forcing her to back up against an old stone wall. “I will honor my brother’s debts and provide for you and my niece—”

“Oh, don’t tell me.” Faye raised her hand to stop his flow of words. “It’s your duty, your responsibility. If you think for a moment I’d marry you just to pay off some debts...do you think I’m that mercenary, Enrico?” Her voice shook as she tried to smother the hurt. “Do you think I’d stoop so low as to *buy* a father for my daughter?”

Ice trickled down her spine. She could never tell him Melita was his daughter, not now. He was monstrous, suggesting marriage purely for financial reasons. Did he think so little of her that he could insult her with such calculating ease?

What if he found out Melita was his? Here he was suggesting marriage as a way to care for his *niece*, just think what lengths he'd go to for a *daughter*. He would make demands she could never hope to fight. He would take charge. Take over. Before she knew it, her desires for her daughter would take second place to his.

Enrico stared at her with something bordering contempt as he retrieved the bleeping cell phone from his belt and spoke into it.

As Faye's mind churned she watched Enrico's face pale. He barked orders in Italian and Faye strained to concentrate on what he was saying. The skin over his forehead and cheekbones had tightened, his long fingers gripping the phone.

Faye deciphered two words.

Doctor and *hospital*.

God...please...no...

She grabbed his arm. "Melita?" Her throat tightened painfully. "Rico, is it Melita?"

He rubbed one hand along her upper arm as the other pushed the phone back into his belt. "She was kicked by one of the horses. We will go straight to the hospital."

"But she's all right?" Faye's voice hitched as emotion closed her throat. "My baby's all right?"

Enrico didn't answer, seemingly only intent on getting them back to the car. He got behind the wheel, turned the ignition and reached across to fasten her seat belt.

His hand moved over hers. "She will be fine, *cara*." He gave her hand another squeeze, as Faye prayed with everything she had that he was right. That her baby was safe.

Twice Faye ordered Enrico to calm down. He hadn't exactly raised his voice or rammed his fist onto the specialist's desk, even though at times Faye feared he might do both. His temper was tightly reigned, evident by the tension in his shoulders and the hard, unwavering line of his jaw. Plus his voice had fallen an octave or two, always a dangerous sign.

"I want more tests carried out before we take her home," he demanded again. "Even if you have to call in extra staff to do them, I want them done now."

The specialist looked decidedly anxious. "But there is nothing wrong with the child, *Signor* Lavini," the specialist said for the umpteenth time, until even Faye was assured. "Just a few bruises and some minor scratches. She is more shaken up than anything else, and more worried about being disciplined by her mother."

She'd be disciplined well enough, Faye thought as she watched Enrico pace the specialist's office. Her daughter would be well and truly punished for sneaking out of her bed to tell the horses that she wouldn't be able to see them for a whole weekend as Uncle Rico was taking her sailing. Yes, she'd certainly be punished, as soon as Faye was through hugging her with relief.

"My niece is not leaving until she has had more tests." Enrico flattened his palms on the specialist's desk and leaned ominously forward making the big man's face lose color. "There may be internal injuries, complications you cannot begin to know about. She is not as robust as other children. She was a premature baby."

Icy fingers raced up Faye's spine as her stomach pitched dangerously. To her horror both the specialist and Enrico turned to look at her and for one crazy moment she thought they'd been party to the sound of her thundering heart.

She didn't know what she was supposed to say, couldn't actually say anything because her mouth felt dry as dust.

The specialist's concerned voice speared through the silence. "How many weeks was your daughter when she was delivered, *Signora* Lavini?" When Faye merely stared at him he prompted, "Did her premature birth lead to any complications?"

Faye tried to swallow. "I..."

She looked at Enrico, at his stern expression and furrowed brow, and wanted to die on the spot. "It... I... She was..." Oh God. How could she tell him the truth right here, right now? How could she just say that, no, there were no complications because her daughter had been born almost to the day nine months after conception? A beautiful, healthy baby girl, with her father's eyes and the same strength of character that had people bending to her indomitable will.

Enrico obviously took her nervous stuttering as a sign of distress over her child because he turned back to address the specialist. "Just look at her records," he snapped. "You must have access to them. I arranged for the transfer of medical records for both my niece and her mother."

He did what?

Instinct flared, pushing Faye to challenge him, demand to know what right he had to do such a thing. But the specialist was typing on his keyboard, deferring to Enrico for correct spellings of names and pieces of information required to access medical records. Faye shot to her feet and moved in front of Enrico, her fevered brain prompting her to get between him and the computer screen, deny him access to the bombshell that would any moment pop on screen and throw everything into turmoil. The specialist's animated fingers continued to tap and Faye feared that in a few moments the secret she and Matteo had long protected would be revealed.

She didn't want it exposed in this way. She needed to prepare Enrico, make him understand the reasons for her decisions. There had to be time to try and make him understand...

But he gently nudged her out of his line of vision, peering over her shoulder at the computer's monitor. Faye knew she had to act fast.

She wedged herself between Enrico and the desk, standing firm when his eyebrows drew together in an irritated frown. "I need to talk to you. Can we go somewhere?" His frown deepened and she knew he was about to refuse. "Please, Rico. It's important."

The specialist provided unwitting support. "This will take some time, I think. There is a small garden at the end of the corridor, you may use that if you wish."

Enrico kept watching Faye but turned his head slightly to reply. "Alert me as soon as you have the records on screen."

The silent corridor echoed only with their footsteps as they made their way to the patio garden. It might have been the late-night air lifting the hairs on her arms, Faye thought, as she pulled the wrap close. But the shivers running over her flesh had more to do with fear and even more unsettling, shame.

When Enrico made to shrug out of his jacket, she shook her head. She couldn't let him make the chivalrous gesture when she was about to confess such cruel duplicity. Couldn't rock his world while his jacket, warm with the scent of him, lay draped around her shoulders.

Gathering herself, Faye looked down at the pond's gently trickling water feature and tried to remember her rehearsed speech. She couldn't seem to recall a single word, but she made herself face him. He deserved seeing her treacherous face when she turned his world upside down.

Her mind felt empty, along with her heart. He looked achingly handsome standing there facing her. So tall, so formidable. And she loved him with her very soul. Every single piece of her belonged to him. Always had. Always would.

But soon he would hate her forever.

Tears threatened, but she swallowed them back through a tight throat.

"I've lied to you."

His shoulders drew back, his hands finding their way into his pockets.

"I've lied to you about Melita. She wasn't a premature baby. She was born right on time and a very healthy weight." The words tumbled out on a single breath, the truth spilling from long years of restraint. She took a breath, keeping her eyes on his as she said the words that would change everything. "She's yours. Melita is your daughter."

He looked at her with a blank expression, as if he hadn't heard her or she was talking gibberish. But behind his guarded eyes Faye knew his brain worked overtime.

Processing...processing...

She filled her own fevered brain with a silent prayer for his compassion.

Then he narrowed his eyes. "It is impossible," he said, his tone flat and businesslike. "Impossible."

Faye shook her head, then covered her throat with the palm of her hand as if to ease the tightness there. "It's true. She's yours. I had her almost nine months to the day after we..."

His face drained of color. "You were using the contraceptive pill."

The cold practicality of his statement was a painful stab to her heart. "I wasn't. I lied about that as well." Her voice broke as she struggled to get her emotions under control. It was hard enough telling him, but watching his almost impassive response broke her heart.

Then his nostrils flared. "Why?" he demanded. "Why are you saying this?"

"I don't want to lie to you anymore. I want you to know the truth."

His eyebrows snapped together in a deep frown. "I do not believe you."

She'd been prepared for that, at least she thought she had. But seeing his fierce expression and the look of contemptible disbelief, she knew that no amount of preparation could have armed her against it. Her courage sank to her feet while her pulse raced alarmingly.

"It's true," she said, making herself look at him. "I didn't tell you at the time because...because I knew how you felt about...I knew you didn't want—"

"You seem to *know* a great deal, Faye." He scrubbed one hand across his jaw, then lowered his arm and frowned again. "If this is some attempt to ensure I continue to provide a home for you and your child, you waste my time. I have already offered you marriage."

"And I was about to turn you down." She wanted to hit back at him for the insult, but knew she deserved it. He had every right to let off steam, and she had to take just about anything he wanted to dish out.

She kept her tone low, appeasing. "Do you think I'd lie about something as important as this?"

His laugh was humorless. "Am I supposed to dignify that with a response?"

She looked away. "I know I lied before, but I had my reasons." She looked back. "This is the truth, I promise you."

Tension speared from his body. "What reasons?" he demanded, his hard jaw lifting. "This I really have to hear."

His tone shifted lower with each word and Faye's stomach gave a terrifying lurch. "You…you didn't want children."

His response was a lift of his eyebrows.

"Well, I thought you didn't," she added quickly, clasping her hands together at her waist. "You certainly didn't want children with me."

His continued silence was more menacing than the harshest of words, his lack of denial more hurtful. Pain stabbed low in her heart. "You…you said it was a mistake."

"It was." He turned then and started to pace the small patio. "*Dio*!"

Now he wasn't close, wasn't spearing her with that uncompromising glare, she could let out a breath. "You said no woman would ever trap you, no woman would ever play you for a fool. What was I to do, Rico? Come and tell you I was pregnant? That I'd lied to you about being on the pill and hey, what do you know, I'm having a baby." She had to stop because she needed a steadying breath. "And what would you have done? *Sacrificed* yourself by demanding marriage, that's what. Then where would we have been? You would have been right in the middle of a loveless marriage, trapped and hating me for it. As for me—"

He whirled, flares of heat scoring his high cheekbones. "As for you? You would have been equally trapped, would you not? Trapped in a marriage with a man you despised, who in a drunken stupor had taken you against the wall. So what did you do? Lie and cheat some more."

"It wasn't like that."

"No?" He moved toward her, nostrils flaring. "What story did you tell Matteo? Did you decide on the premature angle? Or perhaps you told him I took you by force."

When he kept coming toward her Faye took a step back. "Rico...don't..."

"Did he know the baby was mine?"

"Yes."

"Before or after your marriage?" Sarcasm dripped from his tongue, breaking her heart a little more.

"Before." She kept her voice even as her back hit the wall. "Teo knew Melita was yours."

He stopped right in front of her, his hard gaze shooting tiny arrows into her soul. "So it becomes clear, the real reason he demanded I keep away. Not only did he have to deal with the knowledge we had sex, he also knew you were carrying my child."

"It wasn't like that."

"As you keep saying." The leashed anger she'd felt building in him lowered his voice to almost a growl. "Then tell me how it was. Tell me how in hell my brother handled the fact his wife was pregnant with my child?"

What did she say to that? How could she reply? She couldn't tell him the truth, that Matteo married her *because* she was pregnant with his brother's child. Because she knew Enrico didn't love her, didn't want her, although she'd loved him with every piece of her heart and soul. Because she couldn't bear to have him look at her every day of their lives with a mixture of hate and contempt, merely because his fierce Italian pride demanded he do the right thing and marry her.

Neither could she tell him Matteo had his own reasons for marrying her. To throw a smokescreen over his homosexuality and thus deny his father that particular avenue of merciless derision.

"Did you not think I had a right to know?" Enrico demanded, breaking into her silent reasoning. "I understand you loved my brother, but did you not think I had a right to know you were pregnant with *my* child."

What was she supposed to say to that? That she didn't love Teo, that she loved him? It was what she wanted to say, so badly her throat, her heart and spirit, ached with it. But she couldn't. She couldn't risk Enrico knowing how she felt about him, all the while knowing all he felt for her was duty and responsibility.

"Teo and I talked about it." That much was true. "It seemed the best thing all round."

Faye watched as he started pacing again, the tension in his body like that of a big cat preparing to pounce on unsuspecting prey. Although in this case the prey was anticipating being eaten alive at any moment. Faye's stomach revolved and she folded her arms around her waist willing back the nausea.

He stopped pacing. "Is that why your marriage failed?" he demanded. "Because my brother could not handle raising another man's child? Or perhaps because his bride offered herself to another man mere weeks before her wedding night?"

Faye swallowed as tears stung. "Stop it." She dropped her gaze to the hard line of his jaw. "I didn't offer myself." She'd had enough of his cruel sarcasm and harsh words. "I tried to calm you down after the fight you had with your father, I wanted to comfort you. I don't remember offering anything else." Her face burned as anger fuelled her retaliation. "Perhaps you should stop a minute, consider your part in this. You're hardly blameless."

Her words seemed to hit him like a cold blanket. He stared

at her, his expression a mixture of shock and disbelief. Then he raked a hand through his hair. "Why in God's name did you not come to me when you separated? Why did you not tell me then, let me support you and...and...my child...?"

He went to a stone bench and sank down. "My child," he whispered, as he leaned forward and dropped his forearms across his thighs. He stared at the ground. "*Dio*, she is mine."

There was a sense of reverence, of wonder and awe, in his voice and encouraged by it Faye went to sit beside him. "I know you'll never be able to forgive me but I—"

"You have photographs?" He turned to look at her. "Pictures of her as a baby, a toddler?"

"Yes." She tested a smile. "Hundreds."

He nodded. "What sort of child was she?" Before Faye could answer, he raked a hand through his hair again. "*Dio*! What sort of father am I? What sort of uncle? All that time and I never once demanded to see her."

"You sent her cards and presents," Faye soothed, ignoring the stab of guilt and remorse. "Not once did you miss a Christmas or...her birthday."

"Ah, yes, her birthday." His voice was pure stone as he turned on her, anger flashing where moments ago there had been reason. "How exactly did you decide on the date you would use for my benefit? Did you toss a coin? Throw the dice perhaps? A date plucked out of thin air to keep me well off the scent? Or did you celebrate her real birthday then have another for the benefit of the man you decided would have no part in her life?"

They had decided on the latter, and that, coupled with the implied premature birth, had kept him off the scent. But now shame and guilt pressed down on Faye.

"I'm sorry," she whispered, wanting to rest her hand on his

arm but knowing he would throw it off. "I'm so sorry for everything."

"Sorry?" Fury rose in his voice. "You are sorry?" He shot to standing, then reached down and grabbed her arm to yank her against him. "You have denied me my child. You have lied, schemed, cheated. You have let another man raise my flesh and blood. Stolen from me years of my daughter's life. And you are *sorry*?"

He pushed her back and for one terrifying moment Faye thought he was going to strike her, such was the anger pulsing from his tense body. "Rico, please try and understand—"

"You have let her call me uncle," he said in an icy tone. "You have argued about every decision I have made for her since you arrived here, as if I had no right. Did you ever plan to tell me, or was it because you were pushed into a corner?" His face had drained of color except for the slash of heat across his cheeks. "Well?"

Faye stepped back at the sharp demand. "You won't believe me," she said, shaking her head, "but I did want to tell you. I tried earlier this evening when—"

"Spare me, Faye. I no longer wish to hear your lies." He pushed long fingers through his hair, muttered a ripe curse in the language of his birth. When he looked up his eyes were angry slits. "Such deceit, *cara*. Do you hate me so much?"

Faye couldn't speak, her throat had swollen shut. She could only watch as he stormed back into the building. Her whole body began to shake, her muscles trembled uncontrollably. How could he think she hated him? When she loved him with all her heart. That the very reason she had kept silent about their child was because she loved him so much and wanted him to have the life he craved, not the demands of one thrust upon him. Not one he would consider paralleled his father's. Trapped in a marriage with a woman he didn't love.

She shuddered in a breath, tried to quieten her shaking limbs. There should have been some sort of relief about it being out in the open, some lifting of the awful burden she'd carried all these years. But there was just this emptiness in her chest, in her heart.

Enrico would demand Melita be told the truth, and the thought of how that would affect her beloved child made the nausea intensify. Part of her knew Melita would be overjoyed to learn Enrico was her father, but then children didn't always react as you thought they would.

Faye squeezed her eyes shut. Somehow she had to prepare Melita, make sure her child knew how precious and loved she was, make certain she felt safe and secure.

That was her priority right now. Her child.

She trembled in another breath and opened her eyes. She had to go back inside and face Enrico.

The specialist was talking hurriedly on the phone when she entered his office. Enrico stood in front of the desk, his shrewd gaze piercing her like arrows as he said, "It appears Melita's medical records have been mislaid and cannot be traced until tomorrow morning." And his expression told her that heads would roll for it. "So, *cara*, your little confession was perhaps premature, unnecessary even."

Faye stole a glance at the specialist who continued to bark orders down the phone. "You're wrong." She forced herself to face that chilling gaze. "It was very necessary. I know you don't believe it but I've wanted to tell you since we came here. I'm glad you know. It's right that you know."

His eyebrows rose in a contemptuous sweep. "And it has taken you a mere eight years to come to that conclusion."

They both looked toward the specialist as he replaced the

receiver. "I can only apologize," he said with a tentative shrug. "But I assure you the records will be transferred first thing in the morning."

"Good," Enrico snapped. "Although it appears my information was incorrect. There was no premature birth."

The specialist looked nervously from Enrico to Faye and back again. "I see."

"As you have assured me that the child has suffered no ill effects from the incident, I will now take her home."

Assured *me*, *I* will take her home...how soon he had taken control, Faye thought miserably. For now she would allow him that. Because he was right, she *had* denied him his daughter, his own flesh and blood. She had lied to him, the cruelest of lies. All she could do now was allow him a little leeway to assert his right as Melita's father. Just a little.

But fear twisted her insides as she acknowledged everything would be different now.

For Enrico Lavini would never be content with a token involvement in his daughter's life.

Chapter Eight

Melita didn't seem to suffer any ill effects from her momentous adventure and insisted on going sailing as Uncle Rico had promised. If he had any doubts the child was his they would surely have been quashed by the display of such ferocious tenacity, an absolute inability to accept that something wasn't possible or couldn't be done. Indeed, she was her father's daughter. She all but stamped her feet when Faye insisted that they were staying on dry land for a few days to make sure she was fully recovered.

Of course, it was actually Enrico who insisted, just as it was Enrico who insisted that his daughter be told the truth about her parentage that very morning.

Melita slunk around the breakfast table on the poolside veranda and sidled up to Enrico. "Why can't we, Uncle Rico? You promised."

He placed an arm around his daughter's waist and drew her to him, trying to bank down his irritation at her unwitting use of his incorrect title. A fierce and terrifying protectiveness shot through him as he held his child. *La mia figlia bella,* he thought, as his gaze swept over her. His beautiful daughter. With her mother's exquisite complexion, the same delicate bone structure, and while the hair and eyes were unmistakably Lavini, her charm and poise were pure Faye.

He tugged her playfully into his side. "I do not believe any promises were made, *carina.*" His voice was gentle and calm as he softly chastised his daughter. "But perhaps we will do something later that might be even better than sailing."

Melita snaked her arms around his neck. "Ooh, what?"

"We shall see." With a little tug he brought her down onto his lap. As she settled he stole a glance across the table at Faye. Her face was pale and drawn, probably due to lack of sleep. Had she, like him, spent the night in restless turmoil? Most likely. For there was fear in her eyes now as she sat across from him, nervously chewing on her full bottom lip.

As his arms banded protectively around his child he took a deep breath, and prepared to change all their lives once again.

"There is something we have to tell you, your mama and me." He signaled to Faye, waiting as she slowly came around the table to sit beside him.

They both looked at Melita, at the slightly horrified expression that crumpled her pretty features. "We're not going home, are we, Mummy?" She tightened her arms around Enrico's neck, pressed her cheek to his. "Oh, I don't want to go home. I want to stay here with Uncle Rico and Carla and all the horses."

Faye leaned forward and rubbed her hand reassuringly down her child's arm. "Ssh, nobody said we're going home. But as Un... Rico said, we have something to tell you."

Melita looked up at Enrico. "What?"

With his daughter tight on his lap, he shifted. "Well, a long time ago before you were born, Mama and...err...well, we..." He shifted again, swallowed. He thought about testing the water by asking Melita if she'd like to live at the villa forever, preparing the way by asking if she'd like to stay with the horses. But that was the coward's way out. Not his style. Although right now he'd welcome it.

He'd never felt more terrified in his life.

"The thing is, little one, Teo, well, Teo wasn't your real father." He watched as her tiny brows drew together in puzzlement, and strangely he had the strongest urge to grip Faye's hand. But he didn't. "*I* am your real father, *carina*, and I want you to know that you are very precious to me."

Melita looked up at him, a cautious look in her eyes. "You're my daddy?" She looked at Faye, who gave a faltering smile and assenting nod, then straight back at Enrico. "Really?"

He nodded too, tightening his arms around her. "Really." His gaze flew over her face. "And I love you very much."

With serious intent she studied him for long moments during which his heart stopped a couple of times. "But why didn't you live with me and Mummy? Why did Teo be my daddy?"

Faye watched emotion wrench Enrico's face. This was all her fault and she'd let him take the brunt of the explanations to their daughter. It was only fair she step in and take her share of questioning from their fiercely intelligent, inquisitive child.

"Daddy didn't live with us because he didn't know you were his little girl." Faye paused. This was the first time since Melita's birth she'd acknowledged out loud that Enrico was her child's father, and the pleasure of it whispered through her. But guilt at having kept father and daughter apart soon annihilated the joy. "It was very complicated and Teo didn't want you not to have a daddy, so he pretended to be one."

"But why? Why couldn't Daddy live with us?"

Oh, God.

Enrico stepped in. "Because sometimes grown-ups do silly things and people get very hurt and upset. Then they do other silly things and it becomes even more difficult to make things right."

Melita considered that, her young face animated with expression as she sorted everything through. It went from puzzlement to elation and back to bewilderment again. Her satin-smooth forehead crinkled. "But you won't go away again, will you, Daddy? Not ever." It was more a command than a question. A non-negotiable edict. Like father, like daughter, Faye thought, and would have laughed if she hadn't been wracked with anxiety.

Enrico's face was a study in tenderness, wonder and adoration softening the hard edges of his features as he smiled down at the daughter who clung to him. Another tiny arrow in Faye's heart. For seven years she'd had her daughter to herself, had been the centre of her child's universe.

But now...

Melita's brow furrowed deeper. "You won't, will you, Daddy?" she demanded.

He laughed, then rubbed his cheek against his daughter's, hugging her close. "No, my precious child, I will never go away again. Not ever. And neither will you. You are going to live here with me. For always."

"And Mummy too?"

Enrico hesitated before picking up his daughter's hand to plant a tender kiss on her knuckles. "We will see."

Faye didn't hear the rest of the father-daughter exchange because her head was spinning as blood rushed through her veins. *We will see*? Just last night he'd proposed marriage, and now *we will see*?

But then his marriage of convenience had been the suggestion of a benevolent uncle, now he was making proclamations as a *father*. The implications of that soared through Faye's hectic thoughts. It was payback time. He was going to make her suffer for what she had done, what she had stolen from him.

There was no marriage on offer now. He wanted what was rightfully his, without the trappings of a wife for whom he felt nothing but contempt.

Which meant one thing.

He planned to take her daughter from her. He was going to get the best lawyers the Lavini wealth could buy and file a claim for full custody. He was going to make sure she suffered as he had.

She wanted to scream her refusal into his hateful face as he turned to look at her with an expression of cold arrogance.

You'll have a fight on your hands, Enrico Lavini, her narrowed eyes silently warned. Because if he thought for one moment he would...oh dear Lord, no...she couldn't begin to imagine the agony of being separated from her child.

"You do, don't you, Mummy?"

Faye looked to where Melita tugged on her arm. "What?"

"We're going to the beach to swim and have our lunch in a really nice hotel that Daddy's friend owns. You do want to come, don't you?"

"Yes. Yes, of course."

Just try and stop her. She intended to cling to her daughter with the same boa constricting strength with which her daughter presently clung to Enrico. If he thought for one moment she would simply hand her child over to him without one hell of a battle, he obviously didn't know the extent of a mother's wrath.

On the fringes of her awareness Faye heard Enrico say something about telling Carla they were going out for the day, then she watched Melita skipping happily beside him as he made his way back to the villa.

She felt numb, drained. Like everything that just happened, hadn't really happened. If she closed her eyes, took a deep breath, perhaps she would snap out of this awful dream. But when she tried it, nothing happened. Faye felt an emptiness settle in her chest. An awful despair.

She'd known he'd be angry, of course she'd known. Had expected the fury, the anger. She had expected blame and harsh accusation. But she hadn't expected this. Enrico would never be that cruel. Never.

Yet, it seemed the extent of his pain had brought out a part of him she'd never seen before. How on earth was she supposed to fight him? If he'd made up his mind he wanted full custody of his child, he would pull out every stop to make sure he got it.

Well, he could do whatever he liked. He was *not* taking her daughter away.

Propelled forward by a fierce, protective rage, Faye searched him out. She found him in his office, searching through papers.

Swallowing back the fear gnawing at her throat, she stormed to his desk. "You're not taking my daughter away from me." She slammed her palms on his desk. "Know that I'll fight you with everything I have. Everything!"

Like a man without a care in the world, Enrico looked up. Why was it he always looked even more formidable in his office? Dressed in tailored jeans and navy tee shirt he still looked the epitome of a successful and somewhat fearsome businessman, surrounded by state-of-the-art technology that he handled with the confidence and ability of an expert.

"Slightly theatrical, even for you, *cara*." He threw some papers into a tray on the side of the desk. "I have no intention of taking *our* daughter anywhere."

"You told her she was going to live here with you. For always, you said."

"*Si*, I believe I did." He lifted a file from the desk drawer, opened it and examined the contents.

His maddening calm and dismissive tone made Faye's temper escalate. "Put that down and talk to me!"

Pointedly, he took several moments to study the file before closing it and throwing it into the tray with the other papers. "Very well." He folded his arms and looked at her with cold grey eyes. "Talk."

For one mad moment she thought about pleading with him, begging him not to fight her for custody of Melita. She would tell him she would do anything else he wanted, as long as he didn't do that. But something in that steely, uncompromising gaze warned her it would be a futile exercise. Besides, you didn't give a man like Enrico Lavini a glimpse of weakness. He'd pounce on it like a predator.

"You can't expect me to let her stay here with you," Faye reasoned. "She's my child. It isn't right. It isn't fair."

"*Fair?*" His eyes blazed with a savagery that made Faye remove her hands from his desk at the same time he rose to his feet. "You are on exceedingly dangerous ground, and if we are speaking of fair then undoubtedly you must concede that ground to me." His body hummed with barely strapped hostility as he came around the desk and stood in front of her. "And what did you expect, Faye? That I would let my child go? Having been denied her for so long, did you expect me to let her walk out of my life without a fight? You robbed me of my daughter, you lied to me about her birthday, you let me believe she was my dead brother's child." His eyebrows pulled together in a fearsome scowl. "You allowed her to go on calling me *uncle* when all the time you knew differently."

Now Faye did take a step back. It was difficult to breathe with him towering over her, looking for all the world like he'd enjoy nothing more than taking her apart limb by limb.

But she forced herself to hold his gaze, despite the terror that hollowed her legs. "You can't take her from me. It isn't right to keep a child from her mother."

"Or her father." He snapped it out with the full force of his venom. "But it seems you had no compunction on that score." A muscle jumped angrily along his jaw. "I want my paternity legally acknowledged. I want my daughter to have what your lies have denied her."

Faye had expected no less. "I understand, and I have no argument with that, but—"

"She is my first-born child, in effect my heir. I want her safe and protected, in a secure environment where I can ensure she has everything she needs."

"She needs her mother." Faye's voice broke. "I'll fight you so hard, Rico. I'll fight you with everything I have."

"Which is nothing."

Faye stared at him, searching for a flicker of compassion in that hard expression. When she found no evidence of such, she slowly shook her head. "You've become the very thing you feared. You've become the same kind of vindictive, callous man your father is."

The skin across his forehead stretched tight, but he said nothing.

"You just want to make me suffer in the cruelest way possible." Faye went on, as he moved back to his desk. "I can't believe that you're doing this."

He lifted a document from his desk and handed it to her. "You may want your lawyer to check this before you sign. But I think you will agree the terms are more than generous."

"What terms?" Faye glared down at the contract she held with trembling fingers. "What do you mean *generous*?" Even as she formulated the words, the sickening possibility became clear. *He was paying her off? Buying her daughter?*

She threw the document at his chest as if the paper was contaminated with the deadliest virus. "How dare you!" If he'd been closer she may well have taken a swing at him. "What sort of man are you?"

"My terms are disagreeable to you?" His reasonable tone was accompanied by a lift of his arrogant brow. "Well, I am sure we can reach some sort of compromise."

Through her anger and fear, Faye pounced on the splinter of hope. "That's all I want, some sort of compromise. I won't stop you from seeing her, Rico. We can visit whenever you—"

"There will be no visits." He gathered up the document she had thrown at him. "The compromise I suggest will involve an increase in the payment to you."

The flicker of hope she'd entertained vanished with his words. "You're a monster," she choked out. "You're a despicable monster. You think I can be paid off? You think I'll *sell* you my daughter?"

The last words were lost on a cry as her heart knotted with pain.

He started to move around the desk toward her, then stopped. She saw him swallow.

"You seem to be laboring under a misunderstanding," he said in a hard, clipped tone. "I am merely suggesting a monetary settlement for you to pay off Matteo's debtors in full. I assume you will want to take care of this yourself, without my involvement, and that you would want to do so before the legalities."

A chill stole down her spine. "Legalities?"

He remained silent, watching as she tried to make sense of what he was saying. Then his mouth twisted into a derisive smile. "Did you really think I would keep my daughter here without her mother? Did you think I would make her choose between us?"

Faye could barely think at all. "I don't know what—"

"Thankfully, my principles and values are different from yours. I believe a child needs both parents."

"Well, so do I." She knew how hypocritical it sounded, but she couldn't seem to grasp anything. Was he saying that they would have joint custody? That Melita would perhaps visit him for say, Christmas and holidays?

"Then it is settled," he said, as he strode past her toward the door. "As you were legally separated for over three years, it will be perfectly acceptable for the marriage to take place at once. I will arrange it."

Faye managed a tentative grip on reality as Enrico reached the door. "Now just a minute," she protested, grabbing his arm and digging her fingers into hard, implacable muscle. "I have no intention of marrying you."

He looked down at her hand, then slowly back at her. His hard gaze didn't flicker. "Very well. I will arrange for my lawyers to draw up a contract ensuring my daughter spends equal time with each of her parents. Shall we say, six months with me here in Tuscany and the remainder—"

"No!" Faye shook his arm. "I will absolutely not agree to that."

He leaned down, gripped her chin and yanked her face up to his. "I want time with my child," he warned with predatory ease. "You have robbed me of seven years of her life. You will not rob me of another minute."

He bared his teeth. “Know this, Faye. I have not begun to deal with what you have stolen from me. But I warn you, do not push me on something I will fight tooth and nail for. You will have little chance of winning, believe me.”

Her whole body trembled, her voice a strangled whisper. “I was right. You want payback.”

“Indeed I do.” He jerked her chin higher, until her mouth was a fraction from his. His chest brushed lightly against her breasts, and she cursed herself for the sharp bolt of awareness that tripped through her system.

“Fight me,” he dared, with a mocking smile. “You will find me a formidable enemy.”

She had no doubt of that. Just as she had no doubt he was beyond reasoning with.

But how could she agree to this marriage? Knowing he only wanted his daughter, not her. How could she live each day enduring his contempt? Watching him learning to hate her a little more for what she had done to him.

And what of her reasons? If she married him it would be to keep her child close, to let Melita get to know her father. And, heaven help her, it was because she wanted him so badly she'd suffer just about anything to get him. Even enter into a sham of a marriage.

It wasn't as if she were a stranger to the concept. She'd already had one marriage of convenience and look how that had turned out. Yet her marriage to Teo had at least been based on a mutual love of sorts. This one would be based on contempt on Enrico's part and misery on hers. She would spend her life loving, wanting and needing a man who desired only to punish her. How could she want him when he was being this merciless? What did that say about the sort of woman she was?

She couldn't chance losing her daughter. Being apart from

Melita for even a day was hard enough. She couldn't bear six months...

"Well?" Enrico's mouth had set in a hard line. "What is it to be?"

Give me time to think, she wanted to say. *Let me absorb everything that's happened in the past twenty-four hours.* He wouldn't give her that, he'd demand her answer now, and despite all the questions spinning around in her frenzied mind, only one question seemed vitally important it pushed all the others aside.

"How...?" she began, and had to clear her throat. "How would it work exactly?"

Straight eyebrows curved upwards. "How does any marriage work?" Then his mouth quirked dangerously. "Ours will be of the traditional variety."

Faye's whole body shimmered with anticipation, even as she chastised herself for feeling this way about someone so unbelievably treacherous.

His chest pushed against her breasts, crushing her against the closed door. "But just so there is no misunderstanding on your part," he said, reaching for her hips to yank them up against him, "perhaps I should give you an indication of exactly what I expect from our marriage."

Faye barely had time to think how wonderful he smelled, all masculine heat and citrus cool, when his mouth came down hard on hers and crushed away further thought. His kiss annihilated her, stripped away every ounce of resistance and every lingering doubt that urged her to push him away.

She wanted him. Wanted him with a feverishness that stole her breath away, literally. He took what he wanted, making sure he left her weak and trembling against him before pulling away.

"Does that answer your question?" Before she could formulate a cohesive reply he kissed her again, with that same punishing ferocity. When he pulled away they were both breathing heavily. "I expect you in my bed, Faye. Be in no doubt of that."

How could she? After being kissed like he intended to devour her any chance he got.

The thought of it was shockingly thrilling.

"Now, I will have your answer."

"What?" She didn't realize there'd been a question. Besides which her mind, currently filled with images of sharing a bed with this man, was currently incapable of thinking anything rational. "I...I wasn't sure I had a choice."

"You always have a choice. Just be certain you are aware of the consequences. Should you accept marriage to me there will be no bargains made, no compromises in any area." The erotic glint in his eyes ensured no misunderstanding as to what particular area he was referring to. "Should you decline, be certain I will obtain full, or at the very least equal, rights to custody of my child."

His child, the subject of such bitter words between her parents, was racing up the stairs calling for them both with hungry anticipation of the promised trip to the seaside.

Enrico reached for the door, but kept his hard gaze on Faye. "Well?"

She was heading for heartbreak, because as much as she loved him he would never love her. But there was no way out, not if she wanted to be with her daughter. "If it's a case of marrying you or being separated from my child even for a day, there's no decision to make." She made sure to hold his gaze, lifting her chin for a shot of confidence. "So, yes, I'll marry you."

Not that she didn't question her decision over and over during the four weeks leading up to their wedding.

Enrico was distant, cool, aloofly polite with Faye, while a complete and utter pushover with his daughter. Melita wangled just about anything she wanted from Enrico, who in turn lavished attention on his daughter. Faye could almost see the rose-colored hue in his eyes.

On more than one occasion she had quietly chastised him, warning that it was not in their daughter's best interests to be spoiled and that she shouldn't be allowed to get away with some of the things he allowed her to get away with. In return Faye received an icy stare that indicated he couldn't give a damn what she thought, often accompanied by a curt and severe reminder he was making up for the seven years in which she had denied him the privilege.

Now, as Faye unpacked her things in the lavishly prepared bridal suite at the sumptuous *Casa Annot*, she shivered. Not from the air conditioning, or the breathtaking view of the *Cote d'Azur* from the terrace. No. What sent a frisson of reaction through her was the thought that in a few moments Enrico would return from a brief meeting with the hotel's owner, one of his friends from university days.

On arrival at the hotel he had breezily announced his arrangement to have a drink with his old friend, allowing her time to rest following their earlier marriage ceremony in Lucca's civic hall and the helicopter flight along the coast to their hotel. Faye knew she had no right to feel hurt by it. In spite of what Rico had warned, this promised to be no traditional marriage, where the bride and groom could barely keep their hands off each other. This was yet another marriage of convenience. Nothing more, nothing less. She would do well to remember it.

Anyway, perhaps he'd been right, Faye thought, pulling out

a satin padded hanger from the enormous wardrobe to hang one of her sundresses. She did welcome the time to herself. If only to get her thoughts together.

The ceremony had passed in a blur. She barely remembered saying her vows. Although hearing Enrico's clipped tones as he'd said his made her heart dip to her knees. She remembered the well-wishes of Carla and Giovanni who had acted as witnesses. The happiness glowing from her child's face as she swept her arms around her parents and told them she was the happiest girl in the whole world, promising to behave herself for Carla while they spent a few days on honeymoon. And what did a "honeymoon" mean, anyway? Enrico had carefully explained it meant that Mummy and Daddy got some time to talk about things they were going to do now that they were married.

Did that mean they would sleep in the same bed, like her friend Millie's parents did back in London? And if it did, could she still come into bed with them when it thundered, like she always did with Mummy?

Faye smiled, remembering her daughter's barrage of questions, then sank down onto the bed. For what seemed like the hundredth time that day she fought back the urge to weep. This was supposed to be the happiest day of her life, and yet it felt the most wretched. She glanced over to the door. Her husband was out there now, propped against some bar sharing a drink and a few memories with an old friend, while his bride sat alone on their bed willing him to come back and tell her he cared for her and wanted their marriage to work.

Fat chance of that, Faye thought miserably, as she got to her feet and finished sorting her underwear into one of the drawers. Business contracts made no stipulation that either party had to care. She ran her fingers over the scraps of silk and lace she'd bought on impulse. Treating herself to sexy, frilly underwear in the hope that Enrico might weaken at the sight of her in it. How futile was that?

Was there anything more pitiful than a woman trying to attract a man who had shown her nothing but disdain, while simultaneously making clear his intention that she make good her promise to fulfill her wifely duties? For him any lovemaking—no, make that sex, for what he had in mind could never be termed lovemaking—any sex would be payback, the settling of a score. Harsh punishment for her treachery these past years.

What they shared wouldn't be tender or caring. He'd take her in the same way he'd taken everything else. He'd be harsh and demanding, concerned not for her pleasure, but only for his. Once she had thought him tough but never cruel. How times had changed.

All she had ever wanted was for everyone to be happy. To have what they wanted most. She hadn't wanted to burden Enrico with a wife he didn't want, didn't love. Well, it might have taken a few years longer to manage, but wasn't that exactly what she had done now? Trapped him into a marriage he didn't want?

She had absolutely no doubt of his love for his daughter, but it was obvious he wasn't planning on adding to the family. The small box she'd seen him slip into his bedside drawer was evidence of that.

A knock at the door cut short her desolate musing. Faye hurried toward it, realizing as she was halfway across the room that Enrico would hardly knock. He'd just march right in. A waiter, dressed in a cool white uniform, gave her an enormous smile and a discreet apology for having disturbed her, but *Monsieur* Lavini had requested champagne be delivered to his suite.

Faye watched as the waiter placed the silver ice bucket and crystal flutes on the cabinet beside the doors to the terrace, then gave him a shaky smile and a mumbled thank you as he left. She turned to stare at the ice bucket. Champagne? What was that for? They hardly had anything to celebrate. She moved across the room and turned the bottle gently on its carpet of ice, smiling wryly as she read the label. Only the best for Enrico Lavini.

Maybe she should have a quick sample before he returned. A bit of Dutch courage. She certainly needed it. All that musing about how roughly he would treat her in bed had her nerves humming.

She jumped guiltily as the door opened and Enrico strode in. He looked at Faye and then at the champagne, his mouth curving in a mocking smile "Thinking of starting without me, *cara*? You must be more nervous than I believed." He came over to the cabinet. "Did you hope a few glasses of this would dull your senses, help you get through the coming ordeal?"

"No," she lied, watching as he lifted the bottle and began to pour. "I was just interested to see if it was one of your labels."

"It is," he said, as if the very idea of it being anyone else's was ridiculous. "Now I believe a toast is in order." He passed her champagne. "To the future," he said, with a tap of his flute against hers. "To our daughter."

At least she could drink wholeheartedly to the latter, even if *the future* filled her with dreaded anticipation. "To our daughter," she repeated, smiling briefly before sipping champagne.

Enrico kept his eyes on hers. "I have arranged for an evening sail. We will have dinner on board."

"A sail?" Had she heard him right? Surely he didn't mean *that* evening. As if it were just any old evening and not their wedding night.

"Indeed. We will sail toward Monte Carlo. Perhaps you might enjoy a stop-over at the casino."

She *must* have heard him wrong. "Casino?"

He nodded. "I suggest you get ready." A superior smile slashed his face as he surveyed her with enviable cool. "We do not want to keep our guests waiting."

"Guests?" This time she *really must* have heard him wrong. "Tonight?"

"Indeed." He leaned back against the cabinet, arms folded, with the champagne flute nestling in the crook of his left elbow. "I am buying a new yacht, and the owners of the one that interests me have invited us to dine with them. No better way to test sail a vessel than to enjoy a good meal aboard her, would you not say?"

Enrico sipped his wine, watching Faye's eyes widen and her face pale. He may have missed his calling, he considered, as he tried to quieten his overwrought system. Perhaps he deserved an acting award for the performance he was putting on. But the truth was he felt damned awkward about this whole marriage thing. Haunted by the way Faye had looked at him when he'd first suggested it. Stunned, pained...and was there even a glimmer of disgust?

Well, he wasn't exactly proud of himself. But *Dio* she had played him for a fool all these years, she and his brother had laughed behind his back. They'd spent years—*years*—deceiving him. Now it was time to even the score.

He took another sip of champagne, watching her fuss with the tiny pearl buttons of her jacket. She hadn't changed out of the little blue suit she'd chosen for the ceremony, nor did she seem any calmer, any more relaxed. Good, he thought, as venom coursed through his veins. That was exactly how he wanted her. She'd deceived him, kept his beautiful daughter from him, lied, cheated and...fallen in love with his brother.

Shame pumped through him. Heaven help him, that was the crux of his fury, his wrath. Not that she'd lied about Melita's paternity, nor that she'd cheated him out of the first years of his daughter's life. What ripped through him, clawed at him, was that she'd chosen his brother. He'd banked it down all these years, told himself he no longer cared. But now he knew they had a child together it had somehow brought everything to a fierce and terrifying climax.

"What a wonderful idea." Faye's overly-pleasant tone cut through his heated reverie. "And how clever of you to combine two business ventures." She snapped up her vanity case from the chaise at the end of the giant bed. "How exciting, dinner on a yacht and then on to Monte Carlo. I've never been to Monaco. Is it as glamorous as they say?"

She imagined the heavy clink she heard as she closed the bathroom door was the sound of Enrico slamming down his glass. Wickedly satisfied, Faye spun the taps. One up to me, she thought, and tapped an imaginary line in the air. See how he liked that.

Bastard.

It was obvious what he was doing. Keeping her off balance, making her squirm. He knew she was nervous, unsettled by everything. It was all part of his little game. Payback, whatever he wanted to call it. Another attempt to humiliate her. To keep her ground down.

Well, two could play at that game. How about a nice spot of rejection at the end of the evening? See how he'd like that. He'd warned her he'd not tolerate any compromises or bargaining in the bedroom department, but he'd never actually forbidden delay tactics.

She forced herself not to yank at the buttons of her jacket as they stubbornly refused to open. Instead she took a deep breath, told herself to calm down. The man wasn't worth the white heat that had her fingers shaking with fury

How dare he treat her this way?

Anger replaced the nerves and tension. Now she had her own agenda. By the end of the evening she'd have him so hot for her he'd be unable to think straight. And then, *then*, she would pull out one of the stock advantages in a woman's arsenal. By the time she'd finished he'd be the one begging, pleading.

And she'd take great pleasure in telling him where he could go.

Chapter Nine

Enrico shoved open the door to their suite, battling against the sharp desire to commit bodily harm. His temper only increased as his sweet and innocent-faced little wife sauntered past him, yawning delicately.

"What a perfectly lovely evening." Faye plopped herself daintily onto the chaise, sliding the palest pink silk wrap from her bare shoulders. "It was so relaxing being at sea on such a gorgeous night, and I can't believe I actually won my first ever game of blackjack." With a carefree toss, she kicked off cream pumps. "So, are you going to buy it?"

"Buy what?" Even to his own ears, his voice sounded clipped. But he'd had one hell of an evening, no small thanks to the woman draping herself sensuously along the chaise.

"The yacht," she said, after another prim yawn. "Are you buying it?"

He tugged at his tie and threw it onto the dresser, along with his jacket. "No. I am not going to buy the damn yacht."

"What a shame, I thought it was delightful." She smiled at him. "Is there any champagne left? I'm thirsty."

"Then try water. You have had enough champagne." He lowered his voice to a mutter. "More than enough."

"Excuse me?" she said sweetly.

"Nothing." He yanked open the top button of his crisp white dress shirt and went into the bathroom. The woman was driving him insane. She'd been nervous and edgy all day and relaxation personified all evening.

He'd wanted to keep her nervous and edgy, but his plans had backfired. Now, damn it, *his* nerves were on edge. Had been since she'd stepped from the bathroom in that long, pink sheath of a dress highlighting every curve and dip of her sumptuous body. The plunging neckline, with that sexy frill, promised easy access to the full, lush breasts beneath. All he had to do was slip his hand inside...

Enrico leaned forward, pressing his palms against the cold porcelain of the basin. He closed his eyes. *Dio*! What the hell was he supposed to do now? Take her anyway? Even while she seemed not to care one way or the other?

Things weren't going as he'd planned. Nor as he'd wanted.

He came out of the bathroom, muttering a curse when he saw her still stretched out on the chaise, eyes closed and her head propped on one arm. The position made the neckline of her dress bunch, pushing up one plump breast.

Temper and lust fired through him until he thought he might explode.

Faye obviously sensed him. She opened her eyes. "Mmm, I must have dropped off for a few minutes." She gave him that sweet smile that was starting to irritate the hell out of him.

He walked to her, curled his fingers around her wrist. "It is time for bed." He helped her to her feet and she tumbled into his arms.

"I think you're right about the champagne," she giggled. "I have had too much." She looked him straight in the eye and blinked innocently. "I can't possibly have sex tonight. You'll have to wait."

Something snapped inside him. "Do not play me for a fool, *cara.*" His eyes narrowed as his fingers tightened around her arms. He pulled her close. "I told you no bargains, no compromises. You agreed to this marriage knowing exactly what I expect."

As if by magic she sobered up, her blue eyes glaring at him. "Well, I have some expectations too." She pushed at his chest. "I expect to be treated with respect. How dare you treat me like I'm some...some...floozy you can order around? Who will jump whenever *you* say you're ready to jump me." Her voice hitched. "This was supposed to be our wedding night, Enrico. How humiliating do you think it was for me to sit on that yacht knowing those people knew my bridegroom preferred negotiating a business deal rather than being alone with me?"

"They had no idea this was our wedding night." The hurt in her eyes punched straight to his conscience, but he reminded himself of her treachery and fired back, "Not that you seemed too concerned. You flirted and batted your eyelashes at any man who came within blinking distance."

"Too right. I wasn't going to let anyone think I was so undesirable my husband could manage to wait a whole evening before making love to me. I wanted people to think there must be something wrong with *you.*"

Fury raced through his system. "There is nothing wrong with me." And to prove it he grabbed her buttocks and yanked her hips against his erection. "You have spent the entire evening making me suffer, brushing against me at every opportunity, flirting and parading yourself. I will not have it."

"No, you won't. Not tonight." She looked up at him, the hurt in her eyes replaced by a cool conviction. "Ask your hotel owner friend to find you another bed for the night, because you're not sharing mine."

She almost made it to the bathroom, but fuelled by anger, and a sexual frustration that ripped at his self-restraint, Enrico grabbed her wrist and swung her around. "You have no say in the matter." He used his body to push her against the wall as his hands plunged into her hair and tugged until her mouth was a breath from his. Her startled gasp only made him want her more, but he ignored the flash of dishonor that shuddered through him and pressed himself against her. He would make her his, wash the memory of his brother from her head, from her body, with every touch, every stroke, every kiss.

She glared at him. "If you do this now, it will be against my will."

He watched her mouth as she spoke, felt his own burn to cover it. "You think I care?"

"Yes."

There was no fear in her eyes, no discomfort in her expression. But her voice trembled and it was his undoing. He released her so abruptly that her head bumped against the wall.

He held her steadfast gaze, trying to get the breath that heaved in his lungs under some sort of control. He didn't know what was happening to him, didn't know how to restrain the desire leaping in his blood. He couldn't think, couldn't reason. So he turned, snatched up his jacket and stormed from the room.

Faye stared at the closed door that still reverberated from his exit. Breath shuddered in and out of her lungs, hitched at the back of her throat. She had gotten what she wanted, what she had set out to accomplish at the beginning of the evening. She had forced his anger, made him pay for the humiliation of making her spend her wedding night with other people.

So why did she feel this awful emptiness? Why did her

heart feel ripped down the center?

Because it had all been a cover, a smokescreen for the hurt. He'd spent the evening chatting, *negotiating*, for heaven's sake. So she had set out to make him want her, make him ache to have her. And it had worked. She had won. She'd won because she saw the desire in his eyes whenever their glances met during the evening. She'd won because she noticed his scowls as she flirted outrageously with the yacht owner's bachelor son. She'd won because of the way he had pushed against her a few minutes ago.

Yet it was the most hollow of victories, because she ached and she hurt.

Part of her had willed him to just take her anyway. She knew he wouldn't. He was too honorable. She had angered him, tormented him, kept the cruelest of secrets from him for almost eight years, and she knew he wouldn't.

Damn him.

The night air brushed her skin as she stepped out onto the terrace. It was beautiful here, she thought, watching tiny dots of light sparkle against the undulating coastline. Above her the clear night sky mirrored back that light with bright, twinkling stars. Below her, the gentle hypnotic lap of water echoed against rock. It was all wonderfully romantic, sensual and heady.

The only thing missing was Enrico.

Faye leaned against the iron balustrade. She took a long deep breath, letting it out on a sigh as she closed her eyes. How had things gotten to this? By rights she should be in his arms. He should be in hers. But here they were. Her in this huge bed...sleeping alone. While he was heaven knew where. It had all gone so very horribly wrong.

She knew he didn't love her. Never would. But somehow

she'd thought—expected—that they would work things out, manage to get along. Her love for him would have facilitated that.

But the very thing she had tried to avoid when she was pregnant had come back to haunt her all these years later. This was exactly what she had tried to prevent.

Enrico's contempt. His terrifying determination to do his duty, at the cost of his own happiness.

His cool politeness in the weeks leading up to their marriage had been worse than angry words. He had married her for their daughter's sake. To secure Melita's future and make sure he was the one who provided it. He wanted his child. Not a wife.

Faye shivered against the Mediterranean night breeze. What did she want? In the absence of his love, what did she want?

His respect. She wanted—needed—his respect. If nothing else she wanted that. Yet even that seemed impossible.

Faye prepared for bed and tried not to care where Enrico would spend the night. Would he ask his friend for another room? Probably not. Just think what a blow that would be to someone with an ego the size of Tuscany. Perhaps he might drive back to Monte Carlo, spend the night there.

The click of the suite door lock being turned had her snatching her short satin robe from the side of the marble bath, pulling it on as she hurried back into the room.

She found Enrico dropping his keys onto the side table.

"What do you think you're doing?" Faye asked, tying the knot of her robe.

He looked across to her, his gaze flirting over the robe, sending a shudder of awareness down Faye's spine—along with a heady dose of anticipation and fear. Had he returned to make good on his threat? Had she been wrong? Was he the sort of man to take a woman by force?

No. He wasn't. Faye would stake her life—her daughter's life—on that.

He rolled his shoulders. "What I am doing is preparing for bed." He ambled over to stand by it, unbuttoning his shirt. "You may not want me in it, Faye. But that remains your problem."

"But I thought—"

"It seems you're overly fond of thinking." He bent to turn back the covers, then faced her where she stood on the opposite side of the bed, fiddling desperately with the knot in her robe. "If you do not want me to touch you, fine. But this is my bed and I intend to sleep in it."

He shrugged out of his shirt and Faye forgot to breathe. His chest was wide and muscular, a smattering of hair trailing down the centre. He reached down to unhook the fastening of his trousers and Faye had to swallow. How on earth was she supposed to sleep next to him, feel that solid chest brushing against hers, those powerful shoulders, muscled arms? How was she supposed to do that?

She looked away as he reached for his trouser zip, mortified when her gaze met and locked with his. He knew what he was doing, she realized, as his mouth quirked almost imperceptibly. He knew because his eyes narrowed, and a warm flush of heat speared across his chiseled cheekbones.

"I don't think it's appropriate."

He stopped mid-zip. "What is not appropriate?"

Faye moved toward the case she had nervously unpacked earlier and hefted it onto the bed. Enrico didn't move, which at least offered some relief. She'd half expected him to come storming around the bed and snatch the case off, before throwing her down in its place.

He merely watched as she retrieved underwear from the drawer and stuffed it in.

"Going somewhere?

Faye kept stuffing in clothes as hot tears burned the back of her eyes. How could he treat her this coldly? Didn't he know he was breaking her heart? Smashing all her stupid dreams of building a life together? He might not love her but she had enough for both of them. In time he might have come to care for her.

Fiercely concentrating on battling back the tears, Faye didn't realize he'd moved until his hand reached for hers as she continued to pack her case.

"No, *cara.*" He took the tee shirt she held and dropped it onto the bed. "If I have been unreasonable I apologize for it."

Faye took a moment to compose herself, blinking rapidly as she stared down at their joined hands. "*If* you've been unreasonable?" She resisted the urge to shake her hands free of his, because it felt too good to at least have this contact. This simple connection between them. "You think because we're married you get to treat me how you like and I just have to go along with it?"

She waited, hoping for a response. When it didn't come she pulled her hand away and continued to pack. "I was wrong to keep your daughter a secret from you, but you don't get to punish me by treating me like my feelings don't matter. I did what I did because I thought it was for the best. That might be right or wrong, I don't know, but I did it. I can't change anything. But I won't allow you to treat me with such disrespect and—"

"You are the mother of my child and as such you have my respect." He caught her hand again and eased her around to face him. With his eyes on hers he lifted her hand and drew it to his lips, brushing his mouth across her knuckles. "You have it, *cara*. You have my respect."

Faye fought the trickle of warmth spreading across her chest. He might say it, might even try to demonstrate it within the confines of their marriage, but he didn't respect her. Never would. And it caused a sharp tear in her soul.

"Now," He gestured to the case and array of clothing scattered around it, "why not put this away? I will get us a nightcap."

It was all so very easy for him, wasn't it? All he had to do was turn on the charm, say the relevant words and *hey presto*!

Faye lifted her chin. "I thought you said I'd had enough to drink."

He brought her hands to his lips again. "Perhaps another glass of champagne will put you in a mellow mood."

His teasing tone sent angry heat into her cheeks. "So I'll feel inclined to sleep with you? I don't think so."

His fingers tightened over hers. "I have never once had to resort to coercing a woman into my bed, and most definitely not with drink. I will not start now." His voice was rough and low. "If the woman I have married finds it easy to renege on the negotiated terms of what is in essence a business contract, then it is for me to write it off as an unprecedented failure. I will not beg you for sex nor do I desire a woman under me who is anything less than willing."

"I can see why you've never had to coerce a woman into your bed," Faye snapped, as she pulled her hands from his. "You just dazzle them with that amazing charm and humility of yours."

"I do not promise what I cannot deliver. Unfortunately the same cannot be said for you."

The harsh insults mixed with the emotional rollercoaster of a day, now culminating in his confirmation that their marriage was indeed a business contract, proved a lethal combination. She didn't feel angry anymore. She felt downright furious. No small measure of that fury was aimed at herself for agreeing to this ridiculous marriage, and the terms which made up their agreement—specifically the one that put her in his bed. Added to which was the underlying realization that perhaps, just perhaps, he might be a little bit right about her not delivering what she'd agreed to.

Furious with both of them, she marched up to confront him, standing inches away from his naked chest. She jerked her shoulders back, stuck up her chin. "All right," she snapped. "Take me. Go on. It's what you want, isn't it? Take me."

He stood his ground, she'd give him that. Not a flicker of reaction on that arrogant face of his. "It is nothing more than you agreed to," he reminded her, his tone maddeningly matter-of-fact.

But then his eyes slid down the length of her, hovering at the point where her robe brushed her skin mid-thigh before meandering up to hover again at her breasts. Without looking down Faye knew her nipples had behaved shamefully. She felt it in the way they brushed roughly against the satin, saw it in Enrico's predatory perusal. She'd only wanted to challenge him, believing he would storm out of the room again, leaving her alone with her misery. But now, as her mind screamed *take me, take me,* willing him to do exactly as she dared him, she knew she had been lying to herself. She wanted him. Anyway. Anyhow. Even knowing that for him their lovemaking was little more than a clause in a business contract.

She hated herself for it. Hated she had sunk so low as to want a man who stood there looking as if he was weighing up whether or not she was worth the effort. Hated that she could be easily affected by that magnificent bare chest rippling with muscle, the rock-hard stomach beneath sexily unfastened trousers.

Her legs felt boneless even as heat swept through her like a tidal wave. What if he refused now? After she'd all but offered herself on a plate? His for the taking. Literally. She didn't think she could face the rejection. The indignity of being so undesirable to him he could simply refuse her and crawl calmly into bed...to sleep.

Panic edged around the fear as she repeated her challenge. "What are you waiting for?" She thrust out her breasts. "Take me."

His eyes stayed on hers. "Undo your robe."

Faye's pulse raced at the smooth command, realizing he was declaring absolute control over both her and the situation. "No," she said. "You want this aspect of our *business contract*, you instigate it. And don't for a moment think I intend to participate."

She couldn't, she realized, have said anything more dangerous if she'd questioned his very manhood, and the dangerous gleam in his eyes confirmed her suspicion. She'd issued him the ultimate challenge for a sexually confident male.

Suddenly she felt like prey—examined, inspected, scrutinized. His primitive gaze filled with wicked and fierce intent, issuing back his own challenge. He held her gaze for long moments, then he looked down to where her chest heaved with apprehension...panic...excitement...

"I believe you are already participating, *cara mia*. It merely remains for me to finish what I appear to have begun."

All of her senses shot to overdrive. His voice slid over her skin like the finest oil, sensual and seductive. His scent, that special blend of musky, masculine heat, surrounded her in a carnal haze. His physical presence filled her vision, until he was all she saw. She wanted to touch, to explore, to discover.

Intoxicated, knocked off balance, she fought the urge to close her eyes and just give in to him. To simply let him take her where her whole body screamed to go. Now, more than ever, she needed some control. It would take every ounce of willpower, but she needed to stay in control.

But who was she kidding? She'd lost control from the first moment she'd set eyes on him and had spent the intervening years in denial. He was always there, if not in the foreground then on the periphery of her thoughts. Now he was here in glorious reality, and threatening to strip away every rational thought, every last vestige of self-protection.

Perhaps she was a fool to think she would have any control in their relationship, any say in how he could take all her feelings and spin them around until all that remained was how much she wanted him. But she was damned if she wouldn't try.

With a deep breath Faye stepped forward. "Why don't you just get on with it?"

Those grey eyes glittered. "Undo your robe."

He wasn't being stubborn or ensuring he retained absolute control, Faye realized. This was Enrico. Demanding, proud, arrogant but essentially honorable. He was making certain she was a willing partner. He wanted confirmation of her agreement to their union. By untying the belt of her robe she was issuing an invitation, welcoming him. It was a symbol of her acquiescence, her submission.

Although quite why he needed it at this point, Faye wasn't certain. Didn't the physical evidence speak for itself? Her face must be flushed with desire, her pupils all the way dilated by now, and as for her treacherous nipples...

With her eyes glued to his, she let her hand drop to her

belt. Her fingers seemed clumsy and heavy as she fumbled with the knot, then fumbled some more. She used both her hands, lowering her eyes from his to focus on the cause of her predicament.

What was wrong with the stupid knot anyway? She knew nervous energy had caused her to fiddle with the thing during their confrontation but she couldn't have bound it that tightly.

Her face burned, her humiliation complete when Enrico gave a low, sexy laugh then reached out to hook his index finger around the knot. He gave her an easy tug and she stumbled against him.

His eyes smoldered down at her. "Why not let me do that?"

Her heart pounded but she gave a casual shrug. "Do whatever you want."

Another low laugh. "I intend to." His hands got busy with her belt and seconds later, as if by magic, the knot unraveled.

Silk slid against her skin and air brushed over her naked shoulders as Enrico slipped the robe from them. He tightened his fingers around her upper arms, trapping the silk before it could slip any further down.

With another almost imperceptible tug, her breasts brushed his chest. Every precious memory of their first time together didn't come close to how it felt against him now, as if the intervening years had served only to increase her need for him. Her knees trembled, her head spun, everything inside her sprang to life after long years of denial.

"Put your arms around me," he growled, tightening his hold. "Say you want this."

Seemingly incapable of rational thought of her own, Faye brushed her fingers along his forearms. Urged on by his sharp inhale and the jerk of his rock-hard abdominal muscles, she slid them over the granite surface of his biceps, then over the heated skin of his shoulders and around his neck.

"I want this," she confirmed, lifting her mouth to his. "I want you."

He took her mouth in a greedy kiss that told her he felt the same, and her head spun in edgy delight. It didn't matter that her legs had given up the ghost because he was holding her tight...and her breasts were crushed hard against the hot, solid expanse of his chest. Like hers, his heart thundered. The thought of it, the thrill of it, made her tighten her arms around his neck and she slid her fingers into his hair. That she could make him want her like this, as if he couldn't get her close enough, couldn't kiss her hard enough, sent a sharp thrill barreling through her system.

His hands slid down, gripping her buttocks beneath the silk. He didn't end the kiss as he lifted her into his arms. Faye clung to him, her legs tight around his waist, the warmth of cloth, the chill of steel as his zip pushed against her naked core made her squirm and jerk herself closer against him.

He gave a low growl, turning with her in his arms until he could drop them down on the bed.

His mouth slid hot and hungry over her jaw, down her throat. He eased the silk gown away from her arms and threw it aside. She arched into his palm as his hand covered her breast, her nipple incredibly sensitive to the slow roll of his thumb and forefinger. She moaned softly, both in sensuous discomfort and agonizing need. The delicate torture he inflicted on her responsive flesh only intensified when his mouth claimed her breast, his tongue licking and soothing the ravaged nipple.

The quiet night air was ruptured by her appeal for... She didn't know what. All she knew was that she wanted, needed, to say his name over and over.

"Rico..." she ground it out as he licked and teased, showing no sign of acceding to her strangled plea for him to cease the exquisite torture.

He transferred his attention to her other breast as she bucked beneath him, running her hands over his back, his shoulders. Wanting to push him away and yet wanting him ever closer.

It was too good. He was too much.

His hand slid down, over her stomach, her hip, the side of her thigh. She touched his itinerant arm and felt the muscles flex as he stroked and explored. When his fingers danced close to where heat flared she said his name again.

His eyes lifted, found hers, as he pushed his fingers gently inside her.

Faye gasped, her intimate muscles tightening at the contact. He waited, dropping tiny kisses on her mouth, then pushed deeper, harder.

She tensed again, closing her eyes, trying hard to relax. This was what she wanted. This was what she had craved for eight years. Eight long years during which she had never known another man's touch, had never wanted another man's touch. Only Enrico. It was only ever Enrico. Why in heaven's name couldn't she simply relax now they were finally together?

Because underneath it all she knew this meant nothing to him. Nothing more than a means to an end. Keep her happy and he got to keep his daughter with him. It was that simple. For him. They were together like this because of a clause in a contract.

Enrico's hand stilled, but he didn't withdraw it. The warmth of his palm as he cupped her was strangely comforting. And it had tears forming.

She couldn't cry, not now. Her eyes shot open and she saw the tiny grooves between Enrico's.

"You are so tight, *cara.*"

Faye swallowed, stroking her fingers along his shoulder. "I'm sorry." Although she didn't know what she was apologizing for. All she knew was she didn't want him to stop. And right now he looked concerned enough to do that.

"Do not apologize." He kissed her, slow and long. "It is every man's dream."

Although quite why in hell she was *this* tight was confusing in the extreme. But Enrico pushed the enigma away. He had better things to think about right now, better things to *do,* than wonder why his wife was as tight as the virgin she had been when they first came together. But the thoughts wouldn't leave him as he kissed her. She'd had a child, been married. And although separated from his brother for three years, he wasn't so naïve that he didn't know a woman had needs the same as a man. In that respect he wasn't the old-fashioned dinosaur Faye accused him of being. Surely she had taken a lover since the separation?

Don't go there, he warned himself. Not the time, not the place. He had the woman he'd craved underneath him. While she was tense and tight, all the other signs she was a willing participant were there. Perhaps in his desire for her he'd rushed things?

But then Faye arched beneath him, her soft moans bringing him out of his reverie. He hadn't realized he'd resumed a rhythmic stroking of his fingers. Hadn't realized Faye had started responding to him.

Already she was wet and more than ready for him. He was rock-hard. Blood pumped through his system and his entire body throbbed for release.

He rolled on top of her, nudging her thighs apart. Her muscles tightened as he positioned himself between her legs.

Faye had her eyes closed and although her breathing was deep and heavy he saw her jaw clench.

Dio. How in hell was he supposed to stop now?

He took several deep breaths, closing his own eyes as he braced himself on his forearms above her. When he opened his eyes, hers were still closed.

"Faye?"

When she didn't acknowledge him, he said her name again.

Her response was a barely audible "Hmm?"

"Open your eyes."

It seemed like an enormous effort, but her long eyelashes fluttered and lifted.

Nothing on earth could have prepared him for what he saw in those lavender blue eyes as she looked up at him. Any fear he had she was doing this against her will melted away beneath the power of that sultry look she gave him, her pupils dilated, her lids heavy.

"What?" she whispered, her rapid breathing making her voice sound husky. "What's wrong?"

A wave of something indefinable swept through him as he stared down at her flushed face, her tousled blonde hair. He felt his heartbeat pick up again, the blood surging through him. His gaze lowered to her breasts, soft and lush, her nipples plump and ripe. Good enough to eat.

For a moment he thought about tasting his fill, but the persistent throb of a certain part of his anatomy made waiting any longer impossible.

He looked back at her. "Do not close your eyes," he demanded. "I want to watch you as I make you come. I want to see your eyes." They'd go soft and opaque, he thought, just as they had the first time, haunting his dreams ever since.

This time he ignored the way her body jolted as he nudged against her, though he tried to go slow. When he pushed deeper she moaned softly. *Dio*, she was so tight.

He waited, with only their heavy breaths filling the silence. Perhaps he should let her get used to him, he thought, allow her to relax. But she felt so snug, all that heat enveloping him. He pushed into her before he even made the decision, his body somehow taking over in primal and instinctive reaction.

Faye cried out, more from shock than discomfort. She'd tried to relax with each push, knowing he fought to take it slowly. Was he trying to accommodate her nerves? Had he guessed she was still inexperienced in the art of lovemaking?

She'd made love only once in her life. With him. She knew back then, that first time, she hadn't pleased him, hadn't really satisfied him. Then he'd been a sexually experienced male in his mid-twenties, already used to women fulfilling his every need—in and out of bed. She had tried back then to act like she imagined his other women did. Had wanted to please him, make him realize she wasn't the young, gauche little thing she always feared he'd thought her to be. She had wanted him to fall in love with her.

But instead of being the experienced sexual partner she had tried to be back then, she had tensed, whimpered and heavens, she had even cried afterwards. It had been so wonderful, she had cried.

And here she was—tensing—whimpering—

The last thrust, long and hard, took her breath away even as it took him to the hilt. He was moving now, rocking in a slow and rhythmic way, each determined thrust filling her to capacity. And it felt...exquisite.

Faye matched her movement to his, the primitive sway of a woman drawing in her mate.

"Wrap your legs around me," he demanded roughly. "Wrap them tight around me."

She did, keeping her gaze locked with his as he moved above her, inside her.

His shoulders bunched as he pumped into her. His skin hot and taut beneath her hands as they gripped him, pulled him down.

"Rico..." she ground out. *Rico, I love you so much.*

One of his hands slid under her buttocks and with a harsh cry he yanked her hips higher, the movement pushing her legs up high around his waist.

Her breath caught with each relentless thrust as he pounded into her, until, stretched to capacity, Faye felt the exquisite pull of release.

She closed her eyes, her chin arching into the air as she prepared to savor the excruciating pleasure toward which he catapulted her.

Oh, she whimpered all right. Just like last time. She couldn't help it. And she acknowledged that making love with Enrico would always have that effect on her. But those whimpers accompanied the most wonderful sensations she had ever known. The feel of the man she loved pushing her on over the edge into ecstasy, then following her into the abyss.

Chapter Ten

"I hurt you." Enrico lay against her, his hand slowing stroking her hip. He'd pulled the covers over them to waist height, which meant she could still drink her fill of his tanned and muscled chest, with its sprinkling of hair. "You were so tight, I know I must have hurt you."

"No, you didn't." It was hard enough to breathe, let alone talk. But she wanted to reassure him, strip away that questioning look in his eyes. It unsettled her, made her want to put up her guard again. And right now she didn't want to feel that way, didn't want to answer his probing questions.

He hiked himself up on one elbow, rested his head in his palm and looked down at her. "When was the last time you slept with a man?"

His question sounded clinical, or rather the way he asked it sounded clinical, in that flat, harsh tone. For a moment, she thought about saying something like, "not for ages" but this was Enrico, he'd want specifics.

She tried another tactic. "That's not the sort of thing you should ask a woman on her wedding night," she teased, batting her eyelids and reaching to brush back his hair.

His expression remained fixed. "Have you slept with anyone since you separated?"

"No." At least that was easy to answer, and the absolute

truth.

He didn't say anything for long moments, then his hand moved around and his fingers brushed her stomach. "Then I am the first?"

And the last. "You are." She let her fingers play along his cheekbone. "Does that appeal to your macho instinct?"

His mouth quirked. "Considerably."

His hand went exploring, around the plump fullness of her breast, down the side of her ribcage, along the curve of her hip. Then his brow creased. "The last time you ran out on me about now, crying."

Remembering, she turned her head away, but he patted her hip, a silent command she look back at him. His eyes pierced hers. "Why?"

"I was young and it was my first time," she offered lightly, forcing her mind away from the rejection that followed, and how he'd told her it had been a mistake. "It hurt."

His deep frown was thick with skepticism. "Is that the only reason you tensed when I touched you tonight?" His hand slid to the juncture of her thighs. "Because of the memories?"

"Sort of. And, well, our marriage isn't exactly conventional." And he didn't exactly love her. "I wasn't sure what to expect. What you'd expect."

Her face flushed gently as he stared down at her, his hand beginning a lovely drugging stroke where the heat was building again. "And now?"

Sinuously, she moved her hips as he adjusted his hand. "Now I know what to expect." And heavens above, it was wonderful.

She slid her hands slowly over his back, enjoying the warmth of his flesh and the way his muscles flexed beneath her touch.

He purred like a big cat, and sought her mouth. His kiss was slow and deep and—*oh, how could he kiss her like this if he didn't care for her?*

Faye tightened her arms around him, pulling him closer, wanting that hard, lean body against her, around her, inside her.

He rolled on top, using his knees to nudge her legs wide. This time she didn't tense, didn't tighten, but her stomach muscles jerked in response as he kissed his way down her throat, over her collar bone, between her breasts.

Her pelvis surged as his tongue slowly circled her navel. "Rico..."

She wanted to say his name. Seemed she couldn't stop saying his name. As if to reassure herself it was actually him making love to her and not some phantom lover her fevered imagination had whipped up out of thin air.

Moments later she couldn't have uttered a thing if her life depended on it. She shivered and trembled with anticipatory pleasure as he pushed up her knees and draped her legs over his shoulders.

Through a sensual haze, she watched him move up her body, the action lifting her hips, opening her up so very intimately to him.

There was no gentle easing into her this time, no attempt to let her adjust to his size, his strength. Just one powerful and relentless thrust and he was inside her. She felt almost unbearably stretched. Amazingly full.

And it was incredible.

His powerful shoulders bunched as he thrust into her, releasing momentarily as he drew back before thrusting again.

The force of the movement made her hips grind and buck, her breathing staccato gasps of frenzied pleasure.

It was hard and fast and over in a heartbeat.

He collapsed against her and only rolled away when their breathing had slowed. Denied his warmth Faye shivered as the night air wafted through the still-open balcony doors and brushed over her warm, glistening flesh.

Enrico drew her to his side and pulled the duvet around them. He brushed his lips over hers, then settled back and closed his eyes.

Faye waited, hoping he'd say something about what they'd shared. For her it had been the most amazing experience, bringing her closer to him—both physically and emotionally. So she waited.

Her insides took a joyous leap when he turned his head and tucked hers beneath his chin. "Go to sleep now," he said lazily.

As Faye battled with disappointment, the gentle rise and fall of Enrico's chest alerted her to the fact he already had.

But then what had she expected anyway? For him to swear undying love? He'd married her to get his child. Nothing more, nothing less.

Aching both from the heart, and from a body not used to such erotic activity, she watched the movement of his chest and tried to synchronize her breathing with his. When her eyelids became heavy, she cuddled up to Enrico and gave in to the heady call of sleep.

She was still in the same position, tucked into Enrico's side, his arm heavy and tight around her, when she woke during the night. Cautiously, not wanting him to shift away from her, she raised her head to look towards the clock on the bedside table.

Half past two.

She had barely registered the time when hazily familiar sensations whipped through her head, buzzing and humming sounds filling the silence of the room. Then all at once...memories...

Matteo... Edinburgh... The aircraft... *I can't get control, Faye...*

Her body froze with the same fear she'd experienced at the time as the memories flooded back with relentless stealth.

Instinctively she clung to Enrico, tightening her arm around his middle as if to anchor herself. As if to ensure that with these returning memories he wouldn't somehow disappear.

"What is it?" Enrico's husky voice cut through the fear, his hand stroking comfortingly along her arm as it clung to him. "Faye?"

"I...I remember." She hadn't realized she was crying until Enrico brushed moisture from her cheek. "I remember the accident."

"It is all right." He stroked her as she clung to him, letting her cry it out. "Hush now. Everything is all right."

She remembered it all. Every terrifying detail. Matteo's grim, shock-filled face as he struggled to get control of the aircraft. The ground as it zoomed up to meet them. The awful clunk of the engine as it went into its death throes. The ache in her own heart as she realized she was about to die and would never see her child again—or the man she loved.

Powerless to stop the emotion ripping through her, as she relived the horror of Teo's last moments, Faye pushed her face into Enrico's shoulder. Even as grief threatened to overwhelm her she was aware of his strong arms holding like he never intended letting go. For some reason it made her even more wretched.

For eight years she had been the strong one, the one who got on with things. The one who offered support. Teo had tried but it wasn't in his nature. Which meant it had fallen to her to sort things out. She had never had someone to take things over, to tell her everything was going to be all right as Enrico was doing now.

When her racking sobs finally stopped, she wiped her hand over her eyes. "I'm okay now." But Enrico didn't let go, keeping her tight against him so she was aware of his heart thundering. He'd want to know what she remembered but she wasn't sure she could tell him. Not everything.

Desolate, worn out from the sobs, from the memories, Faye drew in a steadying breath.

Slowly he released her, then switched on the bedside lamp and climbed out of bed. "I will get you some water."

Squinting against the light, Faye watched through bleary eyes as his naked body disappeared into the living area. How on earth could she tell him? How could she tell him and not betray Teo?

She sat up, bending her knees and hooking her arms around them. She wanted to tell him the truth. After what they had shared she wanted to tell him the truth. There couldn't be any secrets between them, not any more.

She dropped her head on her knees. She wanted their marriage so much. More than anything she wanted their marriage. But more than anything she wanted it based on trust, integrity—love. While the latter might not happen, at least on Enrico's part, she could ensure the former.

But to do that she had to betray Teo. She couldn't.

Grim-faced, Enrico strode back into the room. He handed Faye a crystal tumbler and sat on the bed beside her.

She couldn't look at him, couldn't stare into his penetrating eyes. How would she be able to perpetuate the lie if she looked into his eyes?

"Tell me," he said softly, taking her free hand in his. "Tell me what you remember."

Faye forced water past the tightness in her throat, but it did nothing to ease the discomfort. She gripped the tumbler and told him about the crash. About how Matteo had struggled valiantly to get control of the aircraft, about how he had screamed at her to brace herself at the moment of impact.

More to force back tears than appease her thirst, Faye took another swig of water. "He said my name," she said, her voice shaking with emotion. "The last thing Teo said was my name."

She broke down again, barely aware that Enrico eased the glass from her hands and pulled her into his lap. He tucked the duvet around her.

The hypnotic rise and fall of his chest calmed her, and she snuggled her nose into his throat, comforted by the steady beat of his pulse. She didn't want to think. To remember. She just wanted to be here like this. With Enrico. With his body sheltering her, protecting her. It felt so good to be held like this.

Perhaps now he might let things go. She had told him about the accident, relayed events as factually as she could. Please God, let him be satisfied with that. Then she wouldn't have to tell him the rest.

She wouldn't have to tell him that she and Teo had been returning from a fruitless visit to Teo's ex-lover. About how the man had threatened to expose their recent affair and Teo's sham of a marriage to the tabloids—unless a huge amount of cash bought his silence.

"Why were you in Edinburgh?" Enrico asked, affirming Faye's fears he'd want to know every single detail. "Why were you together?"

Enrico kept his voice low, trying to soothe her. To be honest he didn't want to know. Didn't want to hear that the trip had been a chance for Faye and his brother to spend time together, perhaps talk of reconciliation. *Dio*, he didn't want to hear that. But the extent of Faye's distress cautioned it was what he was destined to hear.

It was evident she still loved his brother. A woman didn't react like this unless she was in love, unless she cared deeply.

When she trembled against him, he slid his hand down her arm in a gesture intended to comfort. She felt soft and warm and vulnerable.

And he was a fool.

"We were visiting an...acquaintance of Teo's," she murmured against his chest, her words punctured by breathy sobs. "About a...a business proposition."

"Hush," he whispered, when she started weeping again. "Everything is all right."

Pulling her tight against him, he closed his eyes, making "sshh" sounds until she quieted.

He lifted the tumbler to her lips, waiting until she'd drunk. "What sort of business proposition?"

"N...nothing important." Her hesitation, and the way she looked down at the glass, told him she was lying. "Anyway, it...it wasn't viable."

His jaw clenched. Why couldn't she just tell him the truth? Tell him that she and Matteo were considering getting back together? Why all the lies, the subterfuge?

His temper bristled. *Maledizione!* She was so adept at the lies, the deceit. If he wanted proof of that, he had only to consider how he'd been robbed of his daughter for the first seven years of her life.

Faye's vulnerability, her softness, might have gotten to him, but he would be wise to remember how well, how easily, she could play him. Fool that he was, he had even begun to consider that she might *care* for him. She'd responded to his touch, his possession, as if at some level it had been what she'd craved. My, what an actress he'd married.

Underneath it all she was ice. She didn't want him, didn't want what he had to offer. The only reason she'd gone through with the marriage was because he'd blackmailed her. While he wasn't proud of that, some small part of him had hoped they could make the marriage work.

She was still in love with Matteo. She wanted Matteo. He would do well never to forget that.

Lifting her from his lap, he lay her gently back against the pillows and tucked the duvet around. It cost him. He wanted to be rough, he realized shockingly. He wanted to throw her down, take her hard and fast, wash every other thought, every other man, from her mind. He wanted to push her hard, so hard there would only ever be room for him in her head, in her heart. In her body.

But he didn't. Because tears still glistened on her eyelashes, her face pale with grief and exhaustion as she looked up at him with haunted eyes.

The wave of tenderness that rippled through him dampened the anger he would rather have chosen in its place. If he let her get to him like this he had only himself to blame.

He'd just received confirmation of what he'd always known. That for her there was only one man who would earn her tears, only one man who would hold her heart. And while in some ridiculous part of him he ached for it to be him, it wasn't.

"Rico?" Faye reached out to him. He saw her frown at the tense bunching of muscle beneath her fingers, saw the bewilderment flash across her face as he pulled away.

"Sleep now." He removed her hand, tucking it beneath the duvet. "Things will not seem so bleak in the morning. We will work something out."

With that he stood, slipped into his trousers and went into the living area. Faye heard the gentle click of the door closing, saw a snake of light appear beneath it. She heard the clink of crystal as Enrico poured himself a drink.

She wanted to go and join him, wanted to be in his arms. Safe and protected, so that all the memories would find a spot in her mind to settle and heal. But she felt desperately tired and while she didn't relish the dreams, the memories that would surely come with sleep, she knew exhaustion would take over as soon as she lowered her eyelids.

What did he mean about working something out? And why had he pulled away from her? Faye turned her head into the pillow. She couldn't think about it, couldn't think of anything. She was achingly tired.

In the space of a few hours it seemed she had experienced every emotion under the sun. Anxiety and nerves as she said her wedding vows. Happiness and pleasure at seeing the look on her little girl's face as her parents were joined in marriage. Anger and irritation at her new husband's seeming lack of desire to take her to bed. Passion when he eventually did, followed by a soul deep contentment lying in his arms.

And now? Now, there was a strange and gnawing uneasiness, and not only because the final pieces of her missing memory had slipped into place.

No. It was more than that. Something fundamental and scary. Something about the long look Enrico had given her as he'd slipped her from his lap and settled her back in bed. There was tenderness there, but it was strangely distant, aloof almost.

After what they had shared, after what they had done? It didn't fit. She had felt the tension coming off him in waves as she'd reached out to him.

And what *did* he mean about working something out?

Faye couldn't fight the heaviness any longer and knew sleep would claim her before she could find the answers to the questions that nagged.

The last thing she heard was the further clink of crystal as Enrico poured himself another drink.

Chapter Eleven

As Faye expected, Enrico pumped and prodded her for more information over the following days. They spent the remainder of their honeymoon swimming, relaxing, engaging in long leisurely walks—all the activities which to the outsider smacked of two people in love and enjoying each other. But in reality Enrico was cool, enigmatically distant. He was attentive enough and Faye had little outward reason to complain. But she knew things had changed since their wedding night, ever since she had woken with her memory intact.

He had reverted to how he was before their wedding night, before they had made love and she had thought—hoped—everything would change. How was it possible for a man to treat a woman with such tenderness, such passion and desire, and then go back to acting as if he could take their lovemaking or leave it?

Not that he left it very often. Since their wedding night they made love with a fervency that belied the real state of their relationship. Enrico was insatiable and during sex he was passionate and demanding, while equally considerate and attentive to her needs.

Arriving back at the villa Faye learned that Enrico had instructed her things be moved to his suite. She somehow expected they would have separate living quarters, at the very least separate bedrooms, but once again it appeared she had underestimated her new husband.

Enrico strode into their bedroom as Faye unpacked her luggage. Melita was assisting, or rather hampering her, wanting to know exactly when her mother had worn each item of clothing she unpacked and what was it like to have dinner on a yacht?

"You will find out soon enough, little one." Enrico smoothed a hand over his daughter's silky black hair. "Tonight we will drive to the coast and dine on our new yacht. You will enjoy that, no?"

Faye looked up from her unpacking, meeting his gaze for the first time since they had arrived home. The glitter in his charcoal eyes made her insides spin. She loved him so much, and yet he seemed indifferent to her attempts to show him.

She held his solid look. "You bought the yacht after all?" she asked, remembering he had decided against it on their honeymoon.

"I did."

During the long moments their gazes clashed, Faye wondered what was going on in that deep-thinking mind of his. But as usual, he gave nothing away.

She returned her attention to the last of her unpacking, hearing Enrico inform their daughter that if she wanted to sleep on the yacht overnight she had better go on along and ask Carla to help her pack some things.

This was met with much hugging and kissing, exclamations as to how Enrico was *the* best daddy in the whole wide universe, wasn't he, Mummy?

Faye nodded in reluctant agreement and Melita dashed off whooping with excitement. "I would have liked to be consulted," she said, edgy and frustrated about how things were between them. "Is this how it will be Enrico? You making plans for my daughter and—"

"Our daughter," he snapped it out, his shoulders set. "I have much time to make up, and you are in no position to chastise me, Faye." He looked down at the now empty suitcase. "You should have left that."

"What? For Carla to unpack?" Faye slammed the lid shut, then glanced over to where Enrico's case lay untouched. "Would it hurt you to do it yourself for once? Carla and Giovanni have enough to do without waiting on your every need. Or am I to do it? Is that one of my *wifely* duties?"

He turned and strode across the room toward the door. She was about to tell him not to dare leave when she was in the middle of insulting him, when he pushed the door firmly closed and turned back to her.

Fury lit his eyes, barely restrained. "I am aware of how much my staff has to do." The same restrained fury sounded in the low, clipped tone. "And I am no stranger to attending my own needs."

He moved toward her, slowly and ominously. Faye's muscles tensed as he backed her toward the bed.

"As for you..."

Displaying a confidence she didn't really have, Faye resolutely lifted her chin as he stood in front of her. His gaze whipped over her face, a menacing gleam in his eye. "What I meant," he said, glancing toward the suitcase on the bed. "Was that as we are spending the night on the yacht, you might perhaps have left your suitcase semi-packed."

She felt small and unreasonable as color burned her cheeks. What she'd said was stupid and unfair. Even with his vast wealth Enrico never expected people to wait on him. They usually did, of course, but he never made those demands. While it was true Carla and Giovanni had more than enough to keep them busy in the big villa, Faye always sensed most of their work was self-generated.

What she'd wanted to do was attack him, to make him react in any way she could.

"I'm sorry. It's just..."

"Just?" He inched closer, his warm breath brushing across her mouth. "What has really upset you, *cara*?"

"Nothing. I'm not upset." Her heart thumped painfully and all the blood had left her legs. She was actually aroused. All it took was his body pressed up against her, all that honed muscle and warm flesh, and she was aroused. "It's just that you take charge of everything and I...I..."

"You?" he prompted, nudging her further back against the bed.

"I don't ever know what to expect from you." As soon as she said it, she regretted it. It made her vulnerable to him, like he was keeping her off balance. Even though he was, it was stupid to actually admit it. "What I mean is you do things without telling me, without asking me. It's not an equal partnership and marriage is supposed to be."

"Even our marriage?"

"Especially our marriage."

One little nudge and she toppled back onto the bed. Rapier fast his arm went around her waist controlling the fall, so that when they hit the bed he lifted them both further up toward the pillows.

Her breasts were crushed against his chest, her legs falling open and cradling him instinctively. He dropped a brief kiss on her mouth, then went back for another. Lingering this time, making erotic forays with his tongue. Exploring...tasting...

When he lifted his head it took Faye a moment to get her eyes open, her eyelids seemed as if they were weighted, her body drugged and heavy. Heavens above, he could do that with such amazing ease.

"Perhaps," he said, a glittering mockery in his expression, "In the interests of equality and the clarification of my intentions, I should advise you that I now intend to kiss you very thoroughly. Do I have your permission?"

His derision did nothing to halt the shiver of awareness running through her, not even when she admonished herself for it. She couldn't keep on giving in to him like this, like she had done every night since their marriage. He couldn't think he could take her whenever he wanted, like she was a woman he had rights to because of a piece of paper. And that's all it was to him, Faye thought miserably. A piece of paper. One that ensured rights to his daughter. Marital relations with his wife.

"No." She wiggled her hand between them and gave his chest a determined push. "You don't have my permission. Let me go."

After one long, narrow-eyed look, he did exactly that. Levering himself off her and walking toward the wardrobe as if nothing had happened.

Whereas, Faye thought as she pulled herself to a sitting position, she was left gasping, arrows of desire shooting haphazardly through her system.

She had to protect herself. Had to protect her position in this marriage. Let him know he couldn't treat her as he pleased. She focused on his back, watching as he took a couple of fresh shirts from the wardrobe.

Faye willed her voice steady. "I'd like to move back to my own room."

He said nothing, didn't even acknowledge she had spoken.

He just snapped open his suitcase, dumped the pile of used clothes on the bed and replaced them with fresh shirts.

Faye seethed. “Enrico,” she said between clenched teeth. “Did you hear what I said?”

“I heard, but what you ask is not possible.” He didn’t look up, but his voice was deceptively pleasant, as if coaxing an obstinate child. “You will stay here.”

Faye jumped from the bed, storming over to where he was tucking socks into the sides of his case. “I will not stay here. And don’t you dare presume you can give me orders or treat me like some...some...”

“Some what, Faye? You really must practice finishing your sentences.”

A red-hot haze shimmered around the edges of her vision as she yanked away the clothes brush he was about to pack. “You’re despicable.” She flung the brush across the room where it skidded on the polished floorboards before bouncing off the wall with a thud.

They both followed its exhilarating journey then, ashamed she had resorted to such a physical display of emotion, Faye turned red-faced to Enrico. He lifted one amused eyebrow before calmly returning to his packing.

“I won’t stay here in this room with you.” Faye tried to bank down the residual anger still simmering through her system. “I intend to move my things back.”

Abruptly he turned to face her, his expression a stony mask, only his eyes sparking with his own more restrained temper. “You will stay here. Make no mistake about that.” He made a grab for her as she prepared to spin away.

“You will stay in our room,” he tightened his grip on her arm as Faye tried to shake his hand away. “Both because I say so and because it forms part of our marriage agreement.”

"I don't remember any such thing being discussed, let alone agreed."

With a tug he brought her against him. "You agreed to our sleeping together. Which, if I am not mistaken, has caused you little distress so far."

"I honor any agreements I make, whether or not I enjoy their consequences."

He scoffed. "Save it, Faye. You enjoy the consequences of this agreement of ours well enough. That is if the encouraging moans and pleas you give me are anything to go by." He tightened his grip when she made to pull away. "And what am I to make of the way your body writhes beneath mine, the way desire shines in your eyes when I touch you, the welcoming feel of your flesh as you tighten around me, as you take me in."

"Stop it." It was a breathy whisper and Faye damned herself for it.

"You want me right now, *cara*, even as I want you."

She turned her head pointedly away as his mouth lowered to hers, but he gripped her chin with his free hand and yanked her face back. "*Si.* You want me. And tonight aboard our yacht you will demonstrate how much. I have plans for you, *cara mia*, and by the end of this night you will be the one demanding we share a bedroom."

"I won't." She said it for form, because her body said otherwise. Her flesh had heated to near smolder as his words caressed it, her pelvis dragging and pulsing with the need to have him carry out his threats.

He smiled, showing his teeth in the manner of a stalking predator, playing with his prey. In the full knowledge that prey had no escape. Then he released her, gave her one glowering look, and strode from the room.

Faye clasped one unsteady hand to her throat, willing her

body to stop this ridiculous reaction to him. He was a brute, a monster. She should be ashamed of herself for wanting a man like him.

She forced herself to move, busying herself putting a few things together for their overnight stay on the yacht. Remembering his erotic threat she almost wished she owned a pair of flannel pajamas. That would put paid to his devilish plans. But then her body was still reacting in wanton anticipation of those plans, so she packed a flimsy silk teddy, black and scant, the one she knew drove Enrico wild.

Yes, indeed. She was ashamed of herself all right, but not, it seemed, enough to deny herself the pleasure of another night in her husband's wickedly inventive arms.

His threat was right on target it seemed, since Faye hadn't once been inclined to mention returning to her own room after their weekend spent aboard *The Melita.* Its namesake was thrilled when they first glimpsed the new yacht, flinging her arms around her father's neck and once again cooing about his being *the* best daddy.

Since her continual attempts to stop him spoiling their daughter fell on deaf ears, Faye had all but given up. But two weeks later she found reason to take issue with him again.

He had returned from an unscheduled and hastily arranged trip to Paris and the sight of him entering the kitchen, white shirt unbuttoned at the collar and tie loosened, made her head spin with the sheer power of his masculinity. He never failed to take her breath away.

Yet, as he walked closer, Faye saw faint shadows beneath his eyes, the beginnings of stubble darkening his tight jaw. Tiny vertical lines appeared between his brows as he scanned the kitchen, looking anywhere but at her.

"You're very late." And seriously upset about something. She knew him well enough now to recognize the subtleties of his moods. "I can make you a sandwich if you'd like."

He shrugged out of his jacket and dropped it over the back of a chair. "Thank you, no. I have no appetite." He didn't sit, but started to pace. "Is Melita in bed?"

The question was fairly incongruous, seeing it was well after eleven o'clock. "Yes, of course."

Distractedly, he pushed his hand in his pocket and retrieved a small square jeweler's box that he slid onto the kitchen table. "I thought she would like this." He started pacing again.

Faye reached tentatively for the box, mindful of his strange mood. She flicked back the lid, swallowing uncomfortably at the jeweler's name emblazoned in gold. As she expected, inside was a piece resolutely in keeping with the prestigious name, an exquisite silver locket on a delicate chain. A tiny diamond sparkled in its centre.

Faye's gasp had Enrico turning to face her.

"It's too much," she said, shaking her head as she stared at the locket. "This is far too much." He said nothing, just narrowed his eyes as her gaze met his. "Enrico, you really must stop spoiling her like this. She'll grow up to find no real value in anything and I don't want her thinking she can have whatever she wants."

His laugh was thick with derision. "No. We must not have that, must we, *cara*. Far be it for me, her father, to spoil her. Who knows, she may well grow up to be as I am, finding no real value in anything."

"You know that's not what I meant." Faye closed the lid of the jewelry box and placed it on the table. "It's just that you give her too much."

Without a word he turned, leaving the kitchen to stride down the hall toward the library.

Faye stood there for a few moments, wondering if she should go to bed and leave him to it. He was obviously tired, irritated about something, and taking it out on her.

Too bad. He could just get over it.

She was halfway to the stairs when natural curiosity took over. His strange mood had nothing to do with her chastising him about spoiling their daughter, heavens she did that almost every day and all she got back from him was a careless shrug. While he sometimes became frustrated when business matters didn't immediately go the way he wanted, he never let it affect him like this.

When she entered the softly lit library his back was to her as he stared out of the double doors leading to the terrace. One hand was pushed deep into his trouser pocket, the other held a crystal glass filled with what she supposed was whisky.

Taking the bull by the horns, Faye asked, "What's wrong? Has something happened?"

The long silence stretched and she was about to ask him again when he turned. His face was drawn, the cheekbones rigidly set, making the shadows beneath his eyes more prominent.

There was a strange quality about him, the poignancy of a man deeply wounded, unsure of how to handle things, perhaps for the first time in his life. It made her want to go to him, wrap her arms around him and ask him to share his problems with her.

Yet something kept her rooted to the spot. Perhaps it was the accusation in his eyes, or the way he ground his jaw as he pinned her with his gaze.

She wanted to step back, to spin around and go back the

way she had come. Instead she faced him squarely. "Rico, is something wrong?"

"Is something wrong?" he parodied. "Well, there's a question."

"It's a perfectly reasonable one, since you've just got back from Paris looking like you're about to commit murder or something."

He laughed, mockingly. "That might indeed be an option." He moved to the drinks cabinet to refresh his drink. "I did not go to Paris."

Her flesh chilled. "You didn't?"

"No. I had to cancel my meeting to attend another matter."

He still had his back to her, but Faye watched as he poured himself what amounted to a triple whisky. This did not bode well.

She turned away. "If you're going to drink like that, I should at least get you a sandwich to mop it up."

"Stay right where you are!"

The imperious command was accompanied by the slam of the whisky decanter being returned to the table. Crystal clinked and rattled ominously.

"I beg your pardon?" She placed her hands on her hips.

"As well you damn well should." Crystal set to clinking again as he slammed down his refilled glass, making the amber liquid slosh up the sides.

He glared at her, a curious mixture of emotions playing across his face.

She huffed and folded her arms. "Look, if this is to do with the fact I don't want you spoiling—"

"It is to do with the fact you have lied to me for eight years."

"Well, yes. But then we...you...knew that, it's why we got married."

For long moments he watched her, like he was expecting her to add to the statement. When she didn't he picked up his drink, took a swig, then slowly replaced the crystal tumbler. "Do you know where I have spent the day?" he asked, as he stared at the glass.

"No."

He looked up, appraising her through narrowed eyes. "London."

The room seemed to spin a little, not helped when her stomach roiled. "London?"

"Yesterday, I received a call from a man claiming to know Matteo," he said, as Faye's knees went weak. "He wished to meet with me to appraise me of some information he thought I would find interesting. Information he assumed I would pay handsomely for."

Her dry throat contracted painfully. She wanted to stop him, to try and explain. To give Teo's side of things. But although she opened her mouth, nothing came out.

"At first I imagined this man was party to your lies involving my daughter," Enrico went on, in a cold superior tone. "I assumed he was unaware that I am now in possession of the truth, at least regarding my daughter, and expected to extort money for his revelations."

Nausea washed indelicately through her stomach, but Faye warned herself not to break eye contact. When a predator scented blood you didn't act passively. Her hand snaked protectively to her throat.

As she stood glued to the spot, Enrico moved toward the library doors. He closed the doors and turned the lock, increasing her sense of foreboding.

"Allow me to fix you a drink," he said, moving back to the bar and selecting a fresh glass. "I believe you may need one before I am finished."

She wanted to decline, but thought better of it. If he was trying to intimidate her it was working. Her face burned while a chill swept through the rest of her body.

Let's get it all out in the open, she thought. *Let there be no more secrets between us.* Even as she thought it, her heart sank to her feet. How could there ever be a future for them, when she had deceived him in so many ways. "Why don't you just tell me what happened."

"It appears my instincts were correct," he said, moving toward her. "This man indeed had extortion in mind."

Faye willed her hand not to shake as she took the glass he offered. Strangely, it didn't. An incongruous calm swept through her. If there was still a way to protect Teo in all this, she would. As much as she wanted no more secrets between her and Enrico, she would still protect Teo.

For eight years she had kept her side of their bargain, placating Teo's secret fears that his cruel and insensitive father would discover the truth about him and use it to poison Enrico's views. Even estranged from his brother, Teo found comfort in the knowledge that Enrico respected him as a man, as a brother. As a Lavini.

Faye sipped her whisky, letting the heat of it soothe her parched throat. "Extortionists mostly take the truth and twist it to their own ends," she said, hoping Enrico would acknowledge as much. "It's impossible to believe anything they say."

A hint of a smile, mocking and contemptuous, feathered around his mouth. "But I have yet to inform you of the exact nature of his revelations. Why do you so easily dismiss them as lies before knowing what they are?"

The heat in her face intensified. "I...I meant generally, of course. No good ever comes of tattletales."

His laugh held the same mocking derision. "No good ever comes of trusting those closest to us either, or believing them to be the people we think they are."

He knew. He knew the truth.

And his stern, acerbic expression displayed only too clearly what he thought of it. Faye's insides tumbled. Teo had never hurt anyone. He had tried hard to do the right thing. It hadn't always worked, and he was at heart a lost soul. But he had tried.

"You're right about that," Faye snapped. "Because it seems I was certainly wrong about you. Despite your arrogant ways I always felt you were an honorable man, understanding and tolerant. More fool me."

His eyebrows drew together in a deep frown.

"Trust has to be earned," Faye continued, fuelled by a dangerous cocktail of anger and anxiety. "Nobody can just demand it. People, good people, do what they believe is right. What they think is best for everyone."

"Which is why you lied to me on our wedding night," he retaliated, with deadly calm. "Because keeping from me the fact you had been blackmailed was somehow the right thing?"

"That's not the issue, I'm talking about—"

"Damn right it is the issue!" he roared. "When you remembered the accident I asked you to tell me everything, yet you omitted that simple fact."

As her frazzled brain tried to focus, Faye questioned if this whole exchange was simply about her not telling him they were being blackmailed. Perhaps, on realizing Enrico already knew the truth about Melita, Teo's ex knew he couldn't extort any money and had left without revealing anything else. One look at Enrico would warn any would-be extortionist they would be sent packing with their tail between their legs before they even set up pitch.

A crazy sort of joy swept through her. If Enrico thought the reason they had been blackmailed concerned his being Melita's real father, there was no need to tell him anything else.

"I didn't tell you about the blackmail because I thought you might go after him or something," she said with a flippancy she didn't feel. "I knew you would be angry and would want some kind of retribution."

He watched her steadily, during which she had to force herself to meet his gaze. Only the thought of her promise to Teo kept her from looking away.

"And if I had gone after him as you feared, *cara mia*, what other revelations might I have been afforded?"

His pointed tone made her blood run cold. "I don't know what you mean."

"I am merely suggesting that other skeletons might fall from your closet and demand my attention."

Faye shook her head, not sure how much more of this she could take. Her emotions were up and down like a yoyo, while he flicked at them like a big cat toying with prey. "I've had just about enough of this," she said tartly, as anger masked discomfort. She placed her glass on a nearby table. "So I've made mistakes, so what? I'm actually human, Enrico. Of course, you wouldn't know that would you? You're too busy trying to lord it over me with your arrogance, your conceit." She took a moment to drag in a breath. "And in case you're under any illusions let me make it clear. You don't own me and I don't answer to you. I might have entered into this sham of a marriage, but you're not my keeper and most definitely not my conscience."

"I doubt you have one," he sneered. "And this *sham of a marriage* as you call it makes me your husband, and that gives me the right to insist you inform me of potential threats to your safety and to that of my daughter's. If there is even the slightest possibility another stranger could contact me anticipating payment for some sordid disclosure—"

Sordid? Faye didn't much care what snide remarks he directed at her, she would handle them and perhaps even deserved them, but she was damned if she would let him label Teo's personal choices as sordid. But then he didn't know about Teo, did he?

She shook her head again, wearily. "You really are the most insufferable bigot."

The shocked look that flashed over his face gave her a tiny glimmer of pleasure. Serves him right, she thought, taking even more pleasure in the way his jaw tightened.

"Nothing I've done comes close to sordid, and the reason—"

"A wrong choice of word," he grated, pushing long fingers through his hair. "*Maledizione*!"

As he started pacing, Faye took some steadying breaths. She wasn't about to take any more of his arrogance, his righteous indignation or his high and mighty attitude. "The reason I didn't tell you I was pregnant," she said, lifting her chin, "was because you said our sleeping together was a mistake. I knew you didn't want me—" She raised her hand to stop him interrupting "—and it was perfectly reasonable for me to assume you wouldn't relish finding out I was expecting your child. So, I didn't tell you, and I was prepared to bring up my child alone. I didn't know how I would do it, but I would have managed. Then Teo offered me a home, for me and my daughter, and I'll bless him for that until the day I die."

"As will I."

His tone, low and sincere, stopped the rest of her diatribe in its tracks. "What?"

"I owe my brother more than I could ever repay," he said almost wistfully. Then the haughty tone returned. "What I cannot understand is why you didn't tell me, why you didn't give me the chance to act appropriately? Was I so heartless, *cara*? So callous? Was I so undeserving of the truth?"

No, she realized, as she looked at him. At the deep hurt masked well by the hardness in his eyes. "Acting appropriately would have meant marrying me," she said. "You would have demanded it."

"*Si*, I would have demanded it." His nostrils flared as he moved toward her. "It was my right to demand it, and yet you seem to believe you were the only one with rights. You took my child, Faye. You took away my child."

Devastated, Faye thought, as he came up to her. He looked devastated.

The realization hit her like a body blow. *She* was the heartless one. *She* was the callous one. She and Teo. In keeping their secrets they had been dreadfully cruel. They were the merciless ones. Not Enrico. They hadn't given him a chance.

"I'm sorry." She whispered it, as guilt and shame, mixed with a good dose of regret, poured through her. "You deserved the truth. I should have told you."

There was a long, awkward silence, during which she wanted to hurl herself at him, pour it all out. But he stood there, tall and rigid, the proud set of his wide shoulders offering no sanctuary.

She caught her lower lip between her teeth, painfully aware of the huge emotional divide being carved between them. She wanted to weep at the futility of it all.

Then he moved toward the leather chair that had belonged to his grandfather. Wearily, he sank into it and dropped his head back. He watched her from beneath lowered lids.

She wanted desperately to make everything right. But they were too far gone, and from the resigned look in his eyes he knew it too.

"We're never going to get past this, are we?" Her voice, although weak and tremulous, seemed to bounce off the library walls. It seemed fitting somehow, that they finished it here, in the very place it had started. In the place where she'd given herself to him. Heart and soul.

"I do not know." He reached up and squeezed the bridge of his nose with his thumb and forefinger. Lowering his hand, he blinked a few times, then looked back at her. "But I deserve the truth now, Faye." He waited a few beats. "All of it."

Faye sat opposite him on the sofa, a long walnut occasional table between them. Unlike him, she sat poker stiff. "It all seems such a long time ago. Somehow the reasons don't seem as vital as they did then."

She waited, hoping for some small spark of understanding, some tiny sign that they might just weather this. But his implacable expression gave nothing away.

"I knew how you felt about your father, and the way he'd been tricked into marrying Teo's mother. You said you'd never allow that to happen to you. Then, after we'd made love you said it was a mistake, that it should never have happened. So when I found out I was pregnant, it mirrored your father's situation somehow. I thought you'd believe I'd done the same thing, got myself pregnant to trick you into marrying me. I didn't want that. For you or for me. I didn't want you to feel trapped. I didn't want you to hate me."

"Why in God's name would I hate you? There were two of

us that night, Faye. While I admit making you pregnant was the last thing I intended, I would never have abandoned you or my responsibilities."

"I know." She brushed an imaginary fleck of something from her jeans. "But I said I was on the pill, when you asked about protection. I said it was safe. Then when I found I was pregnant, I knew you'd think I lied."

"You did lie."

"I know...I..." Lord, she was messing this up good and proper.

He stood abruptly and went over to the terrace doors, turning his back on her to look out into the darkness beyond. "And what of you, Faye? Did you expect to become pregnant? What of your life, your plans?" He sighed heavily, and she knew he was probably thinking of the naïve young undergraduate he had taken to his bed. "Had you told me I would have done the right thing."

"And resented me for the rest of your life. Like I said, I didn't want a marriage based on duty and responsibility. I didn't want a husband who felt trapped and manipulated."

He turned to face her, his eyes like charcoal ice. "Yet you married a man for the sole purpose of letting him raise another man's child? Did you not once stop to think that he might feel trapped, manipulated?"

The sneer in his tone cut to her core. "It wasn't like that."

She brushed her palms over her face, pushing her fingers back into her hair as if to sweep away the heavy weight of conscience. It was getting almost impossible to keep up the pretence, even if she was doing it to protect Teo.

When Enrico walked back, Faye looked down. She stared at her denim-clad knees while he towered over her, his powerful presence making her chest tighten and her breath come in choppy gasps.

"Then exactly how was it, Faye?" he enquired harshly. "Are you saying you were in love?"

The sheer physical power of him made it difficult to breathe, to think straight. His energy surrounded her, sucking all the oxygen from the air.

Please go away, she begged silently. *Please just leave me alone.*

"Tell me," he demanded, his voice almost a growl. "Did you marry for love?"

She knew he was talking about her marriage to Teo, but the wording of his question left her free to answer truthfully. About her marriage to him. For once she didn't have to lie. "Yes." She raised her head and looked deep into her husband's eyes. "Yes, I married for love."

The skin across his forehead tightened. "Was that love returned?"

Aware he was still referring to Teo she nodded. "Yes, it was returned. Teo loved me. In his own way, he loved me."

For long moments they stared at each other, then his eyebrows drew together.

"How easily you lie to me still." He strode back toward the terrace doors and flung them open.

Something about the sight of him walking away from her after such an exchange left her desperate to make him see, make him understand he was the one she loved, he was the one she wanted with every piece of her heart. Her very soul.

"I haven't lied to you," she said, jumping up so quickly she hit her knee on the coffee table. Ignoring the sharp pain, she hurried out onto the terrace to join him. "Teo and I loved each other, just not in the way—"

"Enough." He swung around sharply, making her jerk back. "Enough of this. I know the truth, Faye. I know about my brother. I might have refused to pay for the information, but his *acquaintance* was bitter enough, hostile enough, to tell me anyway. Even to offer me pictorial evidence should I doubt his credibility."

Faye stood there, her breath hitching.

"Well?" he demanded. "No attempt to deny it?"

Yes, she wanted to deny it. She wanted to protect her dear Teo. But Enrico knew the truth and all she could do now was try and make him understand.

"He didn't want you to know."

"That much I have gathered," he scoffed. "And why did he not want me to know? Was he ashamed?"

"No." Faye's chin jerked up. "He had nothing to be ashamed of."

"On that we are in agreement. I would never have judged him in that way."

"I know, and Teo knew it as well. He was more worried about your father's reaction. He didn't want to give Ruggerio any more reason to hate him."

Enrico cursed. "Had I been in Matteo's place I would have taken harsh delight in telling the bastard just to get a reaction."

"You're not Teo."

His eyes went to slits. "You are very understanding for a wife whose husband decided he preferred a man in his bed."

Before she could answer, he spun away, slapping his palms against the stone railing. Faye stared at his back, at those broad shoulders that always felt so strong and muscular beneath her hands. How she wanted to go to him, smooth away some of the tension that tightened his muscles, run her palm over the hard contours of his face, brush her fingers along the chiseled strength of his jaw.

"You need have no concern about the photographs," he said coldly. "I have arranged for the negatives to be destroyed. You will not be troubled again."

Faye came to stand beside him. "How...how did you get the negatives?"

He scoffed. "Blackmailers are essentially cowards. This particular coward had no stomach for the consequences of *not* handing the negatives over to me. You need have no concern."

Right. Her husband had just pledged to commit bodily harm but she didn't need to concern herself. "What have you done?" she asked on a breathy gasp. "Rico, please tell me you didn't do anything."

He glanced at her, his grin wicked. "Very well, I will not tell you."

When she caught her bottom lip between her teeth, his expression turned to stone. "The money," he demanded. "Why were you flying back with the money? Did Matteo decide not to pay? Did he decide he would not be blackmailed?"

Faye shook her head. "The man asked for more. He said he'd changed his mind and thought his silence was worth double what he'd originally asked. He said if we didn't pay him he would go to the tabloids, he would let them have the photographs. What would it do for the brother of the head of the Lavini Bank to be splashed across the front pages? A man who had left his wife and child to be with his male lover." Faye stopped to take in a breath. "He said he would tell them about Melita, about you being her real father."

"How did he know she was—" Enrico shook his head as the answer to his own question became clear. "Pillow talk," he growled. "A powerful leveler."

Faye moved a few inches closer. “Teo never meant for you to be hurt by all this.”

“No, Faye.” He held up his hand. “Just...”

“I know it’s hard for you to believe that.”

“Try impossible.” He scrubbed his hands over his face, then pushed them back through his hair. “He should have come to me. I would have dealt with it.”

“That’s exactly why he didn’t come to you. He knew he had to handle it himself. He tried really hard to do the right thing, but it never seemed to work out for him.” She reached out to touch his shoulder, but dropped her hand. “He loved you very much.”

His scornful laugh shattered through the quiet night air. “Yet he demanded I stay out of your lives. He knew I was Melita’s father and yet he ensured I had no contact with my child. *No contact*,” he emphasized with a sneer. “What kind of love is that?”

“He did it for me,” Faye said gently. “Because I told him I...I didn’t want to see you.”

The look he shot her was filled with contempt. “And Matteo simply obliged? It was all very convenient, was it not? And what did you tell him?” He pushed away from the railing and straightened. “Did you tell him I had taken you against your will? That you had not opened your legs for me willingly?”

“Stop it.” She’d backed up a little, but now she planted her feet. Her face burned and she felt unbearably tired as the weight of deceit crumbled with each revelation. There was a wonderful release in it, a freedom she hadn’t felt in years. It spurred her on, giving her the courage not to let him bully or intimidate her any longer.

“I’ve apologized for what I did and if it’s not enough for you then I’ll have to accept it. But I won’t keep on apologizing. I won't let you make me into something awful and I certainly won't let you imply that what I did was intentionally malicious." She heaved in a couple of breaths as her heart thundered against her chest. "I told Teo about the baby, about how I didn't want to trap you into a marriage you didn't want...with a woman you didn't love. Teo understood only too well how I felt. He'd lived under the weight of your father's loathing all his life and he knew I didn't want a child of mine subjected to the same sort of misery."

His jaw hardened, his eyes flashed. "You dare to suggest—"

"No," Faye shook her head emphatically. "I didn't think for a minute you'd be like Ruggerio and take your unhappiness out on your child. But I didn't want you to *be* unhappy, that was the whole point."

As the beginnings of a headache pinched above her left eye, she rubbed at her temple. "I was terrified you'd find out the baby was yours, and that you'd come after me and insist we get married. Teo said he would provide for me and my child. That if we got married he would find a way to make it appear the baby was his, and that you'd never find out because he would ensure you stayed away from us. I felt awful about it and said I couldn't let him do that for me. That was when he told me he was homosexual, that he didn't want it broadcast and marrying me would provide exactly the smokescreen he wanted." She heaved a sigh of relief as the last threads of deception fell away. "So he promised me that nobody would ever know you were Melita's father and in return I promised him I'd keep his secret."

Her words fell away at the look on Enrico's face. There was genuine shock mixed with disbelief. "He told you he was homosexual?"

"Yes, of course."

"Before you were married?"

"Yes." It was her turn to look puzzled. "I'm not sure I understand what that—"

He shook his head, cutting her off, then gave an empty laugh. "So he would marry you and you would lie for him," he said wearily. "A pact made in heaven."

Turning back to the balustrade he leaned his forearms on the railing.

"Not such a good track record, have you, *cara*?" he murmured into the night. "Two marriages of convenience, where love has played no part."

"Love has played a part." *In both.* "I loved Teo."

And you. With all my heart.

"Then you must have been disappointed. You had the man you loved in your bed, but his love was directed elsewhere. Love makes fools of us all."

This was awful, Faye thought. From the way he was talking it sounded like he thought she loved Teo *like that.* "Teo didn't share my bed," she said in a hushed tone, both confused by his intimations and uncomfortable discussing Teo's personal preferences. "He couldn't share my bed. We both knew and accepted that right from the start." She moved to where Enrico leaned on the railing. "We were friends, Teo and I, always friends. I loved him as such."

Since there was no turning back now, since there was nothing left to hide, Faye sucked in a huge dose of courage and prayed the words would come out right. "You're the only man I've ever been with."

The silence stretched for so long she wondered if she'd actually spoken out loud. If he'd even heard her. Then he turned to face her, his fathomless eyes unblinking.

Nocturnal creatures chirped and croaked in the distance,

but above them the sound of her heartbeat pounded fierce and relentless. Still he didn't say anything. Did he believe her? Did he think she was still lying to him?

"You never slept with Teo?" he questioned in a chilly tone. "You have never had sex with anyone else?"

Faye swallowed. "That's right." She placed her hands over her stomach, as if to protect herself from his accusatory tone and the dull ache seeping through her middle. He didn't believe her, and even if he did, he didn't seem too bothered either way.

What had she expected anyway? That he'd be overjoyed? That he'd whisk her into his arms and swear undying love?

Something indefinable flashed across his face, although she knew he'd be running everything through in his mind like a movie on a screen. Sifting and sorting...sifting and sorting...

"Where did he get the money?"

It took a moment for Faye to realize he'd spoken. "What?"

"I said where did Teo get the money?"

"Money? I..." Faye's frazzled brain struggled to get back on track and away from where she'd been forming the right words to tell him how she really felt about him.

He shook his head impatiently. "Where did he get the money to pay the blackmailer?"

The truth, Faye thought, as she met his accusatory glare, he deserves the truth. After what they'd put him through, he deserved to know it all. "Teo won it, in a poker game."

He gave a barely audible "Hmm," then demanded, "and where did the stake money for this game come from?"

"I... We sold a few things. Jewelry and...and the paintings my father left me."

He swore, ripe and harsh. "Those paintings were important to your father. They were virtually all he had left to leave you."

"I know, but they were just things. He would understand why I sold them."

Enrico pressed the heel of his hand to his forehead, then half-turned away from her. "*Dio*! My brother was a fool." He swung back with a fury that made Faye gasp. "And you are his equal. Did you think for one moment that paying a few thousand euros would stop the threats?"

Faye opened her mouth, about to protest that it was more than a few thousand, but realized that the situation hardly needed further provocation.

"Did you have more to sell, Faye?" he demanded scathingly. "Did you have more baubles, more heirlooms tucked away?"

His eyes narrowed. "Or perhaps you had something more valuable to sell? Perhaps you were prepared to sell yourself to the highest bidder so you could keep paying—"

With easy grace he caught the hand rocketing toward his face, angling her arm until it was behind her back. Before she could react, he'd caught her other arm and done the same. With both arms pinned behind her, she tried to wriggle free, but the movement caused her breasts to flatten against the hard plane of his chest and he tightened his hold.

"You bastard." Her voice caught on a strangled sob as she tried to pull free. "You don't know how it was."

He silenced her frenzied struggle by yanking her harder against him. "I know exactly how it was, *cara mia*. I know that you did every foolish thing possible to protect my brother." He jerked her even closer as she tried to break free. "Did you spend long nights in agonizing torment craving a man you could never have? Did you commit yourself to a lifetime of aching for the impossible?"

"Yes!" The snap of the word surprised her, as it did him. It was fuelled by a strange and intangible strength that appeared as if from nowhere. Because she was sick of this. Sick of the skirting around, the trying to appease him. Sick of his accusations, his arrogance, his brutish questioning. She lifted her chin until her determined gaze locked with his. "Yes, I did crave a man I could never have, though why in God's name I ever bothered I can't bloody well imagine."

When she jerked her hands, trying to dislodge his grip, she had the unexpected pleasure of seeing him flinch. "You think you can judge me?" she demanded, as her anger built. "You think you can judge Teo? You *don't* know how it was. You never could. Because you do everything right, don't you, Rico? You're so bloody perfect that you don't accept the frailties of others. You don't accept their flaws, their weaknesses. You think that anything that isn't done your way is the wrong way. God, you're so like your father it's frightening."

She watched his throat contract, saw a lone muscle work along the hard line of his jaw. His eyes glowed with dangerous intent as his chest heaved against her, and with each angry breath she felt her breasts press hard up against him.

Lust fired deep and low in her belly. Heavens above, how could he manage to arouse her at a time like this?

"Let go of me," she demanded, bucking against him. "Just let go of me."

When he did, she stumbled back blindly.

Throwing out a hand to steady herself, she watched him stalk to the balustrade where he stood rubbing a hand across the back of his neck. "I don't judge you, or Teo," he grated. "I just don't understand you."

"Well, I don't understand you either, so that makes us even."

There was a long silence as they both stood their ground. Again, Faye found herself staring at the broad expanse of his back. But whereas a little while ago she'd wanted to run her hands over its warmth and strength, now she wanted to beat them hard against the harsh, unforgiving muscle and bone, perhaps pummel some sense into the man.

"I tried to protect Matteo, both because I loved him and because I had promised his mother. I failed." He cleared his throat. "So there you are, Faye, I have a weakness, a flaw. Does that make you happy?"

"No." And it certainly didn't make her happy to acknowledge the sorrow thick in his tone. "But it makes you a little more human."

He gave a low laugh. "Believe me, I am human. Sometimes I wish to the heavens I was not."

When he turned there was the strangest look on his face, and it made what was left of Faye's anger dissipate. He drew in a breath and looked up at the sky. "Do you remember that night you and Matteo wanted to camp out all night?"

The abrupt change of topic had Faye blinking. "You mean, when you set the tent up in the garden down there?"

He looked back at her, a wistful smile playing at the edges of his mouth. "Matteo came indoors after barely an hour, but you stayed out."

"And you came to get me." The memory was a sweet one, and Faye smiled back. "I refused to come indoors, so you got us some lemonade and we lay on our backs and you taught me the names of the stars."

She'd never wanted it to end. Even now she could remember the smell of the grass, the sounds of the night, the warm brush of Enrico's arm as they lay beside each other. She'd been fourteen and had wished upon every single one of those stars that one day she'd belong to him and he to her.

"It was a night much like this one," Enrico said, looking

back at the sky. "It was when I first realized my brother might be in love with you. He did not speak to me the next day. I thought he was jealous I had spent time with you."

"More likely he felt embarrassed. He was probably worried you'd think he was chicken."

"Perhaps." He pursed his lips, then looked at her. "But you were the one thing in life he seemed to want."

Again, there was a long silence as they watched each other. Faye's cheeks heated as his gaze seemed to pierce the deepest part of her. How could he look at her like that and not love her? How could he tear her apart with a gaze that promised much, but delivered so little?

"I never meant to hurt you, Faye."

There was an aching hole in the centre of her heart, but she kept her eyes on his. "I never meant to hurt you."

She kept looking at him as he moved in front of her. "I know I am not the man you would have chosen for a husband, but I will try my hardest to make this marriage work for you."

"What about you?" Faye asked. "What will make this marriage work for you?"

"That I can keep you safe and happy. That I can keep our daughter safe and happy."

"That's not what I meant." Faye fisted her hands to stop from reaching for him. "I meant what will make *you* happy?"

Another of the long silences threatened, but she was damned if she'd take any more of them. "Don't give me any spiel about duty and responsibility, I can't take it. Just tell me what will make you happy, even if it's not what I want to hear. Just *tell* me."

His eyebrows drew together. "I am not sure I understand what—"

"Oh, for God's sake, Rico. Do you want to see other women?"

The frown deepened into a scowl. "No. And I will not allow you to see other men."

"I'm not talking about other men." She wanted to stamp her foot in frustration. "What I'm trying to say, and making a complete pig's ear out of it, is that I don't want you to be unhappy so—"

"Then love me back."

They both froze in place.

Faye stared up at him, her mind spinning until she felt almost dizzy. Enrico looked as if he'd signed his own death sentence.

"What did you say?" She tried to bank down the jumps of anticipation her stomach was making. "What did you mean—"

"I do not know what the hell I mean," he said, rubbing his neck. "All I know is you mix me up and confuse everything."

She inched forward, her heart joining in the festivities as her insides jumped. "Don't do that, don't clam up on me." She moved until their bodies bumped. "I want to know what you meant."

His eyebrows drew together again. "What I meant—what I wanted—meant to say, was that I don't want any other woman."

A little bit closer. "Yes?"

"I want..." He took a huge breath, "I want...you."

She couldn't actually get any closer, so she moved her hips against him. "Why?"

His Adam's apple bounced. "Why what?"

"Why do you want me?"

The muscle in his jaw worked overtime. "Faye..."

Her heart was thumping so hard, he surely had to feel it. “For the sex?”

“No.” When she raised her eyebrows he laughed, and it seemed to ease some of the tension coming off him. “Well, not just the sex.” His expression grew serious again. “I have feelings for you. I know you loved Matteo, but if you give me the chance I swear I will try to make you happy.”

She reached up and cupped his cheek. “You’re a fiercely intelligent man, Rico, but sometimes you can be incredibly dense.” His tentative smile almost broke her heart. “I love you,” she whispered softly. “I’ve always loved you. I’ve never wanted anyone else. Ever.”

He stared at her as if she’d grown two heads, while his hands remained poker-stiff at his sides.

“I’ve loved you since the first time I saw you. I know that’s a cliché, but it’s true. You didn’t even know I was there half the time, but I was always aware of you. Always. Teo and I were friends and I loved him that way, but you’re the man I want. You’re the man I want to spend my life with. I don’t expect anything from you or from our marriage that you can’t—”

Her breath came out on a whoosh as his arms banded around her and she was crushed against him. “I expect much from our marriage,” he warned, his glorious eyes shimmering with something Faye dared not hope for. Her stomach leapt as his mouth feathered against hers. “I have wanted you also, hoped for you,” he said against her lips. “You, my darling Faye.”

Then she was wrapped in him, lost in a kiss that was tender and achingly beautiful. When he drew away, he kept their mouths close. “I love you,” he said softly, his breath whispering across her lips and making her soul leap. “I will do everything in my power to make you happy.”

Faye slipped her fingers into his hair. She was in a dream,

a wonderful floating dream. "You already make me happy," she said, reaching up for a kiss. "You don't have to do anything else, just keep on loving me."

"We have much to make right." His gaze raked over her face. "Much to talk about and plan. And this we will do together." His fingers dove into her hair and he tilted her head back. The fierce look in his eyes was matched by the demand in his voice. "Tell me again that you love me."

"I do," Faye smiled. "I love you. I always have."

He touched his lips to hers...brushed...tasted.

"And I love you." He said it carefully in English, before repeating it in his native tongue. "I will spend every moment, every day, proving to you how much."

"*Ti amo*," she said and clung to him as he took the gentle brush of mouths to another level. Then another. Until there was nothing soft or tentative, just red-hot passion and need. As if every one of the hungry years spent apart needed satiating. Urgently.

Later, in their room, when a little of that need had been soothed, Enrico pulled Faye into his side. The sheets were a tangled mess and Faye giggled as he battled through them to grab her thigh.

"You dare to laugh at me?" he growled, smiling when she laughed again. "You will pay for that."

Faye snuggled in, letting him position her leg so it was draped over his. There was a smug smile on her face as she snuck her arm over his broad, hair-roughened chest. Her whole body was warm, a little tender in places, while her breasts tingled in the aftershock of her husband's greedy attention. And heat still pulsed where he'd been deep inside her.

She snuggled some more. “Rico…?”

“Hmm?”

His hand slid sensuously down her thigh and she had to really focus on what she wanted to say. “We need to get one thing straight.”

“And what is that, *bellissima*?” His voice was husky, his leisurely stroke becoming more dedicated. Faye knew exactly what that meant. If she was going to say this, she’d better be quick.

“I want to carry on working.” Because his hand showed no signs of slowing, Faye hooked herself onto one elbow and looked down at him. He looked all slumberous and sexy, with a smile on his face that managed to be both acquiescent and resolute. “I thought I’d finish off the library,” she said firmly. “There’s this auction coming up in Rome, they have two first editions which will complete your collection—”

“Our collection,” he corrected.

“Our collection.” Faye amended, with a smile. “So I thought I’d bid for them. And I want to finish cataloguing the collection, and… What?”

He had his eyes closed and he was grinning. Faye slapped him gently on the shoulder. “What?”

“You. My wonderful wife.” Opening his eyes, he turned to look at her. “Whatever makes you happy has my support. But I think you may soon have other things to occupy your time.”

Faye frowned. “What things?”

“Well, we have been very…active…for some hours now, and I haven’t used protection.”

Faye settled back next to him, the smug smile returning. “And you think making me pregnant will stop me from working?” She gave a long, reproachful sigh. “Oh, my darling

Rico. And just when I thought I'd succeeded in bringing my old fashioned husband into the twenty-first century."

In one easy movement, she found herself underneath him. "Some things," he growled, "are best done the old fashioned way." He settled himself between her legs. "Some things, when done well, cannot be improved upon. Twenty-first century or not."

And as he prepared to take her to heaven and back one more time that night, Faye could only agree.

About the Author

To learn more about Tricia Jones, please visit www.tricia-jones.com. Send an email to mail@tricia-jones.com or stop by her blog at www.tricia-jones.blogspot.com

Flat broke and desperate, Kate Hartley runs to her ex-husband for help. However, his help comes with a high price. One she can't refuse.

Buying Mackenzie's Baby

© 2006 Kim Rees

The morning after a high society party finds Kate Hartley in her ex-husband's bed. Just a stupid mistake; something to put behind her... Until she discovers that she is pregnant.

Mack had never wanted children; had only married her in a rush of lust. Kate knows this. Nothing would drive her to ask anything of him. Nothing. But she's homeless and flat broke. And it isn't only her welfare now.

However, Mack has his own agenda. Kate had fooled him once; married him for his money. Whored herself... It was why he had divorced her. But now his grandfather has threatened his mother's home if Mack doesn't marry and produce an heir.

He had vowed never to marry again. But Kate Hartley is his only choice.

And payback can be sweet...

Warning: This book contains explicit sex.

Enjoy the following excerpt from Buying Mackenzie's Baby...

She took a deep breath, her hand delaying on the lock. Mack's scent wrapped around her, light, subtle. Kate rested her forehead briefly against the cool wood of the door, feeling Mack's fist pounding on the other side. He was the only man who had ever held her, held her and made her feel completely safe. Tears burned in her eyes, slipping again over her cheeks. It had been an illusion, a fantasy she had created. And then he'd tired of the naïve girl she had been.

She twisted the lock and pulled open the door.

"Kate." Unwilling, she met the hot anger in his gaze. She winced against the fingers biting into her upper arms. "Why lock the door?"

Kate shrugged off his fierce grip. She was numb in the face of his fury. It was stupid to hurt so much. Seven years. Worse was to know that inside her grew a tiny life, a part of the man she still— What? Wanted? Needed? Kate sighed. Now that would be stupid.

She found her abandoned glass and gulped down the rest of the water, wanting the raw taste in her mouth eased. "After I left your expensive hotel room, I wasn't thinking. I thought it would be all right." Her laugh was bitter. "No. Truthfully. I *really* wasn't thinking."

"Your point?"

She held his narrowed gaze and forced out the words. "I'm pregnant."

"Jesus, Kate, that was careless!"

She blinked. "Excuse me?"

He was pacing now. "You were looking for sex that night.

Didn't you at least think to take *some* precautions?"

Her stomach knotted. He made her sound like a whore. "How dare you—"

"What do you want me to do?"

Kate would have loved to have told him that she was simply doing the honorable thing and keeping him informed. But that had never been an option. Her overdraft was strained to breaking and in a few days she wouldn't have anywhere to live. His reaction brought out bitter words. "Give me your money."

Fear washed over her as Mack stalked towards her, his face filled with fury. She shrank back into her seat, but couldn't resist when fierce hands dragged her up. "I will not pay for your abortion."

His words shot through her. She had never once thought of doing that. "I—"

"Or do you think this is your chance to get your claws into me again?" Mack's voice was cold, tight. The familiar burn in his eyes seared her. His fingers uncurled from her arms and she crumpled back into the softness of the chair.

How had she ever felt anything for the cruel, selfish man standing over her? "You think I want this? *Your* baby inside me?" She ignored the brief, unwanted tightening of her heart. She had once thought having their baby was her future.

"If it is mine."

Nothing was worth this. Nothing. She would scrounge somewhere to stay, sell her few possessions. Survive without him. Vainly, she still wished she had her wedding and engagement rings. But Mack, knowing their worth, had taken them back.

Kate leapt to her feet, her spine straight. "*You* were always the slut in this relationship, Mack." She took no delight in the shock that flashed across his harsh face. “I’ll deal with this,” she waved a hand at her flat stomach, “myself.”

“I won’t let you have an abortion.”

“You can’t dictate my life, Mack.” Let him think what he liked. She and her baby would do very well without him. She lifted her chin and turned towards the door. “I’ll be more than happy never to see you again.”

A slow hand clap followed her footsteps. “You always do indignation so well.” The sneer to his voice cut her. “Now, if you’ve finished with your theatrics?”

Anger twisted again in her gut. He had always thought this of her, thought her shallow. Kate stopped and turned, making herself hold his hard gaze. “What’s there to discuss? You already doubt that the baby’s yours.”

“Yes, I do.”

The bald statement stabbed at Kate, pricked tears at her eyes. She had promised herself she would do whatever was necessary to secure money from Mack. But this? She had never thought he would question her, practically accuse her of whoring around. Again.

“But you seem intent on burdening me with the responsibility. Therefore...” He straightened and waved at her chair. His eyes narrowed and Kate forced her slow, reluctant feet to take her back across the deep carpet “...I have to protect my reputation.” His bitter voice turned her insides. “How much?”

Kate sank into the soft cushions. Weary, she pushed down her pride. He had to know the truth. “I’m in debt, Mack,” she said, her voice breaking. “Serious stuff. Up to my neck. In a few days, I won’t have a flat. With that gone, I’ll have nothing.”

Her eyes closed against his cursing. “All right. You want my money? Then it’s an exchange.”

“Exchange?”

“I support you during your pregnancy. After that, the baby’s mine.”

Printed in the United States
141146LV00003B/3/P